MILDRED BUDGE IN CLOVERDALE

DAPHNE SIMPKINS

Quotidian Books

DaphneSimpkins/Quotidian Books

Mildred Budge in Cloverdale/ Daphne Simpkins 2nd printing
ISBN 13-978-0692282656
ISBN 10-0692282653

Contents

This is a story about identity, friendship and exercising the gift of hospitality. This book is dedicated to three women who exemplify that gift so graciously:

Peggy Joseph

Anne Richardson

and

Patty Williams

"Every day is a good day."

–Mildred Budge

ONE

VISIT FROM A CEREAL KILLER

Retired school teacher Mildred Budge was standing naked in her laundry room remembering how her friend Cleo had died in the same state of undress, when she heard her front doorbell ring the first time. It couldn't be anyone she knew. All of Mildred Budge's friends knew to use the back door by the kitchen.

The timing was bad.

Mildred thought maybe she would just let whoever had come to the wrong house go away, when the doorbell rang again. And then, again. Insistently.

There was no ignoring it.

Only Mildred was naked, and everything she had been wearing while tagging dusty, mite-ridden furniture in the hot attic was now rotating inside the washing machine. On top of the clothes dryer were three lone unmatched black socks and one set of long underwear: white cotton Cuddl Duds that Mildred had intended to put away until the following winter.

As the bell rang five more times, Miss Budge decided that any clothes were better than none. Damp with perspiration and gritty with dust, she grabbed the Cuddl Duds and began the arduous task of wriggling into them. It wasn't easy. She looked down at herself in the clingy wintertime underwear that fit like a diaphanous white body stocking.

Victoria's Secret would not be hiring her pear-shaped frame to model lingerie.

"Miz Bulge! Are you all right in there?" A man's voice called out.

Her morning caller knew her, but she didn't recognize his voice. She heard the front doorknob jiggled impatiently. With a start, Miss Budge couldn't remember if she had locked the front door after bringing in the morning newspaper.

"I'm on my way!" Miss Budge called out, and her voice broke. Living alone with no one to talk to for long periods of time, one's voice became, occasionally, untrustworthy.

Tugging at the snug shirt that wanted to rise up and show her unpierced navel, Miss Budge hastily detoured to the foyer, pausing on the other side of her own front door to check the lock.

She peered through the peephole.

Miss Budge had never formally met her morning caller, but she did recognize him. Standing on her front door step was the young father who had moved with his wife and son into the old Garvin house across the street. The young man was wearing the same clothes she had always seen him in--faded black jeans and a black T-shirt. However, this was the first time the young father was close enough for Miss Budge to read the words stenciled on the front of the T-shirt: "Cereal Killer."

He was holding a large Ziploc bag with lumpy grains in it.

As she sent a news flash prayer to Jesus—'There's a cereal killer at my front door and I'm not fully dressed'—she called out, "Another moment, dear boy! I'll be right with you."

Miss Budge scooted to her bedroom and hurriedly slipped into her thick white chenille robe that she had bought for $19 at an after-Christmas sale three months ago. Adrenaline pumping, she clumsily pushed her still naked feet into sage green plastic Crocs.

They were the ugliest shoes she had ever seen, but astonishingly comfortable.

"Miz Bulge! Is everything okay in there?" The Cereal Killer pounded on the door this time. Three hard raps.

Miss Budge cinched the thick robe firmly around her waist and scurried back to the front door, the toe of her right Crocs catching on the rug. She stumbled, and her arms batted the air as she fought to keep her footing. She got her balance back as the doorknob rattled again noisily.

"You haven't fallen or something, have you?" he called through the door.

Miss Budge wrenched the cold brassy doorknob and swung the front door open.

"Of course I have not fallen. Why would I?" Even as Miss Budge said the words, she remembered so many of her older friends for whom the end of their mobility was signaled by a commiserating tsk-tsk-tsk from every messenger who had ever delivered the dreaded news, "Oh, did you hear? She fell."

Cleo had fallen down naked in her laundry room and died alone. And she wasn't the only one of Mildred's acquaintances to begin that journey toward dependence on others in a hospital, nursing home, or assisted living with a fall.

Blinking at the mid-morning sunlight, Miss Budge offered a disciplined, cordial smile, one that had developed over twenty-five years of greeting scared fifth graders as a public-school teacher and which had not diminished in the past two years since her retirement. "Young man, what is it you require so urgently?"

"Miz Bulge?" The Cereal Killer confirmed, squinting downward to meet her brown-eyed gaze. "You're shorter than they said."

"Why would people discuss my height?" Miss Budge inquired immediately, meeting his gaze unwaveringly, though she had to look up to do so. Her neighbor was tall and lanky with the kind of loose posture and untoned muscles that indicates a dearth of exercise.

"No. They said you was a great teacher, and somehow I jess thought you would be taller," he finished lamely. "I'm Kenny from across the street," he announced with a tip of his head toward the old Garvin house. "We been meaning to come say hi. The wife sent this to you," Kenny declared, holding out a gallon-size plastic Ziploc bag of what appeared to be rolled oats with raisins and slivered almonds.

Miss Budge reached politely for the proffered bag. Gifts of food usually came in covered white paper plates or disposable tin pans that she and her friends from the Berean Sunday school class chose to use when taking food to someone's house.

Miss Budge held the cellophane bag of grains up to the foyer light as if it were a bottle of special wine whose color she wanted to check. "How thoughtful," she murmured. "Won't you come in, Kenneth?"

"Thank you, Miz Bulge," Kenny said, stepping into her foyer. A heavy silver key chain slapped against his leg. He patted it companionably as if it were a small pet that was keeping him company. Squared bluish-black marks that reminded Miss Budge of some ancient Celtic designs set off his otherwise unmarred youthful hands.

When she peered more closely Miss Budge saw that the cribbed symbols were not a mysterious message in need of decoding but a single letter tattooed on each knuckle across the back of his hand that ultimately spelled out: L-O-V-E. Although she did not understand the allure of what amounted to inking graffiti upon one's person, Miss Budge, a spinster Christian lady, did believe in love. She smiled beneficently, as she adjusted the beige rheostat light switch in her expansive foyer.

The overhead light grew brighter, illuminating the various black and white photos on the wall of southern bridges that she had collected at one time in her life. Miss Budge had once upon a time loved the sight of aged bridges—loved the lines and arcs and the hope of them, shores being connected so people could cross over. But that season in her life had passed. The pictures were still hung, now a memorial to her previous affection for them rather than a celebration of the old-timey bridges themselves.

Kenny blinked rapidly, confused. She saw that Kenneth's eyes were a weak blue. Underneath the baseball cap that he did not take off, she assumed he was losing his hair prematurely.

"My last name is Budge. You have been calling me Miz Bulge," the retired teacher explained. She patted her mid-section. She was plumper than she had ever been. A frequent awareness of her increasing pear shape had not stopped the pounds from accruing, however. "But it's Mildred—Mildred Budge. Miss...." she declared forthrightly, unashamed of her singleness.

Kenny espied the pictures of solitary bridges on the walls. He blinked some more. The wispy, brown goatee on his chin waved gently when he spoke.

"Miz Deerborn told me about you."

"Will you sit down?" Miss Budge said, waving toward her living room. Her hands were bare of rings. She didn't wear jewelry when she had work to do, and she had spent a sticky morning in her hot attic tagging stored furniture that was to be taken and delivered to The Emporium, a local antique warehouse and flea market. She and her best friend Fran Applewhite were opening a sales booth.

Their initial inventory was the content of their respective attics: two lifetimes of acquired antiques (and a fair amount of old furniture) that would make them a fortune, predicted Fran--or at least enough money so they could travel some.

"I won't stay long," Kenny promised, stepping carefully as if he didn't want to leave footprints on the glossy wooden floor. Kenneth's navy and white athletic shoes made the same small sticking sound against the taffy-colored hardwood floor as her green Crocs. As if mesmerized, her visitor revolved slowly, taking in the room before sitting down on the yellow chintz sofa and saying with wonder, “It’s so clean in here.”

Miss Budge automatically surveyed her living room, pausing to twist the clear plastic prismatic rod that opened her front mini-blinds. The room filled with sunlight. As the room grew brighter, Miss Budge saw that she needed to dust again. There was a small scrap of clipped white paper which must have escaped her paper shredder resting on the border of the large red and blue oriental carpet that defined the floor space. In a culture that necessarily lived with the threat of identity theft, Miss Budge had become a dedicated shredder of her monthly bills on which the numbers, if obtained, could facilitate the stealing of her credit cards, bank accounts, and most importantly, her identity. While shredding was yet another routine chore, Miss Budge liked doing it. She had invested in a sturdy stand-alone monster shredder from Costco that was stationed next to the telephone table, a superior style of furniture made sadly obsolete by cell phones.

Itching to pick up that errant scrap of white paper that disturbed her sense of order, Miss Budge said instead, “Kenneth, are you thirsty?” She had not lost that school teacherly tone. “Do you want a drink?” Her head bobbed up and down encouragingly. When she did, her brown curls caught the light, creating a halo effect that she would have enjoyed if she had known it was happening. She didn’t.

“It’s too early for me,” Kenny said, sitting back on the sofa. “But you go ahead and take a drink if you need a little something. I know how it is. I’ve got a granny who likes her wine in the morning, too.”

Miss Budge’s spine lengthened as her posture aligned itself with the truth. “I do not need something to drink,” she said, taken aback. Her forehead furrowed, deepening the lines that had grown from squinting while grading endless stacks of compositions written by students who did not have good penmanship. Miss Budge absent-mindedly massaged the tender place between her eyebrows that felt now like it retained some perpetual nerve damage. Then, she pressed her brown plastic eye glasses up on her nose; they slipped periodically. Soon, it would be time to go see Mr. Cates. He had been keeping her glasses adjusted for thirty years.

"Me and my wife moved in to that old house two months ago," Kenny said, with a jut of his whiskery chin toward the old Garvin house across the street.

Since Ron Garvin had died of some kind of dementia the legality of his last will had been questioned, and the potential heirs were fighting over his estate. The Garvin house was being rented out by the executor until the domicile could be legally sold and the profits distributed.

"Linda didn't want to live in Old Geezerville," Kenny explained, apparently unaware that the castigation of the Garden District in Montgomery, Alabama as Old Geezerville might be insulting to someone who had lived there her whole life.

The old geezers in reference were the long-time citizens of a southern city that had not only been the birthplace of the civil rights movement, but was also the home place of Zelda Fitzgerald, a famous belle and the wife of F. Scott. For those who cared, country singer Hank Williams was buried over at Oakwood Cemetery not too far from where Nathaniel Coles had lived when he was four years old with his family. In his teens he dropped the "s" and became Nat King Cole.

"I finally talked Baby into it. Our house is awesome. Really awesome, you know. We have what they call an attic fan. You can turn it on and open the windows. The air comes through just like the air conditioner was on," Kenny bragged. "It's going to save us a ton of money this summer, and it's already getting hotter by the day.

We believe in going green." Kenny stared out at his own home through Miss Budge's front window and took a deep breath.

"Me and the wife make organic cereal. That's what I brought you right there. It'll get you going regular. That's our sales hook. These days, you either sell to people who can't sleep, can't lose weight, or to people who can't...." Kenny struggled for the word he needed, pressing his thin lips together, and finally settled on, "Who can't *go.* Cereal can't help you sleep," Kenny added lamely. "Although if that's all you ate, you probably could lose some weight."

There was an awkward pause.

Miss Budge could not discern Kenny's real purpose in coming to see her. Had he caught a glimpse of her and decided she needed to go on a diet?

Miss Budge was an unabashed size-14 woman, but fleshing out the seams of one's garments seemed to happen inevitably as one grew older. The better part of wisdom was to practice moderation in eating, walk as much as you could, and then accept your anatomy as it developed.

Miss Budge eyed the Cereal Killer with curiosity. It seemed unlikely to her that any newcomer would make it his personal mission to infiltrate an older neighborhood and then call on the plumper residents with the goal of putting them on a cereal diet in order to sell his product. Still, she could not recall a time in her life when anyone other than the doctor had ever brought up the subject of her regularity. She decided that the prudent course would be to change the subject.

"I know you are new to the neighborhood. It is actually referred to as Cloverdale—to some, Old Cloverdale," the retired school teacher explained patiently. When Kenny blinked as if he didn't speak English, she explained, "Cloverdale is considered to be the heart of historic Montgomery."

Kenny blinked some more, as if he didn't recognize the name of the city where they lived. Miss Budge smiled encouragingly, and continued politely. "I wonder if you have visited the Fitzgerald museum yet? It is to your left, about two miles that way," Miss Budge directed, pointing, and one more time, saw her mother's hand. She did not mind the vision of her mother's hand extending from her arm at all. Though no one expected a woman of Miss Budge's age to miss a parent, Mildred Budge still did miss her mother and was glad for the company of even the image of her mother's hand.

Kenny eyed the older woman as if she were speaking a foreign language. His eyes morphed to a weak shade of green. Miss Budge wondered if Kenneth was weak or just young. She had taught many young people and had learned that looking into their eyes and making assessments about intelligence or character based on an expression or shade of eye color had very little to do with who they really were—no more than how people once used to feel the bumps on a person's cranium to determine intelligence. Knowing that (and it had taken her a surprisingly long time to learn it) Miss Budge often fought the impulse anyway to a know person's head shape with her fingertips, like a blind person might. Kenny had a rectangular-shaped head. Her fingers began to strum the air gently. If she could know the contours of his head with her hands, what would the arcs and bumps tell her about what was going on inside? She clasped her hands determinedly in her lap and held them there while surreptitiously checking the closure of her robe. Her mother would have liked this robe, too, she thought—and smiled.

"The museum is the old house of a famous Montgomery family. F. Scott Fitzgerald is a famous author. He married a Montgomery girl," she explained patiently. "You may recall from your high school days that Fitzgerald wrote *The Great Gatsby*."

Kenny stared at Miss Budge blankly, and the color of his eyes deepened to the color of an ocean just before it rained. Troubled, Kenny tried to figure out what to say next.

When he didn't immediately speak, Miss Budge continued. "His wife Zelda Sayre was not only a famous southern belle here but a talented writer as well."

Kenny's fingertips scratched the tops of his thighs as if he were getting ready to explain the purpose of his visit. Miss Budge nodded encouragingly, but Kenny did not respond to her cue.

"Or, there's Martin Luther King, Jr.'s church downtown or The First White House of the Confederacy," she added, sounding like one of those volunteer tour guides that some senior citizens become to fill their days after they retired. Though she was retired—prematurely, according to some—she was still too busy to volunteer in that capacity.

Kenny blinked and said, "Awesome." He rubbed his palms on the tops of his jeans. The silver chain with the keys jangled. He petted it.

Miss Budge felt impatient then, though she hid it. Fran and Winston were coming over with the truck in a half hour, and she needed to shower and dress before they arrived. Certainly, the delivery of cereal could not have been Kenneth's primary goal. "Are you sure you don't want some lemonade?" his hostess prompted. She could get it, he could drink it, he could leave.

Kenny shook his head, no, looking as if he might rise. But he didn't. "Miz Bulge...."

Determined to be polite, Miss Budge sat back in the uncomfortable turquoise chair. She had forgotten how unforgiving the chair was. Miss Budge shifted her derriere, struggling for a different center of gravity that might ease the rigidity, but she did not find it.

"Miz Bulge," Kenny said, beginning again, his gaze drifting around the room. "I been watching your house, and you go to church on Sundays. You carry a Bible and everything," Kenny declared. And his nervous hands came to a rest on the tops of his thighs, as he looked to his right at the table with the reading lamp. There were three different Bibles on it.

Kenny's eyes caught hers, and he pressed on. "My son is not a friendly boy. It's like he's not even there sometimes, you know? He's seven. He's supposed to be in school; but Baby---Linda, my wife---thinks Chase won't fit in at school because of his not talking. She's been trying to home school him, but it ain't going as well as she hoped it would. Baby's not a teacher, don't you see?" Kenny said, and his tattooed fingers began to strum the tops of his black-denimed thighs again, spelling out L-O-V-E over and over again.

Miss Budge nodded almost imperceptibly, and the warmth in her brown eyes faded to a wary watchfulness.

"You being a schoolteacher and all..."

Mildred assumed the 'and all' referred to going to church on Sunday and carrying a Bible.

"And I hear you still go to houses of sick kids sometimes...."

"Not anymore," Mildred replied carefully. Initially, after her sudden decision to retire two years ago--and because she needed the money to supplement her reduced fixed income--Miss Budge had accepted short-term assignments as a teacher for homebound students.

But she hadn't done that work for long. The children were too sick and too brave, and they had asked Miss Budge questions that were too hard to answer. She knew the answers; she just didn't want to say them out loud to young children in pain.

Kenny slapped the tops of his black jeans and finally got to his point. "I was wondering if you could help my boy."

"I am not a doctor," Mildred Budge replied, postponing the polite but firm 'no' she would offer Kenny in a moment just as soon as she framed it in her mind. She had left that kind of work behind--cried as many tears as she could. Besides, it was never wise to get caught up in the neighbors' domestic problems, especially if they lived as close as across the street. Before she could say no, her telephone rang.

Loudly.

Miss Budge had only one phone, and she kept the ringer on 'Loud' so that she could hear it ring anywhere in the house. She always answered her phone calls beside her wooden telephone table where a writing tablet and pen were readily available for note-taking and where the small seat built into the table gave her a place to rest in case the caller was long-winded. She sat there to do her monthly shredding, too. Other people thought that speaking on the telephone or shredding the monthly bills were tasks that happened in concert with other activities; it was called multitasking. But Mildred Budge did not like splitting her attention; she liked being focused, had learned as a school teacher that giving one's attention to a person or a job resulted in a better understanding of that person and a better job when work was to be done.

Kenny waited for Miss Budge to move and answer the telephone. She did not.

"I don't answer the telephone when I have a guest," Miss Budge explained simply as the ringing continued, then stopped abruptly.

Kenny laughed. Genuinely. As if the explanation of good manners was some kind of joke. "Miz Deerborn said you was funny and for me not to be afraid of you."

Ah, Belle Deerborn. The well-intentioned woman—and a good friend, too-- who lived just behind Mildred Budge on the other side of the circle that connected their intersecting yards.

Kenneth leaned forward and said in what was almost a whisper: "Miz Belle said you have the gift of healing kids."

Immediately, Miss Budge began to shake her head, no. "I was a teacher. That is all," she replied firmly. "You are wrong—and so is Belle—if you think otherwise."

"Miz Deerborn said you would say that," Kenny replied immediately, his brown wispy goatee wagging.

"It is the truth," Miss Budge replied unswervingly. "I do not glamorize the fruits of determined work by calling it something it is not."

Kenneth nodded as if he were in on the conspiracy of discretion that Miss Budge was determined to perpetuate. "Maybe you could jess speak to my boy then," he said with a wink. "Jest your speaking to him would be good, 'cause Chase don't talk to nobody, even us, sometimes." Kenny took an anxious breath and switched tactics, attempting to persuade her. "That cereal I brought you is all organic. 'S very good for you. No chemicals, pesticides, etcetera, etcetera, etcetera. Let me know if you like it, and I'll bring you a bunch more." Kenny stood up then suddenly. He had finished the job he had given himself to do. The sun shifted from behind a cloud and spilled fresh illumination into the room right where he was standing. The angles of his square-shaped head were easily discerned as bumps inside the baseball cap he had never removed. Miss Budge read his mind then: he had come to see the lady across the street, brought her his offering, made his request, and now he was going home.

Miss Budge was ready for him to go, and she stood more slowly, not because she was older or creaky or less able to stand, but because in her generation one did not rush others out the door by rising too quickly. There was always a hint in every gesture that parting was sweet sorrow—really.

Miss Budge smiled as she followed him to the foyer, speaking in the pace of having an infinite amount of time to get to know other people that others erroneously and inappropriately judged harshly as an irritating habit of an older person, but it was only courtesy.

"That explains why the UPS truck comes to your house so often. He must be bringing you supplies for your organic cereals," she theorized aloud, as Kenny led the way to her front door.

Kenny's voice grew proud. "We sell on the internet a lot, and we take it over to the health food store on the Easter by-pass. We have mucho customers now," Kenny said proudly, as her telephone began to ring again. "Somebody really wants to talk to you," Kenny said. "I'll go on and get out of your way."

He turned in the doorway and said, his voice growing quieter: "My boy's name is Chase, and you don't know him yet, but he's special."

Miss Budge met the young father's gaze, so similar to the faces of so many young parents of young children who had been in her care during the twenty-five years she had served the state in the public-school system. Kenny was a stranger, but Miss Budge knew him. Kenny was a young father who had a son who was special.

"You could come over any time. Any time at all that suits you. Linda would love to meet you," Kenny promised, looking across the street to his new home where the blinds were closed, and no lights appeared to be on inside. There was something in that anxious glance at his own home that moved Miss Budge. She relented.

"I'd be delighted to meet your Chase," Mildred agreed, casting an involuntary glance at the insistent telephone as it continued to ring.

Kenneth fired an imaginary pistol at her with his forefinger and thumb, and Miss Budge marveled at a hand gesture that spoke of a violence that was inconsonant with the nature of his request. Still, she fought the urge born of politeness to mimic Kenneth's hand movement, offering a short wave of farewell instead as she walked toward the telephone. On the way, Mildred stooped over and picked up the scrap of white paper that had been bothering her. It was a piece of notebook paper, not a piece of a shredded bill.

"Greetings to you and yours," Miss Budge said, answering the phone.

"Have you been drinking?" Fran Applewhite asked sharply.

Before Mildred could answer, Fran said, "That was me calling before; but then I thought you might be in the attic, and if I let it keep ringing, you might break your neck trying to answer the telephone. You don't want to die in the attic. It would have been hard as all get-out to bring your body down those stairs. Remember how hard it was to get the broken water heater down? So I hung up and waited a spell. I have news. It's big," Fran warned.

"I was not in the attic. I was in my living room talking with a cereal killer who thinks that the Eastern by-pass is named after Easter Sunday or the Easter bunny. It is unclear which one he has in mind."

Fran interrupted her. "Mildred, she's killed another one."

Mildred didn't have to ask who Fran meant. She knew. Liz Luckie had recently married for the fourth time; and each time, the husbands had died early in the marriage. Mildred had not known the first three husbands, but she had been a special friend of Liz's most recent groom.

"How did Hugh die?" Mildred asked. She sat down heavily in the small seat built into the telephone table. It was a tight fit. It didn't use to be.

"The regular way. Natural causes." Fran reported bluntly.

"Natural causes. Again," Mildred repeated bleakly. She patted her face with one hand. She felt pale. Then, she pressed the same hand to her chest. Her heart was beating fast. The chenille robe was thick. She was wearing long underwear, too, but Mildred felt chilled. Her lower lip trembled. No hot flash conveniently arrived when it might have helped to warm her.

"They all die of natural causes," Fran said quietly. She hesitated before adding, "Today's Thursday. I figure the funeral will be Saturday."

Mildred nodded into the telephone, her throat instantly dry. Yes. That might be hard for someone else to arrange, but for a woman who had already orchestrated three funerals for her previous husbands, arranging a funeral in two days would not be a problem. She wouldn't have the funeral on a Sunday afternoon, and Monday was too late.

"I wanted to tell you before Winston and I got there together with his truck because that's not the kind of news you need to hear in front of company," Fran explained, her voice dropping to a whisper.

Winston must have come inside Fran's house and was now standing near enough to Fran to hear what she was trying to tell Mildred quietly.

Mildred swallowed hard, remembering how before Hugh had married Liz, his fingertips had grazed hers in the church kitchen when he had handed her his water glass to be washed on a Saturday morning. Each had volunteered to participate in the deep spring cleaning of the church building.

And before that, Hugh had sat beside her in Sunday school as if he just happened to land there and how nervous his sitting close had made her feel—and crowded.

And Hugh had asked her to dance after one of the church weddings at the country club, and she hadn't said no fast enough. Hugh had taken her in his arms and steered her around, and while they moved—scuttled crablike is how Mildred described it to herself—about the floor, she had endured an embarrassing hot flash and broken out in a flop sweat of sorts that Hugh didn't seem to notice, but, of course, he had noticed.

"I've got to go now, Millie. It'll be all right," Fran whispered before hanging up. Mildred's best friend said the words with the authority of a veteran widow who had told herself the same thing through many a long night spent without Gritz who had died on her—the husband Fran Applewhite had loved dearly for forty-three years.

TWO

MISSING HUGH

Three days before Liz was supposed to marry Hugh Luckie, the groom had called Mildred Budge at home and said bluntly, without pausing to say hello, "Say the word, Mildred, and I'll call the wedding off."

"Which word?" Mildred asked, standing at attention. At that time, she had only recently retired from her teaching post, still embarrassed that she had worn out six years sooner than she had planned to retire. Grappling with a sense of failure but beginning to enjoy the extended periods of solitude at home, Mildred was—when Hugh called-- not yet accustomed to being at home all the time where people could call her whenever they felt like it.

In that moment of the unexpected phone call and the sound of Hugh's gravelly voice—so strong, so intimate--Mildred had also felt uncomfortably exposed, stripped of the protection of her teacherly persona that she had worn like a comfortable uniform at a school where the secretary took messages but did not promise callers that their messages would reach the requested teacher until the end of the day and maybe not even then. The messages were placed in a teacher's mail box, but teachers were not required to check them daily.

The school's intercom system was undependable in a way that would no longer be tolerated with the ever-increasing heightened security at all schools; but during Miss Budge's career, most teachers didn't worry so much about speedy communication. Important news eventually reached you and when it did, there was time to respond, thoughtfully. Carefully. Prayerfully.

But Hugh had called Mildred at her home on a Wednesday. Mildred had answered the telephone, and there was no other person or a social persona in place to create a distance between them. It was Hugh's voice in her ear, and the intensity of his declaration reached deeply inside of her, touching upon tender girlish feelings that Mildred thought she had outgrown years ago.

"Mildred Budge, don't pretend with me," Hugh said firmly. "You are pretending to be ignorant about what we feel for one another. Or, at least I think we feel something for one another. Am I wrong, Mildred Budge?"

Mildred could not answer Hugh. There had been brief moments when she had actually felt something for Hugh, and it wasn't just admiration for his good head of hair that was often the talk of women in the ladies' room at church. Women admired Hugh's thick salt-and pepper hair. Balding men envied it.

Pressing the phone closer to her ear and feeling rushed in a way that jarred with her timing when messages should be received and the pace of a prayerful response, Mildred tried to figure out in that very moment how she did feel about Hugh. It was hard to know because she lived alone, and no one asked her regularly what she felt about anything. Furthermore, it was not her temperament to dwell on her feelings. To have that kind of personal authentic information demanded of her so suddenly triggered first a deep silence and then puzzlement.

She was always glad to see Hugh, but that wasn't love, was it?

When Hugh was nearby, she didn't feel as lonely as she was accustomed to feeling. In fact, she was aware in a new way that a part of her was always lonely but that was a part of being human. But being less lonely wasn't love either, was it?

And, when Mildred puzzled over the situation further, she didn't particularly want Hugh to dance with her again, though there had been that time when he was sitting next to her at a church luncheon and had forgotten himself and stretched out his arm around the back of her chair. For a thoughtless minute, she had found herself nestling into the circle of it. Later, she had concluded that his strong right arm reminded her of her daddy's protection, but finding a place to sit for a while where she felt safer was not the kind of love one changed the whole structure of one's life to accommodate, was it?

Then, Belle Deerborn, who was stoically married to Sam (a retired Air Force colonel) who in his retirement had become the unofficial CEO of the elders and deacons at church, had seen Mildred sitting beside Hugh and inside that outstretched arm. Given to interpreting anyone else's potential romance as an affirmation of her own persevering marriage, Belle had winked and then did that little salsa step, a kind of hoochie-coochie movement with her hips that Mildred Budge had never attempted in her life. Belle was like that—unabashedly a sexual being in spite of being the wife of an elder.

Immediately, Mildred Budge had stiffened and sat up straighter in the metal folding chair. The squeak of the joints of that chair had hurt Hugh's feelings. As if he were only reaching for a sip of his iced tea, Hugh had discreetly withdrawn his arm. Mildred had missed the feeling of that arm around her but not for long; and that small regret that stemmed more from a desire to feel safe wasn't love, was it?

No, Mildred Budge could not say the word that Hugh demanded she speak in order to stop him from marrying Liz. So, she had replied as honestly as she had known how, still standing and holding the telephone against her ear, her legs feeling wobbly, and her heart pounding drum-like in her chest, "I wish you every happiness, my dear friend. Liz, too."

'Dear friend.' Even Mildred Budge knew that was the wrong way to say it. You can call your dear friends that. But Hugh had been more. She had known who Hugh really was at a deep level, and he had known something true about her. They just didn't talk about it.

Hugh Luckie had hung up quietly without saying another word, the phone making that gentle click that reminded Mildred at the time of the thudding sound of a coffin lid being lowered after a viewing the night before the funeral. The very second she had put down the phone, Mildred Budge had begun to miss Hugh Luckie with more fibers of her being than the small ones that tickled occasionally for a few seconds and then quieted down, but all together they were not love, were they?

Mildred observed that sense of loss in herself and reasoned that she was missing the tickling emotions associated with Hugh, but not necessarily Hugh Luckie.

"Do I turn down opportunities to change that are intended for me?" she asked God, for she believed in unceasing prayer and that was one of the ways that Mildred prayed.

The prayer led instantly to another memory of Hugh handing her his silverware to wash after the last church supper. He had laughingly teased her about doing too much kitchen work, like Martha in the Bible.

Mildred remained silent as Hugh playfully threatened to unplug her Marthaesque sink and let all her still hot and satisfyingly sudsy water drain out. He didn't do it. Hugh had read something in Mildred's face that she would have kept secret if she could by just not talking. The truth had dawned inside of him, slowly, authentically, that Mildred Budge was not pulling a Martha stunt that he could tease her about; Mildred Budge was hiding in the kitchen from him and what she sensed rightly this long-time widower wanted from her.

Epiphanies happened everywhere, even in the church kitchen.

Soberly, Hugh had laid down the silverware on the gold-speckled kitchen counter and excused himself, quietly—embarrassed and rejected. And then Hugh had started sitting next to Liz, and it didn't take any time at all for him to become engaged to Liz, a serial widow. Right before the wedding, Hugh had called Mildred Budge, an act that was totally out of character for Hugh, and he had challenged her to stop him:

"Say the word, Mildred."

And Mildred Budge could not say it.

The phone in Mildred's hand began to beep, reminding her that she had not hung it up after Fran's call. She replaced the phone quietly in its cradle and said in wonder as she had many times about many other people, "I will never hear the sound of Hugh Luckie's voice again."

Mildred stood there a long time, trying to make herself go and get dressed, but the news of Hugh's death had immobilized her. Inertia had not happened to her in a long time. She always kept going.

Mildred gave herself over to the lethargy, rousing only when Fran tapped gently on the back kitchen door before letting herself in.

"You're not dressed," Fran noted with surprise, adding quickly, "It's okay. Winston's backing the pick-up truck into your driveway. I hopped out so I could come in and grab a minute alone with you." Fran studied her friend's face and motioned for her to move away from the telephone and sit beside her at the kitchen table where they could talk. It was an old wooden table that had been in Mildred's family for as long as she could remember. It sat four. None of the chairs matched, but they were all comfortable.

Fran sat down first and watched her friend intently.

"So how do you think Liz did it this time?" Fran asked bluntly. Her blue eyes flashed, and her red lipstick was smudged on her front tooth again. It was every morning. One more time, Mildred pointed, and Fran took her forefinger and brushed her front teeth with it, wiping away the red.

"Winston didn't say a thing. Either men won't mention when your lipstick is smudged, or they just don't see it."

"They don't see it," Mildred replied automatically. "Men don't see what women see."

"I see," Fran promised. She leaned forward and pressed her best friend's hand and said, "I'm so sorry, Mildred. So very, very sorry about Hugh. It was one thing for him to marry her. It is another thing entirely for him to have died."

"We all will miss Hugh," Mildred replied, her expression blank. She felt like she could barely move, barely speak. She needed to pull herself together. There was too much to do, and she didn't have time to be lazy like this. Besides, Hugh wasn't hers to grieve.

"Do I need to make some iced tea?" She asked, as Winston's green pick-up truck slowly came to a stop parallel with the concrete walkway that led to Mildred's front door.

"Not for us. Winston can't drink anything if he has any work to do," Fran replied enigmatically. "Have you marked the items to go in the attic?" Fran asked. There was a tinge of apology in her voice because she recognized that Mildred needed some time to adjust to the morning's news.

"Some," Mildred replied distractedly.

Fran turned, and the morning sunlight caught her. She was a pretty woman who could have been Doris Day's younger sister or one of those models for catalogues that sold clothing to women their age. She wore her gray hair in a 50's flip and was dressed in dark blue denim Capri's and a matching denim shirt that was trimmed at the collar in a red and blue plaid. Her canvas shoes had the same plaid trim around the soles.

"I called and told you first because I didn't want to say the news out loud in front of Winston."

Mildred nodded and spoke in a contrived normal voice that would have fooled Winston but didn't fool Fran.

"My neighbor from across the street came over to bring me that cereal," Mildred said, pointing toward the Ziploc bag on the table. The piece of white paper she had picked up off the floor was beside it. Mildred reached for it. It was a Bible verse assigned by the Berean Sunday school teacher who delegated the reading of the scripture for the day's lesson by distributing hand-scripted verses—not typed-- on small pieces of paper to the ladies as they entered the classroom.

"He rang the doorbell over and over again, and he wears a black shirt that reads Cereal Killer." Mildred read the words that had been assigned to her the previous week from the book of Jeremiah: *'For I know the plans that I have for you—plans for good and not evil.'*

"We ought to get one of those T-shirts for Liz," Fran commented darkly.

"Cereal Killer....with a C. And you don't really think Liz kills them, do you? It's just a kind of bad luck, isn't it?" Mildred asked, refolding the paper. She absent-mindedly stuck it in the pocket of her robe.

"You and I don't believe in luck," Fran replied tersely. "Do you want me to help you finish tagging the furniture to go to The Emporium?'

They turned toward the hallway that led to the attic. The creaky accordion wooden stairs extended from the attic to the floor. The light in the attic was still on, spilling the shadowy light down like a distant spotlight onto the carpeted floor. Bits of dust and black gritty shingle particles had fallen onto the beige carpet when the stairs had been pulled down. Mildred would have to vacuum after the furniture had been removed.

Mildred faced her friend and shook her head almost imperceptibly. "Please tell Winston to take it all. I don't know why I didn't think of that in the beginning. What am I saving any of it for?" she said, rubbing that tender place between her eyes.

Fran studied her friend's face and said carefully, "Think about that, Mildred. You've had a shock. We don't have to do anything today if you don't want to. I mean, really....Winston and I could just leave and come back some other day," she offered.

Mildred shook her head, no. There was no reason for Winston to imagine that she was upset over Hugh's passing any more than any dear friend had a right to be. "Just tell Winston to take anything up there. Take it all. And please ask him to take that turquoise chair from the living room, too. It's a miserable chair. I shall not impose its discomfort upon anyone else. I don't know why I have kept it this long," Mildred said with a vehemence that surprised them both.

Fran paced her question. "You won't regret later letting some of the pieces go? You're sure about what you're saying?"

Mildred held her friend's gaze. The chill had receded. Her legs felt stronger. She could stand again. "I might regret it later but not forever."

The two friends studied each other. Mildred had seen Fran through the loss of her husband. She had not always known what to say to Fran about missing Gritz, as she did not know what to say to many of her friends who had husbands die or had what they called man trouble. Mostly, Mildred had listened. Today, it was Fran's turn to listen, but Mildred was not comfortable talking about her feelings.

Fran reached up and put her arms around her best friend and whispered out of the depths of her considerable experience, "Oh, Millie. We're all of us such fools."

THREE

INSIDE A TIME CAPSULE

There was enough furniture in the attic for the first truckload of merchandise to be delivered to The Emporium and plenty more.

"And we haven't even gone after my goods yet," Fran said with a glint of satisfaction in her eyes.

Fran reported this after Mildred took a fast shower and slipped into her purple corduroy pants set. Winston had quietly moved furniture that he could handle alone and loaded it on to his truck.

"That purple looks as good on you as the sage green one," Fran approved as Mildred joined her in the kitchen.

Mildred often bought her outfits in duplicate. If she liked one of something, she bought another outfit like it in a different color.

"I am going to like having the attic cleaned out," Mildred said, her voice a forced brightness that sent chills down Fran's spine and even caused laid-back Winston, a tall string bean of a man with an old-fashioned crew cut, to stop and look at Mildred curiously as he came back inside. Winston was dripping sweat, but he didn't seem to mind.

"Thank you for helping us, Winston," Mildred said, attempting a smile. It felt false. She rubbed the place on her forehead again.

Winston nodded succinctly and looked expectantly at Fran.

"Do you think that's enough for a first load?" Fran asked, and her face softened as she looked at Winston.

Winston looked over his shoulder out the window at his mostly full truck and said, "Yep." Then, he went back outside where he slammed closed the tailgate of his green pick-up truck that had its share of dings and skinned paint. Mildred wondered momentarily if Winston had bought the truck that way or if he was accident prone. She didn't know him very well. Winston and Fran had only recently allowed themselves to be seen together in public.

Winston had bought the truck that way, Mildred concluded, as she watched him carefully tuck old quilts around the turquoise wingback from the living room and that chest of drawers that Mildred had been storing in the attic for eight years. It had belonged to her Aunt Eileen. Fran had also grabbed two old lamps that in the sunlight turned out to be trimmed in 24 K gold and a portable drop-lid wooden writing lap desk that Fran said reminded her of Benjamin Franklin. They were on the kitchen table ready to be carried out.

"Do you really want to give this up?" Fran asked skeptically, patting the hand-carved wooden lap desk.

The piece had been Miss Budge's preferred paper-grading station. She had taken it to the attic two years ago when she retired. Mildred didn't use the lap desk for writing her bills or the meditations that she sold to different Christian periodicals. She didn't miss the lap writing desk any more than she missed grading papers. She didn't even want to look at it again.

"Take it," Mildred said, as she noted that all of it needed dusting. "Do you think people will really buy someone's old chest of drawers?" She asked again.

"They really will, Millie. This is going to work," Fran promised Mildred and herself.

Winston came back into the kitchen, walked over to the sink, and helped himself to a glass of tap water. While he drank it in two long swallows, Fran waited. When his hands were empty, she handed Winston the wooden lap desk and pointed to a lamp. Winston picked them up silently and looked at Fran again. She smiled.

No. Fran beamed at him, Mildred observed.

"It's getting warm early this year," Winston announced, which was his way of saying it was time to go. "Are you *both* riding with me?" Winston asked, studying his truck through the kitchen window.

Fran looked from Mildred to Winston. She needed to keep Mildred company and motivated to stay positive about their new business, but she also needed to keep Winston happy.

Mildred understood Fran's pressures. "Go on, Frannie. I'll follow in the Coop."

Fran appraised the emotional stability of her friend and decided it was best to give Mildred some space and Winston her undivided attention. Fran picked up the last gilt-trimmed lamp with the small roses painted on it and held it high in a victory stance.

"Let's have pizza tonight to inaugurate the opening of our new business which we have not yet named. You keep thinking about a name for our booth. You're the one who is good with words," Fran nudged, assigning Mildred her duties with the same finesse that she used with Winston.

Mildred flinched, disconcerted. "Pizza?" she asked, her voice rife with surprise. The proposal of pizza with its promise of indigestion that would surely follow felt slightly suicidal to Mildred. The two women regularly compared notes on which foods were no longer prudent digestible choices. Mildred and Fran had given up hot dogs years ago. Pizza had never been in question.

"We're going to have to eat some kind of supper after all the work, Millie, and neither one of us is in a position to cook." Fran handed the second lamp to Winston. He had slipped out, put down the desk and other lamp, and returned for hers.

"Don't you get tired of sandwiches, oatmeal, and soup?" Fran asked before hurrying after Winston and without waiting for Mildred's answer.

Mildred watched as her older friend moved nimbly, levering herself up gracefully into Winston's truck. Sitting next to Winston was already a habit for Fran.

Winston switched on the engine. Fran drew back her shoulders while Winston reached past her, snagged the shoulder seat belt and stretched it across, buckling her in. They really were a couple—more a couple than Fran had let Mildred know. But Mildred saw it then. A man didn't fasten a woman's seat belt if they weren't a real couple.

Mildred took her time locking up the house to allow Fran and Winston more time to gain a lead so she wouldn't trail them too closely. Behind the wheel of her red and black Mini-Cooper, Mildred drove intuitively, trusting her memory, for the neighborhoods along the route had changed. A left here, a right there, Mildred steered her car toward the destination. It wasn't a long drive, and ten minutes later she was on the main thoroughfare that led to The Emporium, which was housed in the big building that had once a long time ago been considered one of the best department stores in Montgomery, Alabama.

As a young man with a growing family, Mildred's father had worked there years ago as the building superintendent. The shoe department had been on the second floor; and when you bought a pair of shoes, you pulled the head of a manufacturer's business mascot-- a goose--and a large plastic egg rolled down with a prize inside. They were the same kinds of prizes you got at the dentist's office for not crying when the dentist drilled your teeth: little plastic rings with fake glass jewels.

Just as Mildred sighted Winston's truck again, she saw Fran standing by the front door of The Emporium waving with both arms for Mildred to join her.

"What have I gotten myself into?" Mildred asked her reflection in the rearview mirror, as she fixed a determined smile on her face. It was hard. For when she drew closer to the building she felt the strange pull of the past to warm memories of her father and her mother.

Because both Hugh and her father and mother were now all dead and together in whatever paradise was designed for souls that belonged to Jesus, Mildred felt that surge of longing that one learns to live with increase. She knew the nature of the feeling but not an exact name for a yearning that was composed of heartbreak and loss and forged together with an illogical hope. For inside the Christian faith paradoxes exist that allow for both grief and a very real solace that feels like a safe harbor—a resting place, really-- and which preachers referred to obliquely as the kingdom of God.

The interior Miss Budge turned in her spirit toward that harbor and murmured "Jesus, I need you," and that rest that is promised in the Bible emerged like a rising tide and enveloped her one more time as she joined Fran.

"Isn't this a wonderful place?" Fran said, waving her arms again to point out the front store showcase windows. Tableaus of furniture and other accessories had been arranged as artfully as if they were a Macy's Christmas window presentation. Fran and Mildred strolled past them in the pace of window-shopping.

"Of course, the people who have the front window spaces probably own the building or something. But isn't it be--u—ti—ful?" Fran remarked enthusiastically.

Before Winston, Fran used to say the word beautiful in the regular way. Now, Mildred's best friend split the syllables of that word the way Winston did. Sometimes Mildred missed the way the old Fran used to speak.

"It's so us, isn't it, Mildred?"

Mildred felt overwhelmed by the flood of so many items that represented the past and the powerful emotion of nostalgia. "This place is like a big time capsule," Mildred observed. That idea was not an unfamiliar one to her. She had been writing a devotional for one of her Christian magazines about people as living time capsules. Since her retirement she had earned extra money writing un-bylined devotionals for a magazine that paid her a hundred dollars for seven meditations. That's what Mildred called her 450-word reflections on Bible verses—short essays that were, as her editors requested, "preferably linked to themes and seasons. You're like every woman who reads us. Mothers and wives. Our readers will connect with you."

Mildred hadn't explained that she was neither married nor a mother. She just wrote her seven meditations at a time, sent them in a bundle, and waited for the check that often took six weeks to arrive. It was immediately deposited into the bank account that she liked to refer to as her travel fund, but which was inevitably tapped to fulfill her Faith Promise pledge or some other need.

Fran continued animatedly as she directed them to the entrance, "As wonderful a place as it is, we don't have to be present at The Emporium any more than we want to be."

Although she had explained how the operation worked before, Fran described the process again. "We tag our merchandise. Customers find what they want, take the tag off the item up to the front desk where they pay, and an assistant goes and gets it and helps the customers load their car or truck. At the end of the month we get our cut, and it's direct deposit right into the bank. None of this waiting around for a check." Fran pivoted suddenly. She signaled to Winston with a nod of her head, and one significant finger demonstrated where he was meant to take the merchandise.

"Winston's got to take the truck around to the back-loading dock where the deliveries come through," Fran explained. "I told him to let me out here in front so I could take you through the showroom. How long has it been since you were here inside, Millie?" Fran asked, for she knew the story of Mildred's father's tenure as the building superintendent. And why he had quit. Mildred's father got sick and missed one day of work after thirteen years. The company docked his pay. He went looking for another job the next day.

Her legs heavy with memories that anchored her to the past, Mildred replied, "Yesterday. Yesterday I was here, and I was ten years old. Today I'm here, and I'm sixty-one."

"Sixty-one is nothing these days, Mildred. You like to imagine yourself as older than sixty-one."

"No, I don't. I feel sixty-one because I am sixty-one."

"What does that mean? I am older than you, and I don't feel sixty-one!" Fran declared vigorously as they passed through the open front door and stopped for a moment in the foyer to get their bearings. The cavernous store was packed with arrangements of furniture and glass display tables. It was clean and well lit. Someone kept the glass tops sparkling so that the costume jewelry inside the cases could shine through.

Fran smiled approvingly, waving her hand again for Mildred to take a look. "You retired too early if you ask me. Besides," she said, "Today, you feel sixty-one, but tomorrow you could feel thirty-four again. Last week you had a day when you felt thirty-four. Remember that?" Fran prodded.

Fran believed in seeing the positive; sometimes her optimism wore on Mildred.

"Those days are getting fewer and farther between," Mildred replied dourly.

"Well, I feel twenty-four again today, and I plan to enjoy it," Fran declared. "There's free coffee," she said, but Mildred had already smelled the old coffee that had been made earlier in the day and had now grown stale. The coffee pot was positioned in a customer reception area on a work station that fit behind a circle of chairs and a small black leather sofa. On a coffee table in the middle were stacks of magazines and an open package of cheap vanilla cream sandwich cookies.

"Sometimes the men who come with their wives don't like to shop, so we provide free coffee and cookies to our visitors who just want to sit here and take in the ambience," Fran explained brightly. Dropping her voice, she added, eyes glinting, "We don't personally pay extra for the coffee and the cookies. It comes out of the rent we pay to The Emporium." Fran leaned over, picked up a stale cookie, and nibbled a bite with her front teeth in that perfect way she did when she chewed without losing any of her red lipstick. "Men would eat these cookies," Fran concluded, and then she discreetly tossed the rest of it into the nearby trash receptacle.

"I don't want any coffee," Mildred said before Fran could arrange for her to taste the scorched brew in the pot that was missing its lid.

"There's a drink machine in the back where the vendors' restrooms are," Fran reported. "Fifty cents a drink. How long has it been since you paid just fifty cents for a soda?"

Mildred shook her head. The price was irrelevant. Neither one of them drank sodas regularly, although Mildred had a secret stash of the small bottled Coca-Colas that she drank sparingly. Carbonation caused digestive problems, too. Mildred stopped to appraise the long glass counters that contained all kinds of costume jewelry for sale. Even she knew it wasn't real jewelry. But the sparkling pieces were pretty. Mostly rhinestones and other kinds of colored glass. The jewelry reminded her of a brooch she had inherited from her Aunt Eileen. Mildred's heirloom pendant was very Joan Crawfordish, too big and heavy to wear. But sometimes, Mildred took out her Eisenberg Original, and looked at it and thought about her Aunt Eileen and wondered if her aunt had ever worn the heavy piece of jewelry either, or also only looked at it. How many valuable pieces of jewelry got passed down through members of families with no one really using them because while they were valuable, they were no longer in style or even practical? Mildred wondered one more time if she should sell the brooch because there was no one to leave it to. She took it out and looked at it occasionally; it was something physical that connected her tangibly to her mother's sister and in its way, her own mother, gone so long now. That made it priceless. She could never sell it.

Two older men stood near the cash register. One of them was moving a chair to a place underneath the florescent light. Mildred watched as he stepped up and began to tug at the four-foot elongated plastic cover that needed to come off before he could change the long cylindrical bulb. Dust flew. The light cover stuck.

"Excuse me," Mildred said, stepping over. "That cover has a lip that needs to be pushed up and back."

He followed her instructions, and the thick plastic cover popped loose immediately. He handed it to his buddy and then reached up to take down the burned-out bulb. He pulled. Nothing happened.

"That type of bulb has two small metal feet that fit in a groove," Mildred explained. "You have to rotate the bulb first up and then out and backwards toward you."

He did.

"Just install the new one by reversing the process," Mildred advised. Why was it you could remember how to change a particular light bulb in a particular building from years ago because you had seen your father do it and couldn't remember how to tell which side of a fitted sheet was the top or the bottom of your own bed? Each week Mildred changed her sheets and had to do it wrong before she could do it right. Why was that? Was she losing her wits? She repressed that question one more time as Fran called out a cheerful greeting to the two men who were working.

"Hi, boys!" You remember me? I'm Fran, and this is my best friend Mildred Budge. She knows how to do a lot of stuff like that. We have a new booth in the back over there." Fran pointed and beamed.

Mildred had a sudden start of realization that Fran knew she was pretty and had always known it. What would it be like to be pretty and know that about yourself?

The two men nodded. The one on the chair asked Mildred and listened hard for the answer. "How did you learn about these florescent light bulbs? They're the devil."

Mildred offered a gentle smile of her own, and the light from the florescent bulb doused her in the achingly cold glare of ungenerous illumination. It showed the lines around her eyes and revealed the small crinkling of wrinkles that crested her top lip, but it also showed with great clarity the integrity of her gaze. Miss Budge was not as pretty as Fran, but she had a clear-sighted, brown-eyed gaze that others recognized as trustworthy. "A long, long time ago, my father used to be the superintendent in this very building," Mildred said, and she liked saying it. She didn't have many opportunities to mention her father.

"Thanks for the instructions. I've been fooling with these bulbs, and I can eventually make them work. That tip of how to turn the feet, I'll remember that," he vowed.

Mildred and Fran didn't wait for him to put the cover back on, although Mildred wanted to take it to the back restroom and wash it off before he did. Feeling Mildred's interest moving toward the homely chores of housekeeping that would keep her in company with her missing father, Fran gripped Mildred's elbow firmly and said,

"It's time to stop lolly-gagging. We've got real work to do, Mildred. Let's get to it."

Their booth's floor space was in the back and marked off with strips of yellow tape. They were situated between a booth dedicated to memorabilia for "Gone With the Wind" and Scarlett O'Hara on the left and a display of vintage pastel flapper clothes and hats on the right. Very Zelda Fitzgerald.

Fran grew resolute, undaunted by the almost obscure location so far from the front door and sandwiched between two other flashy vendors. "It's farther back than I remember. But this is our spot for now," Fran declared firmly, stepping inside the area marked out with the yellow adhesive tape. Both names were written on alternate strips of the thick tape that marked the dimensions of their booth's floor space. Applewhite. Applewhite. Applewhite. Budge. Budge. Budge.

Mildred read her own name and inhaled the mandate that seemed to be her inheritance: It felt time for a change. A small change, but it was, she thought, time to look at her life—and budge.

"It's not a very big space," Mildred observed quietly, but she wasn't complaining. The small designated area made her feel inexplicably better. This adventure wasn't a large investment after all. No one was going to stop at this small space in the vast warehouse of vendors whose merchandise was more glamorous than theirs. Fran would get tired of this project soon. Then, they could have a big garage sale, use the money to fulfill their Faith Promise pledges to support missions, God willing, and get back to their respective daily routines.

There was plenty of church work to keep both women very busy. There was the Lydia ministry for visiting homebound people; there was the Barnabas ministry, which focused on discovering people who needed acts of mercy from the church; there was the Fishes & Loaves committee that took condolence casseroles to grieving families; there was Vacation Bible School that taught young children the gospel and gave their parents a break from them in the summertime; there was the Sunday morning flower ministry that culminated in redistributing Sunday's sanctuary's flowers on Monday morning and taking them around to people who were in the hospital; there was the choir which led the worship service; there was teaching Sunday school that imposed the discipline of small-group studies of the Bible; there was filling in as a receptionist one afternoon a week so that the church could save money by not hiring a secretary; and there were a multitude of hostessing opportunities that emerged with the Fall Bible Conference, the Missions Conference and any of the monthly women's circle meetings.

"Twenty feet by twenty feet is all we need to get started," Fran declared emphatically as she began to step off the area with heel-to-toe movements, making sure of the size and that they weren't being cheated. They were paying rent for floor space. It was just the kind of thing Fran did before fellowship suppers when she double-checked the placement of tables and chairs that she had designed to fit the size of the crowd anticipated.

"It is small, but think of it this way: we can grow. Try to think of it that way, Millie," Fran urged.

"I could try to think of it that way," Mildred replied, and she rotated around slowly, extending her gaze. She could see the heads of early milling shoppers moving slowly through the store, remembering and browsing, and she wondered how many of them still cared about either Scarlet O'Hara or Zelda Fitzgerald. Would anyone want old-fashioned furniture that would be too big for small rooms in modern houses?

Almost as soon as Mildred framed the question, someone tapped her determinedly on the shoulder, pointed a long pink-polished fingernail toward the chest of drawers that Winston was positioning in the corner of their space, and asked bluntly, "How much do you want for that?"

Mildred surveyed the woman in low slung, skinny jeans. Mildred didn't have to look down to know her belly button was on display.

"How much do we want for that?" Mildred repeated the question loudly enough for Fran to hear.

They hadn't priced the items yet. Their inventory was not even in place. Fran stepped over beside her business partner and answered enthusiastically, "That's a wonderful piece, isn't it?" Fran eyed it with great appreciation and a kind of fervent admiration that Mildred did not share.

It was an old chest of drawers. Mildred was glad to have it out of her attic. On a different day in a different situation she would have paid someone to take it, and now this woman wanted to know how much it cost.

The pert blonde nodded, reaching out to stroke the wood. She wore a pink baseball cap, and her small pony-tail swung perkily through a hole in the back. The cap matched her pink-striped Ralph Lauren shirt.

"And that's not particle board, like you find now," Fran pointed out. "That's genuine oak. It'll shine up be-u-ti-ful-ly." As if to prove her point, Fran whisked out a waxy cloth from an orange cellophane packet she had thought to bring and rubbed the top drawer's surface. It was one of those pre-oiled disposable cloths. The wood instantly gleamed.

"We are especially proud of this discovery and are asking only three-seventy-five. It's our Grand Opening Special," Fran added, grandly.

"Our Grand Opening Special," Mildred confirmed, nodding. She watched fascinated, as Fran came to life selling furniture.

"Three seventy-five," the woman repeated thoughtfully. She reached out and patted the wood, leaving her fingerprints in the fresh residue of oil.

Smiling, Fran wiped them off and shot the woman a reproving look that meant *Don't do that again.*

"Would you consider...?" The customer began, leaning over to study the chest's knobby feet.

Before the woman could finish offering an alternative price, Fran shook her head. "It'll go for five hundred, I'm pretty sure. It's a bargain at three-seventy-five," Fran confirmed to the woman, who did not seem disappointed or surprised that Fran would not dicker.

The customer changed tactics. "I do wonder if it will fit my space. Will you take it back if I get it home and it doesn't fit?"

"No," Fran said easily, still smiling. "Why don't you go home and measure your area and then come back? If it's still here...." Fran said the words easily, dangling the possibility of the woman's losing what she wanted.

"No. No. I want it," the woman said with conviction. She looked around as if she thought some mysterious other buyer would appear before she could write out a check. Then, she opened her purse and took out a red plastic-covered checkbook that had a name embossed in gold on the front.

Mildred surreptitiously read the words: *Home Designs*. It was the business name of a prominent home decorator.

"To whom shall I make out the check?" the woman asked hurriedly, as if she didn't know. She wrote out the amount quickly.

"To The Emporium, of course," Fran explained, filling out the sales chit that she had not even had time to tie to the chest. "You pay the boys at the front counter. I'll have the chest waiting for you on the loading dock. Thank you."

The woman nodded, noting the amount of the check in her checkbook ledger, and then before leaving, in a voice lowered so as not to be overheard, asked, "Will you be bringing in more pieces like this?"

"All week long," Fran promised, looking around for Winston. "Come and see us again real soon," Fran said, as their first customer turned and without even a second glance at Scarlet's or Zelda's stuff, marched her check over to the boys at the front.

Mildred watched it all happen and then deducted 32% from the price and divided the remainder by two. "I would have to write a lot of devotionals to make that much money," she concluded soberly.

"I don't know how you have that many words in you," Fran said, her hand busy with the cloth again as she readied the chest of drawers for Winston to collect and transport back to the loading dock.

Mildred sat down in a rocker that was part of the next booth's display and took a deep breath and nodded. Then, for the first time, Mildred looked up at Fran and predicted, surprising herself, "This Emporium idea is going to work, isn't it?"

"You bet it is," Fran said, slapping her hands together. "Now, let's go get the rest of our gold unloaded and see what else we need to bring over here to make our booth look better than anyone else's."

"I didn't realize you were so competitive and ambitious," Mildred said as she began to rock gently. The movement was comfortable, like a boat nestled against the dock of the harbor.

"I've got enough ambition for two people, shoot, maybe even three people," Fran promised, clapping her hands at Winston, who looked up and at Fran as he navigated the corridor with his reloaded two-wheel truck. He was wheeling in the turquoise wingback.

Mildred closed her eyes then as she had a sudden image of how her daddy used to clap his hands together like that and what it felt like to stand in front of that golden goose in the shoe department and wait for the prize to roll down through the chute and land in her hands. The prizes caused an immediate start of joy, but that delight faded quickly. The cheap, plastic prizes dulled quickly and broke easily.

Fran kicked the side of Mildred's rocking chair playfully and said, "Budge, Mildred Budge. You don't want to spend your days in a rocking chair."

Fran smiled to soften that statement. Mildred stood up.

"What do you think about three hundred dollars for this chair?" Fran asked. "That color would make a great accent for a certain kind of room. The upholstery is perfect, and the feet are real wood. Someone will really like that chair."

Mildred didn't mention that the chair was uncomfortable. Fran wasn't really asking her anyway. Her question was another one of Fran's decisions that masqueraded as a question—the kind of question that Fran used like a second language to keep other people who needed to be organized moving.

Mildred nodded and reached for another disposable waxy cloth from the orange packet Fran had brought; and though Mildred Budge really did not like dusting, she got to work shining the turquoise chair's real wood feet.

FOUR

ALWAYS A BEAUTIFUL WIDOW

There was no doubt about it. Liz Luckie made a beautiful widow. She always did.

As the organist played the old version of "Rock of Ages," Liz Luckie sat stoically in the front pew surrounded by members of her Seekers Sunday school class.

Mildred was four pews behind Liz Luckie and close enough to admire the widow's freshly dyed blond hair.

An indentation in the back of Liz's hair recorded that a widow's hat had been tried but ultimately rejected, Mildred saw.

"Do you think she has a wardrobe especially for widowhood that she just rotates the same way you and I switch out our closets from summer to winter? Or maybe she stores her black outfits in a hope chest?" Fran asked tartly, as Mildred noted the stylish big black Audrey Hepburn sunglasses that Liz had selected instead of the traditional widow's veil to hide her grief-filled eyes. "Looks like everyone here is on the groom's side of the family," Fran observed, her gaze sweeping the room.

Mildred shook her head for Fran to be quiet. But Fran was feeling itchy. She had been fond of Hugh, too, and part of her adjustment to the loss of their mutual friend was a kind of acerbic running commentary on the occasion. Mildred took a deep breath and prayed silently that she would not experience one of her heaving crying spells that had blessedly receded in recent months.

Someone passed by Mildred and placed a hand on her shoulder, pressed down in a friendly way, and moved on. Mildred looked up to see Sam Deerborn. His wife Belle leaned over—her breath smelled of garlic-- and whispered, "This too shall pass."

Fran and Mildred nodded affirmatively and watched Belle as she navigated through the crowd of other mourners, catching up with Sam to pay their condolences to Liz, whose shoulders shook slightly as she pressed one of Hugh's white handkerchiefs to her mouth.

"How exactly did the other three husbands die?" Fran rasped. The question came out louder than she intended. The people on the pew in front of them stole quick glances over their shoulders.

"Cancer. Heart attack. Old age," Mildred replied, keeping her face composed. "I'm not sure if they passed in that order...but....cancer, heart attack, and old age." Mildred fought a wave of sadness and tried to change the subject. "That Belle Deerborn told my new neighbor across the street that I have the gift of healing. I wish she wouldn't tell people that."

"That's just Belle talking too much. You don't have the gift of healing," Fran said dismissively. "If you did, we wouldn't have so many people dying all around us."

Fran repeated the litany of words that had taken out Liz's first three husbands. "Cancer, heart attack, and old age," Fran mused, as if the terms were vagaries.

Her own husband Gritz had died of pneumonia in a time when pneumonia was not supposed to kill you. Miracle drugs had failed. Fran had learned how to repeat the words, "It was the will of God," but, occasionally, that benediction which was supposed to put perplexity and bitterness in its place did not succeed.

"They *could* have died of those conditions. They are all natural causes," Mildred said, wondering if Hugh had suffered before dying.

Hot unwelcome tears of an insistent grief brimmed momentarily. Mildred batted them back.

"Liz Luckie is a "Lifetime" movie waiting to happen," Fran said as she took an appraising view of the closed coffin. It wasn't a top-of-the-line model. Hugh could have afforded a Grade-A coffin.

"The thing about death is that it doesn't feel natural at all. You always have to adjust to the surprise of it, no matter how many funerals you attend," Fran said, and then laid the printed funeral service bulletin on the burnt-gold pew cushion beside her.

Sensing that the setting was dredging up a deep reservoir of heartache and loss in Fran, Mildred turned around on the pew and faced her friend. There were no words that could be said to ease Fran's loss. Fran was a widow. She had learned to live without her husband, but she still missed Gritz. Mildred placed her hand upon Fran's and squeezed. Fran attempted a wan smile and said, "At least Hugh died in his sleep."

Looking up at Mildred, Fran added, "They performed an autopsy anyway."

"They won't find anything," Mildred predicted, as the song shifted to "Shall We Gather at the River?"

"Doesn't mean Liz is not guilty of something," Fran replied flatly. "We just don't know what it is."

Mildred shook her head again as the music finally stopped. Brother Joe ascended to the pulpit. Mildred closed her eyes, tamping down the rising emotions. Once again someone patted her back. This time Mildred didn't look up to see who it was. It was time to pay attention. The restless crowd found a point of stillness and responded gladly as the preacher asked them to recite in unison the 23rd psalm.

Mildred didn't remember when or if she had ever sat down and memorized this psalm which was recited at most funerals. The words spilled out.

"Though I walk through the valley of the shadow of death, I will fear no evil."

The psalm reached its conclusion, and the preacher led a prayer. Brother Joe's brightly-lit eyes swept the audience, finally connecting with Mildred; he let them warm as if speaking only to her.

"We have all of us met death in its many forms, and this is one more way—this loss of Hugh Luckie. Most of you already know what I am going to say. Anybody who knew Hugh could say what I am going to say, because he was the same with everybody. If Hugh Luckie was your friend, he was truly your friend. And if you were in that very large circle called Hugh Luckie's friends, you were less lonely than you had ever been before. Hugh Luckie had a way of being with you that was real. When you were with him, you weren't alone in those ways that many of us feel all of our lives off and on and which some of you are feeling again today in a God-honoring, profound way, for our friends are gifts from God, and God has given and now taken away."

The preacher nodded to Mildred and then shifted his gaze to Liz.

"You'll have some rough days ahead, Elizabeth. Today is a hard day. But they won't always be this hard. You know that."

"Boy, does she know that," Fran said darkly.

"You have known loss before. But each loss is fresh and new in its way. Ask Jesus to help you. All of you." Joe's gaze swept over the congregation of mourners. "Jesus has helped you before. Jesus will help you again. Our Jesus is like that. And our Hugh knew Jesus. They are together today in ways that are new and fresh to Hugh and in ways that we who have called upon the name of Jesus as Savior and Redeemer will know too. Praise the Lord. "

"Praise the Lord," the congregation replied, and inside that disciplined response there was a growing sensation of something that could not be reached out and touched but which was felt by Mildred and Fran and others whose shoulders began to relax. Deep breaths were taken. Heads that had been lowered in a kind of mournful defeat were raised.

Sensing the shift, Brother Joe said the words again, "Praise the Lord. Praise Jesus."

"Praise the Lord. Praise Jesus." The congregation repeated after him and began to come to life in a new way, and Mildred was a part of that. She didn't question it. Neither did Fran. Only Liz still looked held together with a kind of invisible barbed-wire.

"Hugh and I never talked about his funeral. Some of you have talked to me about your funerals. Others...." The preacher shook his head, changing his mind about what he was going to say next. "But Hugh didn't tell me the songs to have played or which psalm to read or what to say about him. I could remind you of the biographical facts of his life. But some of those facts—those details-- seem irrelevant now. Don't they? All that stuff we spend so much time building and cultivating and being proud of—."

Joe waited, and the friends of Hugh and Liz Luckie considered the question. It was a sobering idea. It was meant to be.

"Like the flowers of the field, our personal glories fade. What matters is that Hugh Luckie knew the name of Jesus and that he served his Lord in the ways that faithful men do in our church. Hugh was a deacon; he did many important jobs, but the one that stands out to me is one that was never assigned to him. On Saturday afternoons, Hugh swept the church's sidewalk so that people walking into their classrooms on Sunday morning wouldn't skid or trip. If a child was barefoot, he or she wouldn't step on broken glass or hard acorns or rocks because Hugh swept the church sidewalk on Saturday afternoons.

"In meetings when we planned the Mission Conference, which is coming up in three weeks, Hugh would be the first man to suggest that we pray before getting down to the nuts and bolts of the arrangements. He was a praying man, a faithful man, who found his second prayer partner here at church in our Elizabeth, who is grieving today."

Liz's shoulders shook gently again, and people on either side put an arm around her.

"Our Elizabeth is a woman who has known loss."

"Boy, has she known loss," Fran muttered.

Mildred shot her a silencing glance. Fran raised her eye brows innocently in response.

"Liz is a very brave woman who has not let loss stop her from loving again or from choosing life. I pray that she will honor Hugh by continuing to be that brave woman Hugh loved and married."

"Look out number five," Fran whispered to the heads of the people in front of them.

Across the room, Belle turned and stared at Fran, who shrugged.

"If you do not know the Jesus that Hugh Luckie served--if the words I am saying don't make sense to you—that's perfectly reasonable. For if you have not accepted the promises of God to be reconciled to your Maker in Jesus Christ these words about him as a Savior and as a very present help in time of trouble don't add up. If they don't make sense to you, that's fantastic. In fact, be thankful for your confusion. Be alert. That confusion means that you are being prompted to reconsider who you are and who Jesus is, and anyone in the room who knows Jesus would like to answer that question with you.

"And Hugh would be glad to know that today—this sad and glorious day that the Lord hath made—is the day of your salvation. Salvation is an old-timey word that simply means you don't have to live out this life alone. You were not created to live like that. If you are lonely and losing your appetite to be with people, talk to me. I'll tell you more about the One who can change you into the person you were born to become with Him and in Him, and you will meet the Love that never fails."

And then the old preacher raised his hands, smiling now, his face a-lit with a joy that defied the physical reality of the moment.

The crowd stood and sang, "I come to the garden alone while the dew is still on the roses. And the voice I hear falling on my ear, the Son of God discloses. And He walks with me, and He talks with me, and He tells me I am His own. And the joy we share as we tarry there, none other has ever known."

The pallbearers moved up to the waxy brown casket and lined up on either side. Mildred saw that they were the men from the Gathering of the Saints fellowship group that didn't like the confinement of a Sunday school classroom. Mildred knew four of them. They met for coffee while their wives went to class.

There was Sandra's husband Mitch Harper, who was a detective with the Alabama Bureau of Investigation, and Wallace Tidmore, whose wife was a good friend of Mildred's, and Jake Diamond, the building superintendent at the local university and the first black man to start attending Christ Church. Hovering authoritatively nearby was Sam Deerborn, the retired military colonel, who was signaling where each pallbearer was to stand alongside the coffin.

The remaining two men were young deacons who had been tapped to help carry the casket and get their hands-on training in the never-ending church business of funerals.

All six men were dressed in dark suits with white shirts and dark ties, and each man held himself in a stance of composed strength that had always made Mildred Budge feel secure. For all of the on-going arguments about the division of labor in a church divided by gender, it never failed to comfort Mildred Budge to see men who served at times like these.

The congregation waited for the widow to leave first. Fran and Mildred stood in attendance as Liz filed out after the casket. Still, the congregation did not move.

"Come on, Mildred," Fran said, tugging at her friend's arm.

Dully, in a stupor that was unfamiliar to her, Mildred clasped her classic brown leather Grace Kelly handbag and moved out of the pew and down the center aisle after Liz. When they were almost at the end, the rest of the congregation shifted to exit.

Talking began.

Mildred walked on outside and headed to her red and black Mini-Cooper so that she and Fran could join the funeral procession and follow the hearse to the gravesite. Once she was in the car, Mildred looked over at Fran. "Why wouldn't they move until you did?"

"They weren't waiting for me, Mildred Budge. They were waiting for you," Fran explained simply, staring ahead. "Mildred, Liz is Hugh's widow—and he must have loved her-- but you were the one." Fran turned then and said consolingly to the surprised Mildred Budge, "Everyone knew that Hugh loved you dearly, Mildred, except, it appears, you and Liz."

FIVE

COME PLAY WITH ME

"The boy is playing his computer game right now. It's kind of hard to get him to stop. That's why we need help, Miss B.," Kenny said when he opened his front door and found Mildred Budge standing there.

Kenny appeared to be wearing the same pair of jeans he had worn before when he had come to visit her and the same T-shirt. Or maybe he had several Cereal Killer T-shirts. The whiskery patch at his chin was not any longer, and Miss Budge had the most amazing thought that he trimmed it to look exactly the way it did: thin and unkempt. Undefined.

Mildred stepped through into the dark house out of the sunlight and into the gloomy confines of a living room that was a mess.

"Linda-girl, we've got company. Miss B. is here." Kenny had apparently decided to call Mildred by her last initial since distinguishing between budge and bulge was too much of a tongue twister for him.

Linda, dressed in the same outfit as her husband, was sitting on the black futon, and her face immediately registered anxiety. And perhaps displeasure. Mildred had the distinct impression that Linda did not think they needed some help from the older lady across the street who was likely to become a nuisance now that she knew the way to their house.

Mildred tried to smile reassuringly—a friendly smile that would make Linda feel safe in her own house-- while she prayed inwardly, `Help me to be a help, Jesus.'

Kenny was oblivious to the instant tension between the two women.

"The boy is in his room. We can't get Chase to come out this time of day," Kenny said bluntly.

When Linda shot her husband a look that said, *shut up*, Kenny shrugged and added, "It's the truth. That's why we asked you to help."

Only *we* hadn't asked. Only Kenny had asked, and his wife didn't look happy about it at all.

"My son comes out for lunch," Linda interjected, standing up. She was pale, as if she needed to spend some time in the sun, and Miss Budge noted that there was a stain of some kind on the front of her matching Cereal Killer T-shirt. Reading the expression on her husband's face, the frazzled young mother relented and added, "Sometimes."

Linda pointed toward a dark room where the sight of her son's small back was illuminated in front of a computer screen. "He's in there if you want to talk to him."

"Couldn't *we* talk first?" Miss Budge asked Linda. "And perhaps switch on a light? My eyes aren't what they used to be."

The request caused a stricken expression to pass over the younger woman's face; it was the response of someone being summoned to the principal's office for misbehavior. Miss Budge regretted that. Often her speech to younger adults had the effect of a disciplinarian, when really, Miss Budge was simply trying to talk.

"I don't have much time for house cleaning. I run our home business, you know," Linda said, her youthful single chin jutting upward. She needed a haircut and some new clothes. The younger woman had the appearance of someone who had forgotten herself.

Miss Budge recognized Linda's condition: she was a caregiver for her special son, and Mildred thought, perhaps her young husband as well.

"Women these days have too much to do. I don't know how you do it all. Don't worry about your house," Miss Budge assured the younger woman.

Linda tried to smile then, but only her mouth contorted. Her eyes were filled with pain and shadows.

"You want a soda?" Linda asked suddenly. "It's got sugar in it." She laughed self-consciously. "We like sugar even though we sell health food."

"I'm not thirsty," Miss Budge replied truthfully. "Is your organic cereal business thriving?"

"We're making it," Linda replied defensively, sitting back down on the futon.

Kenny perched on the edge of a seedy old recliner that was apparently loaded down with stacks of mail that had been left there day after day. As if an urge to tell the unvarnished truth had suddenly come upon him, Kenny announced, "Linda may have to go back to work if things don't get better. Our boy needs to be in school, but he can't do well in school if he won't talk," Kenny explained. "That's one of the main reasons we need you to do something."

Mildred Budge understood. Linda was not home-schooling Chase because she believed in that choice. It was her only choice. Chase was most likely a special needs child who had not been mainstreamed and now perhaps could not be.

Kenny stood up suddenly. "I'll go check my e-mail orders and let you two girls get to know each other."

Mildred nodded okay, and Linda shot Kenny a desperate look that faded as soon as he was gone. Once Kenny was out of ear shot, the dam broke, and Linda began to talk openly and feverishly with

Miss Budge. Once she had someone to listen to her, Chase's frustrated mother did not stop talking for forty minutes.

Miss Budge was afraid that soon the young woman would notice that her uh-huhs had changed to, "Oh my" and then to her last resort, "Goodness!" By the time Linda got to the part of the story where she had said yes to marrying Kenny when they learned they were pregnant, Miss Budge had begun to wriggle uncomfortably on a chair where she had eventually sat down without being invited because it was the only place to sit that didn't have something piled high on it.

It was a strange rattan chair shaped like a big bowl that held a massive cushion, and Miss Budge was worried that she might not be able to get out of it again.

"I better go check on the boy," Linda said suddenly, as if running out of steam. "He's got to be thirsty by now."

"Why don't I do that for you?" Miss Budge inquired gently, preparing herself to get up out of the chair. Her left foot had gone to sleep; and when she moved, the bowl of the chair seemed to tip with the movement of her weight. "Why don't you sit down and read that magazine and relax? I know little boys," Miss Budge assured Linda as she struggled awkwardly to her feet. She made it with a single groan and pretended not to need to stamp her left foot, which was now tingling uncomfortably as the blood rushed back to it.

"Relax?" Linda asked in wonder. She looked at the stack of magazines about selling organic foods that were piled high on the coffee table and other furniture. Perhaps there would be a less serious magazine somewhere under the pile.

"Little boys don't scare me," Miss Budge promised the young mother, and she smiled, as if to prove that she didn't always sound like a school principal. And having said that, Mildred tugged at her shirt, adjusted her bra strap as surreptitiously as possible, and went to the kitchen. She found a glass that could have been clean, filled it with water and carried it to the dark room where the small boy sat with his back to the world.

"Excuse the mess!" Linda whispered hoarsely after Miss Budge, and then the young mother fell back against the black cushions of the futon that had seen better days; and as if she had just run a marathon and could finally stop, Linda began to take deep breaths of air.

The boy ignored Miss Budge at first. His eyes were fixed on the flickering computer screen. His right hand moved the mouse as he played. Miss Budge repeated his name, "Chase. Chase. Chase."

No answer.

Miss Budge increased the volume of her speech and said, "Hello. Hello."

The boy's aloofness could be an undiagnosed hearing problem.

She tried his name again. "Chase? Chase?"

Nothing.

Miss Budge drew closer and placed a hand on his uncombed hair. She felt the shape of his head. It was a good shape. She had forgotten how fine a child's hair could be. In that moment the school teacher remembered a thousand young children over the years running on the playground, the sunlight catching their hair and lighting it up.

She experienced again the yearning to know how their lives had turned out—and that heavy grief, too, for she had seen them in families with problems—so many problems that it appeared their futures would always be anchored to the past. And because the other adults in their lives—the teachers like Miss Budge—were limited by their own weaknesses, they often failed the children too.

Miss Budge had tried to finish her race, but she had failed to reach the finish line. She had just stopped. Quit. Retired. *'Jesus, I'm sorry,'* she prayed, as she used her forefinger and middle finger to press on the muscle at the nape of Chase's neck.

He tilted his head responsively to the left. His right hand released the mouse.

Miss Budge reached around Chase and pressed the "off" button on the computer screen. The screen's light went out. She leaned down close to the boy's ear so that her breath was in his ear.

"Come with me," she said gently. "Come and see."

Chase didn't move. Instead, he grew stiff and made himself heavy the way children who fought learning often did, holding themselves back against being tested for fear they couldn't pass the test. Miss Budge could feel that something inside of him went into hiding, deep, deep within himself where the dark shadows of the room fit the darkness of his aloneness. Miss Budge understood it, but she didn't know the name for the condition. There were not enough clinical names for the many conditions of the children she had known through the years. Some were classified as hyperactive or slightly autistic or learning disabled or reading disabled, but the terms that medical people used did not cover the undercurrent of emotional needs that were often inside the condition as well. The medications doctors often prescribed as an antidote sometimes dulled the symptoms without solving the problem.

"Help me to be a help, Jesus," Miss Budge prayed again. She inhaled, then breathed again, and her breath grew deep. With each breath, Miss Budge felt a calm rise up in her, warm her, and spread from her heart through her hands and to her face, which relaxed in a way that it didn't when she was Miss Budge, church lady. Miss Budge, the school teacher, had a different face. And in the beginning of her career and for a long time, the school teacher's face had been a genuinely happy one.

Miss Budge tapped the boy's shoulder repeatedly with one finger, as if establishing a beat for movement.

The repeated tapping didn't move Chase, but Miss Budge could feel the boy thinking about it. A part of the child began to resurface, but not as talk or as an actual presence in the room.

Miss Budge placed both hands under his arms and lifted the boy, shifting his body to turn away from the computer. Finally, the boy stood up unsteadily. But the child wouldn't meet her gaze, and his hands hung down at his sides limply. His knees stayed bent. The school teacher reached down and took his hand and led him quietly out of the room.

They passed Linda, who was now prostrate on the couch. Miss Budge recognized the young mother's condition, too; it was a fatigue so great that she hadn't known it was there until someone offered her a respite.

"Chase is going home with me for a while," Miss Budge announced. "I'll bring him back later," she promised. "You keep resting. You need it."

Linda had gone into that silence that was so deep she couldn't even say, thank you. Her eyes followed them out of the room, and then Linda allowed the current of her fatigue to overtake her and carry her out to that place she had not dared go before: to the place of acknowledgement, where she had to admit she had gone too far alone.

Out in the daylight, Miss Budge could see the boy's eyes. The pupils were still dilated from being so long in the dark. But as his eyes began to adjust to the light, Miss Budge saw that Chase had his daddy's eye color: a light shade of blue that reflected the color of whatever he wore.

The boy's clothes were days old, and he needed a bath.

Her observations were not judgmental. Chase was a boy who needed attention. The conclusion brought Miss Budge to attention, tapping into something deep inside of her that had been dormant for two years. It was a familiar sensation of being needed, and she did not resist it any more than Linda had stopped herself from going into that zone of acknowledged fatigue.

Miss Budge heard her phone ringing before she opened the front door. Chase looked surprised by the loud sharpness of the sound. Miss Budge was glad that the sound startled him. It was a positive sign. Chase's response answered one question: the problem wasn't in his hearing.

Chase looked baffled as he stood inside Miss Budge's house. His large eyes shifted focus, slowly, moving from one point of interest to the next. He studied the pictures above him of bridges.

That was good, too, Miss Budge observed. He had the capacity to be aware. That moment of his attention to the new surroundings did not last for long. Chase saw her silent TV in the other room and walked through the living room to the den. He plopped down onto the floor in front of the dark screen and grunted.

Miss Budge ignored the ringing phone and went to the kitchen, where she began rattling pots and pans. She opened the cupboard doors and closed them loudly.

The boy barked in the living room. She ignored it.

Chase barked again.

She went to the den. "One. Two. Three. Four. Five," she counted, as she tapped Chase on the shoulder with each number. "Come with me. Come and see."

Chase stood up uncertainly, not moving at first. She tapped his shoulder again, and then he followed her with shuffling feet to the reading room where stacks of children's books waiting to be reviewed by Miss Budge for the *Library Journal* were piled high. She sat down in her reading chair and opened a book with a bright red cover. Chase stared at her blankly. She held up the open book and asked, "What do you see?"

The boy grunted more quickly this time, which Miss Budge decided was another sign of progress.

After three books and three more grunts, Miss Budge puckered her lips and wished regretfully that she had some red lipstick on because it was funnier with lipstick. She sucked in her cheeks and crossed her eyes while she made a sound that most children found very satisfying.

Chase stared blankly, tipping his head to the side as if he wanted to look inside her mouth and could see better from that angle.

Next, Miss Budge whistled a long-held, single-pitch note.

Curiosity surfaced in the boy's light blue eyes.

Miss Budge let the long note escape again. On the next breath, she whistled the opening bars of the old song, "I've been working on the railroad."

Chase didn't blink in recognition. He didn't know the tune. But the boy watched her mouth in wonder to see what she would do next. He stepped closer. Miss Budge reached an arm up around him in a loose embrace. Then she sang,

"London bridge is falling down. Falling down. Falling down. London bridge is falling down. My fair laddie." As if she were twenty years younger, Miss Budge dropped to the floor with a harrumph, and the little boy, surprised, plopped down beside her. She giggled. Chase cocked his head.

She sang the song slowly again, and this time, with no room to fall, she simply raised her shoulders and let them fall. Holding her gaze, Chase raised his shoulders and let them fall.

Sitting in a huddle with her on the floor, Chase wriggled closer, his eyes averted as if he didn't want her to know how close he had gotten. She did not move closer to him; the retired school teacher waited for him to establish the boundaries. They sat there together adjusting to the new sensation of being close while she tried to think of another song.

"Let's go to the piano," she said, pointing toward the dark Baldwin upright that she had owned for forty years. It was still in very good shape, for with the exception of the time when her parents had been ill and she had been so absorbed in caring for them that she had forgotten about the piano, Miss Budge had kept it tuned annually. After their deaths, she had called in the piano tuner. She had not seen Mr. Belvedere in four years; but when she was finally able to call him to come, he arrived still wearing his signature red plaid vest with a black bow tie. He had maintained a petite, tidy black moustache that repeated the bow shape under his nose.

Sitting with his plump derriere on her padded piano bench, Mr. Belvedere had asked the same question he always had: "Which tone do you prefer—brassy or mellow?"

Something perverse inside Miss Budge had kicked in, and desiring a change in her routine, she had replied, surprising herself and the piano tuner, "Oh, brassy, I think, for a change."

Mr. Belvedere must have been waiting for years for Mildred to say that, because he had an immediate response. Turning immediately, Mr. Belvedere had taken hold of her hand and said without preamble, *"Ahhhhhh....Now you and I could make beautiful music together, my Mildred."*

She had instantly withdrawn her hand and said, "No, we cannot."

She hadn't seen Mr. Belvedere since and couldn't call him again to tune her piano. He would have misunderstood.

Leading the boy by his hand, Miss Budge walked over to the piano, wondered whom she could call to tune it now instead of Mr. Belvedere, and lifted the heavy lid. She trilled a few notes with her right hand.

Chase stood beside her, staring at the white keys first, then the black keys.

"Do you sing?" she asked, playing the first few bars of "Jesus Loves Me."

Chase stared up at her, more light growing in his eyes as his curiosity intensified. Miss Budge smiled, was tempted to make the fish face again, but decided not to distract him with too much stimulation. *One thing at a time.* She then played the Middle C octave, one note after another very slowly. It made a very nice complete sound, moving from one C to the home sound of the next C in the higher octave. She repeated it. The next time, she played the first seven notes only, letting the last completing note hang unplayed, unresolved in the air. The tension to find resolution was irresistible. Finally, after she played the seven notes again and again, Chase reached over and with one small, delicate finger played the correct eighth note to complete the sound of the octave as a whole. Then, as his finger rested on the note while the sound hummed in the air, Chase looked up at Miss Budge to see what she would do.

Miss Budge smiled broadly, the light in her brown eyes glowing with approval as she ruffled his golden brown hair. "Young Master Chase. You are a smart boy. A very smart boy."

Chase's face didn't register the meaning of what Miss Mildred said. She catalogued his response: it was as if he were watching her, as if she were a program or a character on the TV. The realization felt dehumanizing to her. But Chase was the one in some kind of interior quicksand.

"I am not going to let you go all the way down. I am going to pull you up and plant you on firm ground," she promised Chase, as if announcing a lesson plan.

Chase didn't know what the teacher was talking about.

Miss Mildred returned his watchful gaze, and declared truthfully, "I wish I had some bubblegum in the house. I believe no one has ever taught you how to blow a bubble."

Chase's gaze faded back into a benign lack of expression; and suddenly, the lack of animation was more than Miss Budge could bear. She reached over and placed her arms around Chase and drew him to her. His body was rigid at first inside that embrace; but as her hand rubbed the center of Chase's back and moved up to the nape of his neck and massaged that muscle, the strain of reserve and watchfulness receded in the child. Seconds later, the small boy's chest rose and fell dramatically, and then, his small arms went up and wrapped around Miss Budge's shoulders. The little boy who liked to sit by himself in a shadowy room with a computer held on tightly to Miss Budge.

SIX

RAIDING THE MISSIONS CLOSET

Mildred passed the gray metal wall rack with all the brochures and pamphlets on it that members and visitors were invited to pick up on their way to the sanctuary or Sunday school. You could read up on baptism, election, and a number of topics that used the word millennium now. None of the brochures' subjects were on the top of Mildred's to-think-about list. The topics were on a secondary list that Mildred mentally filed under "paradoxes of belief" that she might get around to evaluating if she lived long enough.

She dallied by the rack when she saw a new manila pamphlet bordered in black that had been added to the collection: "Preparing for Death." Underneath the title was the sub-heading, "How to Build the Kingdom Through Your Bequests to the Church." It should have read: "How to leave your money to the church in such a way that your expectant and now bitter relatives cannot have the will revoked."

Mildred didn't take a brochure. She had a grave plot bought, her will was up to date, and Fran knew to request "What a Friend We Have in Jesus" as the congregational hymn. Additionally, the two best friends knew the other's 'If-I die-before-you-do instructions, here's what I want you to do at my house.' When the time had come, her best friend was to get herself over to her house and do what a best friend did before even the pallbearers were called: make sure that the kitchen counters were wiped down and that there were fresh hand towels in the bathrooms before the visitors whose job it was to roam through the house of the newly deceased traipsed through for an inspection of the goods that needed to be distributed to remaining relatives or marked for an estate sale.

Mildred didn't know what Fran would think when she found Mildred's secret jar of bacon grease that she used for cooking, but Mildred knew what Fran would do. Her best friend would quietly, discreetly throw the jar away in a trash can not associated with Mildred's house. And Fran would pour out the small decanter of sherry Mildred kept in her upper right kitchen cabinet behind the Maxwell House coffee. When Fran found the small Coca-Colas in the fruit drawer of the fridge, she would wonder who had drunk those because Mildred Budge was not supposed to be drinking carbonated beverages. Fran knew that. But Mildred let herself have a small Coke from time to time.

Except for these small artifacts of life that Mildred counted on Fran to handle after she was gone, Mildred Budge was prepared to be found dead any day of the week, though hopefully not naked like Cleo, and she did not need a brochure named "Preparing for Death." She knew Jesus, and she was ready.

Underneath the rack was a cardboard box that had once held cans of Dinty Moore stew and which now contained the materials that were arriving for the ministry displays for the Missions Conference. The church spent a lot of money on printed materials for the conference, and Mildred wondered what percentage of the occasionally controversial Faith Promise pledge was designated for the cost of printing publications. Some members of the church didn't like the tithes to be spent that way. Other church members were great advocates of publications that spread words about the Word.

The glossier the paper, the better. This particular controversy concerning the amount of money spent on publications belonged on another 'I-could-think-about-it but-I-don't-want-to' list that Mildred regularly crossed a line through when the question occurred. It was irrelevant to her. Blessedly, approving of how the elders and deacons spent church funds wasn't her good work to do. The responsibility for decisions about how church funds were allocated had been offered to and accepted by elders who had been voted into their positions of authority within the church, and they would ultimately be held accountable by God for how they did their work. That was enough for Mildred, who didn't worry about arguments like that anymore than she fretted over the regular arrival of utility bills; they kept coming and they had to be paid.

Mildred Budge paid her utilities promptly and dutifully supported missionaries sponsored by the church. Dragging the net around the world was work that had to be done. The long-time church lady knew all of the arguments about original missionaries who reportedly supported themselves through some kind of profession like fishing or tent-making work, but her church had sorted out the various aspects of individual missionaries' callings and allied with the organizations that recruited and managed them. She was grateful for the structure in the same way that she liked tithing. Free will was not all it was cracked up to be. Submission was simpler.

"Give me a good commandment any day of the week, and I'll obey it with gratitude," she whispered to Jesus.

Yes, obedience in the church had its benefits. There were always the small rubs, like negotiating other tasks known inside the church as doing your good works. The question for any believer was: which good works are mine to do?

Each person had to find out those good works for herself and do them. And that did not mean that other people could point out tasks for her to accomplish by calling them her assigned-by-God good works. Mildred drew a firm line by saying, no, when people looked at her life and tried to assign her their good works to do, as if delegating good works was a good work. Mildred Budge had scant patience with people who called themselves idea people or inspired-by-God people and who shrugged off their responsibilities by telling other people what to do. They were the God-told-me-to-tell-you to-do-this people. She had met her share of them, listened to them, and walked away from them without guilt. Mildred had her own leadings from the Lord about the good works appointed for her to do. They were her responsibility just as it was her responsibility to learn how to discern the Lord's leading. She had felt led to create the mission's clothes closet: a small room in the building where members of the congregation could deposit their best used clothes and to which missionaries could help themselves during the conference.

There wasn't a verse in the Bible about having a mission's clothes closet, but the idea of recycling good clothes for the visiting missionaries made sense to Mildred Budge. It didn't feel like work to her either. She liked tidiness. She enjoyed keeping the donated clothes in order and the closet ready to be perused. Garments could be selected for use by missionaries who needed respectable clothes and who were coming to the annual Missions Conference soon to offer reports, raise monthly support, and find refreshment in all kinds of ways, including adding to their wardrobes.

The door to her missions' closet was open. That surprised Mildred. The light was on, too. When Mildred was close enough to peer inside, she felt a strange sensation in her stomach, as if she had been kicked. Someone had emptied some of the hangers, shoved other hangers back, and made a gaping hole where once her arrangement of the clothes had been. Vandals or thieves going through the mission's closet! In a church! Mildred had heard of such a thing and even the news reports of thieves stealing the copper tubing from industrial-sized air conditioning units at churches, but it was hard to believe that someone had broken into the church and vandalized the mission's clothes closet. She remembered the video camera on the outside of the building and understood: the church was a natural target for a roaring lion bent on devouring or destroying, and it appeared that he had gotten into the mission's closet.

Mildred spotted some of the discarded clothes right away. Apparently, she had caught the devil in the act, and he must have made a run for it, leaving behind the goodies' bag. For at Mildred's feet was a black plastic lawn bag—the kind you put winter leaves in on the floor. Some of the garments had been balled up and jammed into it. Mildred leaned over. One of her own contributions, a white blouse she considered a better blouse—a white polyester blend that had worn like iron and that she had donated after a great deal of soul-searching--had been stuffed in the garbage bag. It still looked brand new, and it had been a sacrifice to let it go. Mildred had its twin hanging in the closet at home. She planned to wear the other blouse during the Missions Conference at the ladies' luncheon with a pair of black slacks.

As if it were a small kitten being rescued from certain death, Mildred lifted up her donated blouse and placed it on a hanger. As she did, she saw Liz Luckie walking down the hallway toting a brown leather suitcase that kept beating against her left leg with each step she took. Mildred wanted to call out to Liz and warn her, `Watch out! Intruders could still be nearby!' But once again, Mildred was made mute by noting how surprisingly wonderful Liz looked.

Like her non-widow clothes, Liz's black pantsuit was fashionable and sophisticated. Liz had tied a glamorous red and gold scarf around her throat and fixed it in place with a diamond-studded clasp. Mildred didn't wear jewelry very often because she didn't remember jewelry until she saw someone else wearing it; but when the idea of jewelry did surface, Mildred discovered inside herself a weak-kneed desire for diamonds that her inherited Eisenberg Original rhinestone brooch could not satisfy.

Instantly, Mildred felt a start of envy at the sight of the sparkling diamond brooch at Liz's neck, and the general and familiar pall associated with feeling outclassed settled upon her. Mildred clutched her own exposed throat and wondered if she should explore the advantages of wearing a scarf there. Her rhinestone brooch at home was too big and heavy to use with the delicate material of scarves.

"Hello, Mildew."

"Mildred," Mildred replied tightly. Liz Luckie knew what her name was.

"That's what I said," Liz replied, lowering the suitcase in front of the open closet. "I've been working in here this morning. It was a mess."

Mildred had seen her missions closet a week ago. Her mission's closet had not been a mess. She squinted, discomfited, and attempted to adjust to the idea that it had not been vandals or thieves who had destroyed the work of her hands but the very woman who had stolen Hugh Luckie. Thinking of Hugh gone—gone forever--caused Mildred's eyes to mist over. Mildred attempted to hide her emotions by replacing her retrieved blouse on a hanger and then fastening the top button on the blouse.

Liz made a small expression of dismay at the sight of the blouse back on the hanger.

"What is it?" Mildred asked, reading her expression.

Liz bent down, and snapped open the suitcase that was neatly packed with carefully folded garments, most of them men's clothes. She looked up at Mildred, her blue eyes astonishingly vivid.

"It's nothing," Liz said. "I was only wondering if we might weed out some of these pieces that are so long out of style that it would be embarrassing to have a missionary that represents our church wear them anywhere in the world."

Mildred silently counted to three. "Might keep someone warm," she replied tersely.

"That old-fashioned mink jacket would keep someone warm. But I can't believe that any missionary with a sense of style will actually take that fur jacket and wear it somewhere."

"No missionary in his right mind would wear or let his wife wear a mink jacket. It's hard to raise financial support from churches while you're wearing mink. Nobody will believe you need the money," Mildred snapped. Then, she repented. Liz was a new widow: a vain widow who was not privy to the inner tensions still part of the back stories of so many ministries inside the church.

The mink jacket had belonged to Thelma Boartfield, who had left her entire household goods to the church. The ladies who had organized the estate sale could not bear to hang Thelma's jacket outside on a Saturday morning to be pawed by strangers who would offer a measly ten dollars for it. Instead, they had hung it in the mission's closet, and no missionary had ever been fool enough to take it. The jacket was now a problem no one wanted to solve.

"This poor mink jacket is not getting any younger," Liz said. "They should have just buried the old lady it belonged to in it."

Mildred's jaw dropped. Thelma Boartfield had not been much older than Mildred or Liz when she died. Mildred still missed Thelma. It had taken six months after her death for anyone to sit in the regular spot on the left side of the sanctuary on the fifth pew from the front where Thelma had always sat. People left her place in the sanctuary vacant out of respect the way sometimes people who have lost a family member continue to set a place at the family dining table. Thelma had been remembered in other ways, too. Thelma's signature banana pudding was still made on the final night of the Missions Conference. The girls took turns making Thelma's pudding. It was Belle's turn this year.

Liz slipped Thelma's jacket off the hanger and slid her arms through it. She ran her manicured hands up the front, pressing the neckline higher and higher until it was under her powdered chin. She closed her eyes, leaned her head back, and inhaled with satisfaction.

"Mink does make a girl feel safe," she said. "Of course, it's too big for me," she said, shrugging off the fur and placing it back on the hanger.

The fur jacket hadn't looked that big on her.

"It's more your size," Liz said. "Why don't you try it on?"

"I'm not a missionary," Mildred replied, staring at the mink jacket. "We should have sold it when it was first donated and put the funds in the missions account," Mildred concluded finally. It was what Thelma would most likely have wanted. "What are you doing here today, Liz?"

Liz smiled wanly. "Hugh had all these clothes, and the church has so many missionaries coming from out of town; and I thought if I put his clothes in here, someone might like them and use them. His closet had to be cleaned out some time, and this job doesn't get easier to do over time, so I just got up this morning and decided to do it."

Mildred swallowed hard and with a kind of grudging admiration. It was the practical and tough decision a seasoned church lady would make. "You shouldn't have to do that job alone, Liz. Any one of us would have come over and cleaned out the closet for you."

Even as she said the words, Mildred knew that Liz didn't have a friend like that in the church, and she obviously hadn't felt free to ask anyone. The plain truth was: men liked Liz, and women did not.

"I have to do something. I can't just sit at home and do nothing. What do you do with your days since you retired? Doesn't time pass slowly?" Liz asked, continuing to lift out garments and smooth them, then hang them up. Her hands found a blue flowery Hawaiian shirt. Liz smiled when she lifted it out. "Hugh and I wore these matching Hawaiian shirts on our honeymoon. We didn't go to Hawaii. I had already been twice before. We just drove down to Point Clear and stayed at The Grand Hotel on the gulf. It was almost back to normal since the hurricane." Liz caressed a large sterling silver heart-shaped pin that was still affixed to the woman's matching sea-blue Hawaiian shirt. Liz's blue shirt was a shade lighter than Hugh's. "This sweetheart pin held a big silk orchid on my shirt. I kept the flower. I can't keep the pin or my shirt either. Maybe a missionary couple will take them and wear them where I don't have to see them again."

Mildred reached for the shirt. "You shouldn't have to hang this up." Mildred felt wrong touching it, but she couldn't resist either. It was a `dry clean only' shirt. Extravagant. Mildred never bought any article of clothing she couldn't launder herself. Paying five dollars an item to dry clean something was like never really owning a garment outright. It was more like renting it.

"Are you sure you don't want to keep your matching shirt? You could let Hugh's go," Mildred asked, and she had the strangest thought of taking Hugh's shirt home and using it for a summer night gown. The idea shocked her, and the inner voice that prayed without ceasing sent a silent apology to God, *'Sorry.'*

Liz shook her head definitely. "It's better just to let it all go, really. Believe me, Millie, I know."

"I believe you," Mildred said, as she fell into the other woman's rhythm and helped finish unpacking the suitcase of clothes. She had never worked with Liz before. There was a gentleness in Liz's moves and an economy in her motions that revealed a loneliness that was so deep it was expressed like this—carefully, not willing to let her guard down so that others might also see that sometimes the motions of her hands were all that she had to stir the air around her for company.

"It's nice—being here like this," Liz confessed suddenly, timidly.

"Is it?" Mildred inquired, as the light in the closet flickered briefly and went out.

"Oh," Liz said. "I hate it when that happens at the house. It's so hard to change light bulbs when you live alone."

Mildred didn't respond, except to reach up and tighten the bulb with quick twists of her hand because the bulb was hot to the touch. The light returned.

"It jiggles loose sometimes when the building settles or the wind blows, or maybe it's someone walking upstairs, I don't know," she explained to Liz.

Liz nodded seriously as if Mildred had just said something profound. They continued their work and when Liz wasn't paying attention, Mildred took her own old white blouse off the hanger and placed it discreetly back in the lawn bag.

"Sometimes people think a church is only a place where we all get together on Sunday mornings and sometimes Wednesday nights. But for other people, it's the only place left that feels like home," Liz confessed suddenly.

Mildred looked around. She had her own key to the church building. She had her own set of chores—a routine of responsibilities at the church that she enjoyed maintaining, but she didn't see church life as a replacement for a personal life. It was simply another part of her life.

Mildred knew what was in the church pantry, how well the clean-up crew actually cleaned up and where she or one of the Bereans needed to come back and use a Brill-O pad and scrub the drain in the sink and around the faucet handles. She knew how to use the industrial-sized oven and why, occasionally, there was an oven-mitt fire. One of the burners was tilted, and you had to learn how to hold your hand just so to avoid catching it on fire.

Mildred knew where the vacuum cleaner was stored, and she knew which height should be used on its floor roller for the nap of the church carpet. She knew where the small silver wrench was stored, and she knew how to use it when the garbage disposal jammed.

Mildred knew where the extra rolls of paper towels were, where the toilet tissue was stored (they bought it by the hundred-roll box) and where the various sizes of light bulbs were kept. She knew how to take one out and put a new bulb in every light fixture all over the building. Mildred Budge was not afraid of burned-out light bulbs. She knew how to change them.

"Yes," Mildred agreed, after taking her mental inventory. "It is a second home."

"Hugh loved it here," Liz said, and there was a small whimper inside the mention of his name. Just that quick, Mildred could have fallen on her knees and sobbed the way she used to after coming home from teaching school. All the faces, unmet needs and neglect of the students would overwhelm her, and she would cry and cry and cry.

Taking a deep breath, Mildred repressed the memory and said, "I'm sorry about Hugh. That must have been quite a shock." Her voice sounded colder than she felt. It was the tone of voice she had used as a teacher when one of her students had mentioned that a grandparent or other family member had died. School teachers heard many sad stories.

Liz didn't answer at first. When she finally did, the widow's voice sounded small and scared, like a child's.

"Do you ever see things, Millie?"

"What kind of things?" Mildred asked, working the colors of the garments around so that the reds were sorted with other reds and the blues were matched with other blues.

Liz began to do the same, nodding in agreement that she understood the organizational strategy and explained, "Like out of the corner of your eyes. Flashing shapes?"

"Of course," Mildred said.

"And then when you look hard, nothing is there?" Liz asked, hopefully.

"Sometimes something is there. But light can play tricks on you. And as we get older, we have more and more floaters in our eyes. Those black things that squiggle by when you hold your head a certain way? I swat at floaters sometimes, thinking they're some kind of insect."

"I don't like seeing things that aren't there. I don't like getting older, and there's nothing I can do about it," Liz said soberly.

"I don't mind getting older," Mildred replied truthfully. "And there are a lot of things about it I really like."

"What is there to like?" Liz asked. The light bulb seemed to glow brighter, and Mildred saw that Liz was very young inside and that she would always stay that way.

As if Liz were one of her former school children, Mildred considered how to respond. Mildred knew that she could not say to Liz what Fran would have understood instantly: that a practiced faith resulted in a very real hope, and hope itself is priceless. A lived-out trust in God was incomparable—made any place you were home. And often there was a kind of joy that bubbled inside the serenity that is given by God in what He calls entering His rest. There was less fear of pain, but sometimes there was a deeper experience of more kinds of pain, like the grief Mildred had known before she had suddenly retired because she could not bear the children's pain. But Jesus was always there, and Mildred Budge was increasingly less afraid of pain and of the tears that were not coming as often now. It felt to her as if she was almost cried out.

When Mildred was her best self, there was a deep sense of awe at the complexity of life and in so many instances, its simplicity. Some days, she woke up happy. Often, she went to bed feeling snug and safe. These days, since her retirement, she felt somehow like she was getting well from some illness that had never been diagnosed by a medical professional who might have called it depression or menopause. Mildred wasn't depressed, and she was not defeated by menopause. She simply felt from time to time a grief that needed to be expressed, and it moved through her like a sudden afternoon thunderstorm. When it did, she cried. The tears were the reason she had stopped working with homebound students. She had reached a point when she could not promise herself that she wouldn't cry in front of the sick children. But she hadn't cried in several days like that, except for Hugh.

Except for Hugh. And she had no right to cry for Hugh. Not really.

Mildred readjusted the last of Hugh's shirts on its hanger, unnecessarily stalling for time as she fired off an emergency prayer to Jesus to help her answer the question that Liz had posed.

Finally, Mildred said, "It's easier just to enjoy each day as it comes—to try and find the adventure in it."

Liz stood up again and nodded thoughtfully. "Do you ever feel like you know something is going to happen before it happens?"

"Sure," Mildred said. "You live long enough, and you feel things like that. You can't explain it, but you feel it."

"I felt funny going to sleep Wednesday night. And when I woke up, Hugh was gone. Just gone. He just left me, like all the others have." Her voice had a self-pitying quality. "I sort of knew Hugh was leaving. I learned that from the others," she explained mysteriously, looking at Mildred as if she could understand.

Mildred nodded, though she did not understand.

"But even if I had admitted that to myself, I couldn't have done anything about it, could I?" Liz peered at Mildred soulfully.

The serial widow felt guilt, and she was confessing to Mildred. What would Fran say?

"Nobody can save anybody," Mildred assured Liz. "We're not in charge of life and death. It's comforting knowing that."

And as Mildred said the words to Liz, a great wedge of ice, like some part of a heavy ice floe that had been trailing her since her retirement when she had deserted all her children, seemed to break off and simply float away.

"It is," Liz agreed readily, as the door in the hallway slammed. They heard footsteps. The two women turned and waited in silence to see who would join them.

"You two gals keeping busy?" Sam Deerborn asked, coming through the side door with his usual determined jollity that often rang false. Sam entered any room as if he expected the troops to stand and salute, and he always appeared not only surprised but disappointed to find himself in the company of civilians. He was a retired Air Force colonel who had liked the discipline of the military and tried to recreate that order at church. He never succeeded.

"Keeping busy is harder than it looks," Liz said, and she aged from bright-eyed child to teary-eyed widow in one breath. "Do you want me to take that trash bag away, Mildred?"

Before Mildred could answer, Sam offered gallantly, "I'll take care of that, Sweetie."

No matter what other people in the church said about Sam's need to be in charge, he was not lazy.

"Thank you, Sam," Liz said, and she smiled at him warmly with appreciation. "Thank you for everything, Sam. I mean, about the funeral. All your help with planning it. I don't know what I would have done without you."

Sam waved away her gratitude, as he scooped up the trash bag. Liz smiled approvingly one more time. "Do you need any more help, Mildred?" she asked, turning back to Mildred.

"Not today," Mildred said. Liz's face fell. Her expression was so pained, her dread of going to her own home was so great that Mildred couldn't refuse to offer her a refuge. "But there will be more clothes coming in. Probably a lot before the conference. People use the missions conference as a motivator to clean out their closets. Could I call on you to help, Liz?"

Liz brightened momentarily. "When do you think that will be?"

Mildred shook her head uncertainly. "I can't predict that, but I'll call you. It can be a lot of work."

"I'm available," Liz said with an intensity that pierced Mildred.

"You're out and about pretty soon, Liz," Sam said, patting her on the shoulder awkwardly. "You doing okay?" He surveyed her crisp pants suit and the colorful scarf. "You look real nice," he approved.

Liz was one of those women who liked to hear a compliment, and Sam was the type of man who believed that it was his duty to give it. Sam never mentioned her appearance to Mildred; she never missed not hearing a compliment.

"Just passing along some of Hugh's clothes," Liz answered, backing toward the door. "The good thing about giving old clothes to missionaries is that they leave the city, and you don't have to see them worn by anyone else again. Call me, Mildred. Ta."

"I will," Mildred promised. She closed the closet doors as Liz disappeared.

Sam and Mildred stayed quiet for a few seconds after Liz left, as if they thought she might listen at the keyhole to what they were going to say. But they weren't going to say anything about her.

Finally, Sam broke the silence, drawing back his shoulders as he planned his strategy of persuasion. "Now don't say no, Mildred."

"Why do people always think I will say no?" Mildred said, moving toward the sanctuary. She always spent some time in the sanctuary after tidying the mission's closet. It was a reward for the labor. She loved the sanctuary when the lights weren't on and there was no one preaching. Mildred Budge loved the quiet when other people weren't there.

Oblivious to her desire to be alone, Sam trailed Mildred into the sanctuary, stopping as he always did to look around and get his bearings. Mildred felt the pace of Sam's movements, which had slowed since his hip replacement surgery a year ago. Like some of the older women and men, Sam was losing his height and his hair. However, he still wore the same type of eye glasses, and they were very similar to Mildred's: brown, plastic, old-fashioned sturdy glasses that could hit the floor and not break. It was not the only kind of eye glasses Cates Optical sold, but Mr. Cates did approve of them.

"Because everyone knows how you feel about busy work, Mildred Budge. But sometimes you don't stop and think that not all work that you don't want to do is busy work."

"A lot of it is," Mildred said, sitting on the first pew. "Do you suppose we have been wrong about Liz? Do you suppose she's just lonely?"

But Sam was planning what he was going to say to Mildred, and he didn't hear the questions.

He spoke more loudly than he needed to after sitting down beside her. "Committee work can be a kind of busy work sometimes, but I'm not here to ask you to be on a committee."

"Good. Because the answer is no," Mildred said with a smile. She closed her eyes to pause and then opened them again. Sam was still there.

Sam flipped open one of the sign-in registers that were passed along on each pew for visitors to sign during the morning service so that the church could follow up with a visit or a phone call, but the page was empty. Frowning, Sam closed the book.

"Mildred Budge, you're the kind of person who does it all, but you don't like to say yes right away. There are times, Mildred Budge, when you are just plain ornery."

The criticism did not displease Mildred. "There are worse things to be called," Mildred commented, unperturbed as she spied a layer of dust on the Lord's table. Why didn't that get dusted regularly? Mildred hated dusting. Still, it needed dusting. The church lady stood up again, walked over to the table, reached around below for the small cotton cloth kept there, and wiped the surface. Sam watched while she worked. Mildred hoped Sam would leave by the time she finished. He didn't. She sat down beside him again.

"That's just what I mean," Sam said. "You're helpful. But you don't want to be seen as helpful. I don't know why. Belle is like that sometimes, too," he added ruminatively.

Sam always made his requests the same way. He worked up to it by offering an employee evaluation first. Mildred waited patiently, exulting in each moment between each spoken word where silence was. She observed her need for silence in that moment: it was like a different kind of thirst. She needed a drink of silence often.

"You are a capable woman, Mildred," Sam began again.

The silence was gone. Mildred took a deep breath and asked, "What do you want, Sam?"

"It's not what I want. It's what the church needs."

"Don't try that with me, Sam," Mildred warned. Sam patted her on the leg in a gesture that suited them. There was no sexual harassment in the move, no resistance on her part to being touched. They were old, old friends who bumped along together in the faith.

"Now don't say no right away, Mildred. At least think about it."

"Just ask it," Mildred said, closing her eyes briefly. She would go home in a few minutes, and the rooms would be clean, the house quiet. There would be shadows and lights that shifted as the day passed. Yes, she could go home and have the twilight to herself in the quiet.

"The Polks have cancelled. They were supposed to host a missionary couple in their home, but they can't now."

The idea dawned slowly in Mildred Budge, and it was an unbelievable idea. "You don't want me to host a missionary couple in my home? You just can't mean that," she confirmed, her voice rife with disbelief. How could any real friend of hers ask her a question like that? Everyone who knew Mildred Budge understood that she did not have the gift of hospitality.

"It's not for long, Millie. The missionaries come in on a Wednesday and leave on Sunday."

"That's four nights and five days. No, Sam. It is most inconvenient. Fran and I have just started a new business, and there's a little boy who lives across the street from me that I'm just getting to know. I will be spending a couple of hours each day with him teaching him to read. Hosting a missionary couple is not my good work to do. Find someone else. Ask Liz," Mildred suggested suddenly. "She's very lonely and would probably like having people in the house."

Sam waved away Mildred's objections. "I know all about The Emporium, and there's no way we're going to ask a new widow to take in company. Besides, Liz might end up crying on their shoulders, and we don't want our missionaries coming here and being burdened. You don't cry, Mildred."

"I don't?" she asked softly, her body finding the stillness where quiet could be.

Unaware that a part of Mildred had retreated and was simply watching herself with Sam, he continued, "You don't have to be at The Emporium very often. We all know how The Emporium works. And you can bring that little boy to the Missions Conference. We'll have some activities for children. You already know that."

"No," Mildred replied staunchly. "What you are proposing is not my good work to do," she repeated firmly.

"Millie, I know you don't like having people in the house, and I know that you think because you don't like having people stay with you that inviting them to stay is not your appointed good work."

"Don't go there, Sam," Mildred warned. "Don't tell me what my good works are."

Sam pressed on relentlessly, like a soldier with a hill to climb where he needed to plant a flag.

"Sometimes we have to do some chores we don't like to do, Mildred Budge. Since Hugh is gone, we're going to have some work gaps to manage until we can get someone to take his list of chores."

"Hugh wasn't scheduled to keep the missionaries. You said the Polks were."

"That's right. But Hugh was in charge of arranging their housing. I'm asking in his place," Sam said, and then he coughed self-consciously. "I don't really mean it like that, Millie," Sam said, his gaze softening. His left eye glass lens had a big smudge on it, and Mildred fought an impulse to go get the dust cloth and wipe Sam's glasses for him.

"I know you don't," Mildred conceded.

"Al and Janie Jones are coming a long way from Seattle. They are a young couple, Mildred, trying to make their way to Bogotá, Columbia to serve the Lord. You know how dangerous Bogotá is. When they are not scheduled for a Missions Conference activity, they will need to visit other churches to try and raise financial support. They wouldn't do much more than sleep at your house, Millie."

"I can't take the noise," Mildred said.

"I'll tell them to pray quietly," Sam replied, allowing his eyes to twinkle.

He almost lost her then. When someone else confessed a need or a weakness, others respected it. When Mildred confessed a need for quiet, it was brushed off as some kind of an excuse to avoid doing a good work.

Mildred looked up at the cross on the wall, and Sam followed her gaze. Sometimes just staring at the cross gave you the rare courage to tell old friends and strangers the truth: *No. I just don't want to, and I don't think I'll go to hell for it. As for earning stars in my crown, I don't wear the jewelry I have now. Why would I start in heaven?*

Sam felt the words building in Mildred and spoke first, his voice a long sigh laden with heavy words.

"Mildred Budge, I am worn out," Sam confessed. "Something's going wrong with Belle, and she won't admit it. She's been eating garlic as some kind of cure-all, and you don't know what that is like to live with. I've got to get Belle to the doctor, and so far, I haven't been able to talk her into it. She's behaving weirdly too—doing stuff that isn't like her."

"Maybe it is like her. It's just not what you think Belle should be doing," Mildred replied, but Sam paid no attention to her argument.

"Janie and Al need a place to stay. And you have a guest room and a second bathroom."

Mildred didn't answer him.

"Will you do it for me, Millie?" Sam asked. "I'll owe you."

It was the undeniable request. Personal. *I'll owe you.* They were the words of last resort—uttered only after all the people who did have a means and a responsibility to host the couple had been asked and had turned him down. Only Sam Deerborn and Mildred Budge were such old friends—such veteran Christians-- that they didn't waste time criticizing or judging others' responses to the challenge of finding one's own good works to do. They simply acknowledged the truth of the problem and worked out a solution.

Mildred Budge understood Sam Deerborn. And while she always said no to busy work, she never said no to a friend who needed help badly enough to say, "I'll owe you." Her old friend would never have to pay because it had already cost Sam too much to ask.

"I do have a second bathroom," Mildred agreed grudgingly. "And I guess the Joneses can use it."

SEVEN

MILDRED, YOU'VE GOT COMPANY

Al and Janie Jones looked relieved and nervous to be standing on Mildred Budge's doorstep Tuesday afternoon at four o'clock because they had had a long trip from Seattle.

Only they weren't expected until Wednesday afternoon.

Mildred's smiling houseguests were a whole day early, and they didn't seem to know that.

Further, the missionary couple looked so healthy that Mildred felt quietly let down that they obviously did not need the determined care she had decided to give them. After repenting of her own lack of enthusiasm for the good work of hosting a missionary couple—God's appointed evangelists!-- for four nights and five days, she had resolved to have a better attitude about the good work, which had now become five nights and six days.

Mildred Budge checked the clock on the wall and moaned to God in her spirit: 'Why didn't I sign up for HBO when they called here last week with a special offer? What are we going to talk about?'

Nope. Janie and Al looked fine. Well fed. Rosy cheeked. Janie was a red head, and Al was a dish-water blond. Her hair was thick and glossy. His hair was thin and receding.

But his smile wasn't. Al Jones could not stop smiling. He pumped Miss Budge's hand vigorously, and said, "I'm happy as a clam to be here. And you're a honeybun to take us in." To prove he meant it, this perfect stranger kissed Miss Budge loudly on the jaw. The kiss made a smacking sound and left a damp place on her cheek that Mildred strongly desired to blot but didn't because Al was still looking at her, smiling clownishly.

"The missus," Al said with a self-conscious chuckle, "and I are eager to see where we are gonna be kicking back for the next couple of weeks."

Icy fear penetrated Mildred Budge. She turned wide-eyed to Sam, who avoided looking at her.

"One day at a time," Sam said abruptly. Turning his back on Mildred's piercing glare, Sam marched soldier-like back to the car for the missionaries' suitcases. There were two good burgundy leather cases that some wealthy church-goer must have donated to them because no missionary Mildred Budge had ever known could have afforded to buy those suitcases for themselves.

"Help me, sweet Jesus," Mildred whispered, as she stepped back from her front door and pointed a welcoming hand toward the living room.

"A couple of weeks?" she repeated bleakly as they passed through. When Al offered only a grin in response, she attempted to fill the moment of awkwardness. "You must have a number of churches to visit then?" she probed hopefully. Surely, Al meant he was going to be in the area two weeks. That's all he must have meant.

Al's brow furrowed, as if he were remembering his itinerary; then, he shrugged as if to say his plans weren't firm yet. Muscles rippled in his neck and shoulders. Al must have done some yeoman's labor in his day. Mildred approved. Sometimes preachers and missionaries had health problems that stemmed from a sedentary lifestyle of Bible study. Al had done more than hold a Bible.

The front door opened again, and even though he knew the answer, Sam called out, "Where do you want these bags?"

"In the yellow room," Mildred answered, and the three waited while the sound of Sam's footsteps marked the time for them.

Mildred's thoughts were racing. Could she call the cable company and have HBO turned on? Could they do that over the telephone, or would a serviceman need to come out? What would constitute an emergency for the cable company? Mildred thought she might be willing to pay extra if they would come out after business hours this very night. She looked at the clock again. Three minutes had passed. Forty-seven minutes until 5 PM. She could squeeze in a phone call, maybe.

Sweet Jesus. Help your old Mildred.

As she was finishing that emergency prayer, Sam called out loudly as he hurried back out the front door, promising just before he closed it after himself, "See you tomorrow. Goodnight, folks."

And then Sam was gone, and it was another minute more past four o'clock, and Janie hadn't said a word. Al Jones was still smiling broadly, waiting on Mildred Budge to do something.

Her thoughts darted. What does one do with houseguests who are complete strangers? It was too late to take them on a tour of historic Montgomery sites. What time did the Fitzgerald museum close? That was close by. The Alabama Shakespeare Festival? Her thoughts racing, Miss Budge asked instead: "Would you care to see your bedroom?"

Five more seconds passed.

"And the powder room," Mildred added, referring to the second bathroom that had gotten her into this trouble.

Janie leaned closer to Al and translated, "She means the bathroom." The young woman smiled.

Janie's smile stayed in place as Mildred showed the couple her home. Though she was usually happy with her house, when Mildred began to see it through the eyes of younger people who had traveled the world, her two-bedroom bungalow on Cloverdale Road looked different then.

The living room grew smaller.

The den was close, not cozy.

The reading room was too dark, and the piano needed tuning.

The small kitchen wasn't warm; it was stuffy.

The hallway that led from the second bathroom to the yellow guest room was narrow and seemed more so because Al Jones was a big man.

"If you're wide, turn to the side." The tour guide's voice from Mildred's recent outing to Ruby Falls in Tennessee hallooed in her aural memory. Mildred stopped herself from stupidly repeating the instructions. Instead, she fired off another plea to heaven.

Sweet Jesus, help your old Mildred.

Mildred prayed unceasingly as she pushed open wider the door to the guest room, which she had decorated in pale yellow with a border around the ceiling in jonquils and daisies. The bed was freshly made; the buttery yellow bedspread had been rewashed and hand-patted into place just as the pillows had been hand-plumped and, after some thought, not scented with lavender.

Rather, fearing that one or both of the missionaries might have allergies, Mildred had only rewashed the pillowcases that had been embroidered by the mother of a former learning-disabled student who Mildred had successfully tutored. The child had been able to reenter school and was now on track to graduate from high school.

Since that time, the mother had sent Mildred special hand-embroidered linens each year for Christmas. They were very pretty, and if Mildred had aspired to be a bride she would have kept them in a hope chest for her marriage. Instead, she used the linens as soon as they arrived.

"I've cleaned out that side of the closet for you," Mildred explained. "And those two top drawers in the dresser. And there's fresh soap and towels in there. Ivory, in case your skin is sensitive. It's not a big bathroom, and there's a little gas heater if you get chilled in the morning. Sometimes I do. The matches are in the medicine cabinet there, and if there's anything you want...." Mildred's voice trailed off as she revolved back toward the door and unexpectedly caught a glimpse of Janie in the dresser's mirror. She saw Janie's smile fade as the young woman surveyed the guest room.

Mildred hurriedly excused herself. "I'll just leave you two to freshen up," she said, backing out of the room.

And as Mildred left, the expression in the younger woman's eyes remained with Mildred. While water for iced tea boiled, Mildred plucked a few mint leaves from the plant in the windowsill for the tea and arranged on a plate the chocolate chip cookies fortuitously made from a Betty Crocker mix the night before. 'What expression was that?' Mildred thought, before answering it almost immediately: the girl was young, and her expression said she was trapped. Oddly, it was how Mildred Budge felt, too. Rather than feel angry or hurt, Mildred felt a quickening of compassion.

Mildred took a sprig of mint, chewed thoughtfully, and as she heard the voices of the missionary couple making their way down the hall, she tossed the mint into the trashcan. Then, in a moment of determination that she would not be defeated by the challenge to be hospitable, Mildred Budge walked softly over to the telephone table and dialed the number of the cable company. A live person answered.

"Could you by any chance turn on HBO from where you are?" Mildred asked hopefully, as Al and Janie noisily made their way to the kitchen. She listened, said yes three times, and then, "Thank you."

After hanging up the phone, Miss Budge asked, a smile fixed stoically on her face.

"Are you two ready for some iced mint tea?"

Tuesday, fifteen long minutes later

"So how did you two meet?" Mildred asked politely as the iced tea grew watery in the glasses. She had already refilled everyone's glass twice, and now no one needed any more. The lack of necessary domestic service made Mildred nervous, and she tried to fill the space with the easy conversation that many church women possess, but which Mildred did not have in abundance. She had already given them the F. Scott Fitzgerald speech. They had endured it.

It was back to personal questions now.

Janie waited for Al to answer. She was a shy girl with a round face, gray eyes, and short curly red hair. Mildred smiled encouragingly and waited for Al.

"We met in a chat room," Al said with a sheepish grin. His front left tooth was chipped.

Mildred sort of knew what a chat room was.

"The internet?" Mildred clarified. She had a computer. She just didn't like to turn it on except to type her devotionals. It operated faster than she liked to process information; and more troubling, Mildred was sometimes informed quite bluntly by the messenger balloons that popped up that she had performed an illegal function. After making that accusation, the computer did the equivalent of slamming the door in her face by shutting itself down to punish her. Mildred Budge had never knowingly performed a criminal act in her life. One day, she was going to find out what that message meant in technological terms, but Fran had strongly urged Mildred never to ask a young person how to use a computer.

"Because it's just giving away your power, and you have less and less personal power anyway as you grow older."

Mildred didn't argue, but she did wonder: 'If you can't ask a young person, who can you ask?'

Al added a second packet of artificial sweetener to his glass of diluted tea and nodded yes. "It's lonely in the field," he explained, stifling a smile. He was one of those men who smiled when he was revealing something personal or when he was nervous.

"And how did you become missionaries?" Mildred inquired politely. "Were you already missionaries when you met in the chat room?"

Janie spoke up unexpectedly. "When I was little, I wanted to be a missionary. I love to travel!"

Mildred nodded encouragingly. She hoped the girl would feel free to give her testimony, but Janie retreated immediately. Shy.

Al reached over and patted Janie's hand, then held it. Janie moved over on the couch closer to him.

"I never set out to be a missionary. It just kind of happened," Al said with a modest shrug. "We love people." He looked to Janie to confirm this.

She nodded, and repeated that message. "We love people."

"And you don't have children?" Mildred asked unnecessarily, because the fact sheet for the missionaries had plainly stated: No children. Childlessness was as unusual for missionaries as it was for preachers.

Ordinarily, Mildred would have been very careful not to bring up the subject of children after learning information like that as she surmised that some unmarried couples were sensitive about a lack of fertility; but in this instance, conversation was so halting that even making one of the missionaries cry would be a nice break in the way the visit was going.

"Nope, no children," Al replied, still smiling. The expression in his eyes changed though. When Miss Budge peered deeper, she thought that her missionary looked more tired than he wanted others to see. Yes, Al was hiding a deep tiredness underneath that determined smile. 'It must take a great deal of energy to smile so much,' she thought. 'And to travel around asking for money. And to stay with strangers who use old-fashioned, embroidered pillowcases and grow mint in their windowsill pots.'

Mildred tried to smile back at Al with an understanding that was void of sympathy because most men couldn't tolerate sympathy, and the effort made her feel tired too. It was going to be a hard few days. He had said two weeks! She couldn't let it come to that. As soon as possible she would have to call Sam and confirm that he would straighten out that misconception right away.

The room grew silent again, and Miss Budge looked around the room for another catalyst for conversation. Attempting to alleviate the awkwardness, Al asked, and there was a wistfulness in his tone, "You are not on cable, are you?"

Mildred nodded.

"Whoo-hoo!" Al grinned, and pivoted toward the room with the dark TV screen. "Tuesday night and cable TV." He waited expectantly, and his enthusiasm caused Mildred to speak.

"There's even a possibility that..." she said, "that we have HBO. I called a lady, and she said she had turned it on from where she was, but that doesn't seem possible, does it?"

"Miracles happen!" Al said, and Janie smiled with relief.

"Would you care to watch some television?" Mildred asked hesitantly, for while she had been longing for the escape from the awkward conversation and his enthusiasm was obvious, it was also against her upbringing to turn on a television when company was present.

"We'd love to watch anything at all," Al promised instantly.

"We love TV," Janie said, looking hopefully toward the room that had been identified as the den. It was one of Mildred's favorite rooms. The sofa was an orange, brown, and yellow tweed. You could spill anything on it, and the stains never showed.

Of course, they would love to watch anything. Young people loved TV. Many young people liked to watch television in the daytime. For a second Mildred was sorry that she had committed to spending $9.50 more a month for the next three months. Perhaps they hadn't really needed HBO, but she had panicked. If she had been a better Christian, if she had trusted Jesus more, she wouldn't have added HBO. Mildred repressed the acknowledgement of her failings, and led the way to the den and the TV console that sat in the corner of the room near the fireplace that she had not used the past winter because it was too much trouble to clean up afterwards.

"Thirty-six-inch screen," Al said. "You go, girl!"

Miss Budge looked at him quizzically and picked up the remote control. Then, in a move that was inspired, Miss Budge handed the TV's remote control to Al, whose eyes lit up as if she had just told him she would become a financial sponsor for his next mission tour.

Al began pressing buttons. He didn't even aim it at the TV before punching the buttons. His fingers flew, and the TV responded by coming alive. He began to zoom through images. Miss Budge was terribly impressed. She always took careful aim with the remote, trying to find that place on the set that corresponded to the invisible signal that was supposed to leap from one instrument to the other.

"Are we going to have supper? I know it's early, but we missed lunch," Al asked, while the channels flipped by. His and Janie's face resembled the bright expressions of children at the State Fair, which had once upon a time been a popular field trip for fifth graders.

Miss Budge had a selection of mixed deli meats for sandwiches that she had planned for snacks over the next couple of days; but before she could offer this as supper, Al asked, the expression in his eyes hopeful, "Could we order a pizza?"

Miss Budge had never ordered a pizza to come to the house, although the delivery man had stopped by a couple of times and asked directions to other people's homes. But since Mildred had shared a pepperoni pizza with Winston and Fran, she had been wanting another one. But Mildred thought it was wasteful to order a pizza just for herself, and she hadn't wanted to inject herself into another social occasion with Winston and Fran.

Almost overjoyed to have the problem of dinner settled with her deli meats still maintained in reserve for a later time, Miss Budge answered carefully, "I would enjoy eating a pizza, but I do not know how to order one to come to the house."

Al clapped his hands together and didn't wait for her answer. "Show me the phone book. I can handle that."

Miss Budge pointed to the telephone table where the phone book was stored. He thumbed to the business directory, found a listing that was familiar, dialed the number, and then called to Miss Budge, "Honeybun, what's the address here?"

Mildred told him.

"We're going to need a twenty or a credit card, Mildred," Al said, when he returned to the den where Janie and Mildred had been waiting quietly for him.

Janie handed the remote back to Al, who surfed until the signature opening bars of one of the versions of "Law & Order" signaled an episode was about to begin. "The pizza will be here in thirty," Al promised.

Sitting in her regular reading chair and pleased with his television program selection, Miss Budge asked, "How did you know this show was on?"

Al threw his head back and laughed as if she had said something very funny.

"Honeybun, this show is always on."

In an attempt to keep alive the congenial atmosphere that had begun with the shift to the TV room, Miss Budge added, "That movie about Josey Wales comes on a lot, too."

"Ain't it the truth?" Al confirmed, settling back on the sofa. "I love that movie."

"I love Clint Eastwood," Miss Budge breathed as if it were the most deeply held secret of her life. She wasn't supposed to love Clint Eastwood. He played violent characters, but still, Mildred Budge loved Clint Eastwood. Loved, loved, loved him. Loved Clint's quiet speech. Loved the planes in Clint's face. Loved the way Clint stood and faced bad guys.

"Come on. Make my day," Al said huskily.

Janie giggled again.

Both were happy people in their way. Al was a determined smiler. Janie was a nervous giggler.

Janie reached behind her on the back of the sofa for the pumpkin-colored throw that Miss Budge had almost forgotten about. The girl placed it over her knees. She must have experienced a chill, but she felt at home enough to help herself to the covering. Good.

Miss Budge felt herself relax just as that poor jogger was once again bopped on the head in Central Park in New York City and left for dead. It would be this case the Law & Order team would solve again tonight.

Miss Budge had seen the episode a couple of times before. She remembered who did it, but she did not admit to this. Watching a rerun was so much better than trying to make conversation.

She was knowing greater and greater levels of relief until the commercial came on advertising accident-proof underpants for adults. The advertisement featured an older bride getting married and suggested that the star of the commercial was wearing their product under that wedding dress. The commercial was illogical. Mildred was just about to explain that a bride that woman's age would not be wearing a long fancy wedding dress in the afternoon, when the front doorbell rang.

Al instantly muted the volume and stood up.

"Honeybun, if you'll get that twenty, I'll pay for the pizza."

Embarrassed that she had forgotten to ready the money to pay for dinner, Miss Budge rose and went to the kitchen and her drawer where she kept an envelope for coupons and petty cash. She found twenty and two ones for a tip. She moved to go back to the den, but Al intercepted her in the doorway where he stood waiting.

He took the money from her hand, and patted her on the back, "You get the napkins, and I'll bring the food. We are eating in the den with the TV, aren't we?"

Mildred was not accustomed to having a man take charge in her house. She didn't mind it, and the place on her shoulder where Al had patted her felt warm. It was Tuesday night, and she felt like she was having a party in her own home. Miss Budge was smiling as she placed three saucers on a serving tray; and in a fit of inspiration, she also retrieved three of her small Coca-Colas that she kept in the fruit crisper drawer. She added some paper napkins left over from a baby shower she had helped host (they had little blue baby bottles printed on them, but who cared?), and returned to the living room where Janie and Al were already eating their first slice of pizza without her.

Bless their hearts, they must have been hungry.

Miss Budge placed the tray in front of them and watched as Al ignored the saucers. Sliding a large slice of pizza on a napkin he handed it to Mildred, and said, "Let's make a deal. Whenever possible, let's not dirty up any dishes for anyone to wash."

Then, Al pressed the mute button again to release the sound because the show was back on, and he didn't want to miss anything. Miss Budge took a bite of her pizza. Cheese oozed. There were bell peppers and black olives and twice as much pepperoni as Fran's pizza had. And there was more: onion and some pineapple and some goat cheese, too. The concoction was heavenly. Mildred took a sip of her Coca-Cola. It was icy. Al tipped his own frosty drink toward Mildred and said with robust fervor, "Cheers!"

Mildred looked up at the clock on the wall. Time had passed. "God is good," Mildred replied in response to Al's exuberant one-word blessing.

In that instant, fear of the coming nights and days began to ease, and the most amazing thought popped up. It wasn't a Sweet Jesus prayer; it was a message of reassurance that felt to her like a cozy throw which she had forgotten and which was now wrapped snugly around her, and the message was: everything is going to be all right.

EIGHT

DAY 1
THE MISSIONS CONFERENCE

Miss Budge awoke the next morning earlier than usual, with a meditation topic that surprised her. She lay in bed long enough to see the whole idea. Then, she sat up, and with her legs hanging over the side of the bed, her slipperless feet getting colder by the minute--and before coffee or prayers--she wrote out the meditation.

When it was finished, Mildred laid the three sheets of paper on the bedside table and announced to herself, "Five down, and two more meditations to write." She placed the essay near the water glass that she always prepared and took with her to bed at night, but from which she rarely drank. Then, she went to the bathroom and splashed her face and combed her springy hair so her morning self would be presentable to the two people who were still asleep in her yellow room.

The first cup of hot coffee was waiting for her, thanks to the timer on Mr. Coffee. Taking her pink stoneware mug—the last of its set that she had inherited from her mother--Mildred adjourned to the back-sun porch for her Bible reading time rather than to her regular place in the living room, where surely her company would go upon waking and most likely need some time by themselves without the attention of their hostess.

Although she had replaced the screens on the back porch with double-paned glass windows, the exposed brick room with its red tiled floor was still colder than the rest of the house. It was not yet fully light outside. Miss Budge wrapped herself in a portable electric blanket she kept on the old settee and turned the temperature to low, not because she was particularly cold, but because she liked the coziness of it. Then, she opened her Bible and read, for writing a devotional was one kind of activity and not a substitute for private prayer time when she positioned herself to listen to Jesus.

She was abiding in the book of John, coming and going in and out of the verses that took her in and out of memory and prayer and meditation to that desired and promised place where she could lay down her tensions and even her curiosity and let Jesus speak to her in that still, holy place where he communed with her—convicting and nudging, leading and calling in a way that is not known to those outside the faith. It is learned step by step, day by day, word after word, breath by breath by those who have said the name of Jesus and then say it over and over again every day of their lives until Jesus, in a way that defies human logic, becomes the Author and Translator of one's life.

Mildred's consciousness receded. Her prayers sprouted, showing up as thoughts, combined with feelings and then were shaped into words, like some piece of clay being given form by a potter who was using her voice as the spindle that held it. She had strange ideas, remembered old names, saw faces, and in response, she prayed.

"Help Belle. And Sam. And bless the Missions Conference. And help our business at The Emporium to thrive, and make us grateful rather than proud. And help Winston. And comfort Fran who must be missing her husband in regretful ways, even while appearing not to as she spends more time with Winston. And help Janie and Al to find the financial support they need to get out in the field wherever that may be, and help me to arrange their meals and to not mind their being here so much, and could we have more pizza? Help me make my dishes for the fellowship suppers and to do my part in dragging the net, and don't let me grow so tired that I am unwilling to love You above all else and others as myself. I'll have no other idols before you," she declared.

"Miss Budge, I can hear you talking, but I can't see you. Where are you?"

The sound of another person's voice in the house startled her. Miss Budge did not jump, but she did return to the present temporal moment with regret. As she refocused on the physical reality of her home and houseguests, she heard the faint yearning, murmur,

"Don't go too far."

And that always surprised her for it was difficult to believe that with all of the people in the world who were talking to Him at the same time that Jesus would call to any one special person to stay close. However, as incongruous as it sounded, Miss Budge heard that from time to time. It filled her with wonder and gratitude every time.

"Do you have any milk?" Janie asked, appearing in the kitchen doorway that led to the back porch. She was wearing only a pair of lavender cotton pajamas—no robe and nothing on her feet.

It wasn't very cold, but Janie's teeth almost immediately began to chatter, and Miss Budge stood up immediately and wrapped the electric throw around her.

"Take my place right here, my dear, and I'll get you some milk. Would you rather have cocoa?"

The girl squeezed the blanket tightly up to her chin. Her short red hair framed her face in ringlets. How could she possibly be a missionary? She was only a child. Miss Budge wanted to pat her head and ask where her mother was.

"I haven't had cocoa in a very long time," Janie said, teeth still chattering. She tried to stop them, and that made it worse.

"Do you like cocoa?" Miss Budge asked, for the girl had not answered her.

"Yes, but I hate to bother you when you are busy," Janie explained, pointing toward the Bible which was still open.

Miss Budge's attention, which just seconds before, had been removed from the physical moment, returned. The former school teacher said warmly, fresh with love given and received during her quiet time, "It's no trouble, my dear. We will not put marshmallows in, I think, because you would not want so much sugar this early."

"Okay," Janie agreed, although the answer lacked sincerity, and Miss Budge wondered if she had been correct. *Didn't young people love sugar the same way they loved TV?*

"Sam Deerborn—the gentleman who delivered you here—lives just over there with his wife, Belle. See their house?" Miss Budge said, moving back into the kitchen. She found a mug with a picture of Keats' house on it, deemed it special enough, microwaved the milk, and then added the Ghirardelli double chocolate cocoa. Mildred stirred, stopping for a moment to marvel again that her hand was so like how her mother's had looked at the same age, and Mildred gave thanks that she could still use it. Many of her Berean girlfriends had terrible arthritis and trouble stirring. Marion had said the other day that she could not lift the gallon-size milk jug anymore and had to buy her milk in quarts.

Carrying the hot liquid carefully, Mildred delivered the cocoa to the girl with a cloth napkin under the cup to insulate the heat from the girl's hands.

"You're very nice," Janie remarked, blowing across the liquid and taking a slurping first sip. The girl closed her eyes, and the knuckles of her slender fingers grew white with gripping the cup. She seemed a delicate child, and Miss Budge wondered how Janie would survive in a foreign culture. But the Lord calls all kinds. You had only to look at the apostles to shake your head and know that the Lord had a special fondness for the inexperienced.

Miss Budge sat down in the white wicker rocker in the corner of the sun porch.

"Did you rest well?" she asked, as the lights in the Deerborn house began to flicker to life. Miss Budge watched placidly as the darkness in her neighbors' house was replaced sequentially room after room: the back bedroom, the bath, the hallway, the den, and then Sam moved into the kitchen where he would read his morning newspaper, *The Montgomery Advertiser,* and look out the back window and across their shared field and see Mildred's lights on and wonder how she was doing with the missionaries. Sam was probably worried about her.

"I'm all right," she whispered to Sam as if he could hear her.

"I never sleep very well in a different place at first," Janie said, and it was almost an apology. "But the sheets felt so cool, and they smelled so very nice. So clean. You must use a special soap."

"It's the Clorox," Miss Budge replied. "Some people like Chanel No. 5. But I like Clorox. Were you warm enough last night?"

Janie nodded, yes, but something inside the motion seemed ambivalent—a yes offered out of politeness and not wanting to complain about anything. Miss Budge determined to add an extra blanket, for Janie did not strike her as the sort of guest who would complain of being cold. Sweet.

"Would you like to have your quiet time out here?" Mildred asked.

Janie took another sip of cocoa, preoccupied with her drink. Maybe she didn't hear her.

"Or would you like breakfast first?" Miss Budge prompted.

"I don't think I can eat just yet," Janie said slowly, staring across the field at the Deerborns' house. Sam had come outside and was dropping a sack of trash in the garbage can. Mildred purposed to remember to collect the trash from around the house. The city clean-up crews collected the garbage on Wednesday morning. That was today, Mildred remembered with a start. How could she have forgotten that?

Jesus, don't let me lose my mind, she prayed automatically, wondering instantly how the burden of self-doubt had come with ageing. When Mildred was younger and forgot something, she had simply believed that she was too busy to remember everything; now, forgetting gave her a start of worry.

'*How do you lay down that worry*?' She asked Jesus one more time, and then that part of her that waited on him to reply moved to that interior place where one communes with one's Creator, while at the same time, she continued her conversation with the young missionary in her care.

See? I haven't gone so very far, she told Jesus. *I'm right here.*

"You could use my Bible," Miss Budge said, returning to the question of morning prayers.

Janie looked down at Mildred's Bible, and her gaze veiled the way a school child's did when she didn't have her homework ready and didn't want to admit it.

"It may be as difficult for you to have a prayer time in a different house as it is to sleep in a strange bed," Miss Budge offered delicately.

"I'm going to have a baby," Janie announced suddenly. "I am going to have a baby of my own," she said with wonder in her voice. Janie placed the almost empty cup on the small table in front of her, and then folded the electric throw around her so that it was across her belly. "It's all I can think about, Miss Budge. A baby!"

Miss Budge automatically began to rock. "Sweet Jesus," she said solemnly. "A baby."

"Exactly," Janie confirmed, almost immediately picking up the cup. It was mostly empty. The remaining milk was forming that film that Miss Budge found unappetizing.

"Do you want another cup of cocoa, my dear?"

"That would be awesome." Janie asked, her voice growing tremulous and childlike. She held the cup up, her bottom lip offering one last tremble before quietening back down.

"It's no trouble," Miss Budge assured her, taking the cup. But she didn't use it. She found another clean mug and made a fresh second cup of cocoa and came right back.

As Mildred handed Janie the hot drink, she deduced aloud, "You haven't told very many people your news."

Janie shook her head, no. "I only told Al two days ago. He's happy about it," she declared with determination, but there was a hint of uncertainty. Miss Budge saw it as Janie took another sip of the fresh cocoa. She had added a sprinkling of miniature marshmallows after all because the girl was drinking for two. Janie spooned one into her mouth right away. *Yes, young people liked sugar in the morning.*

Miss Budge felt great compassion that someone so young had been carrying around such weighty news. Here she was in a strange woman's home, preparing herself to raise money from strangers in order to serve in a strange mission field, and the mission field was dangerous Bogotá, Columbia, where violent men kidnapped people off the street and held them for ransom. Well, surely not! Surely, Al would consider his family first, prayerfully reconsider what he must think of as his calling in the mission field. Surely, Al would have better sense than to take his dear young wife and a new baby to such a place. Surely, God did not expect either of them to place themselves in harm's way.

But no sooner had Miss Budge acknowledged her own concerns for the young couple—and especially the young mother-to-be and the baby to come-- then her memory supplied many an example of just how a young person had been sent and hurt and often killed for the sake of building the kingdom.

"Sweet Jesus," Mildred repeated softly, as Belle came out the back door of her house, and sat down outside where she always did to have her prayer time under the pecan tree that had known a bumper crop this past year. Mildred had shelled four pounds of Belle's pecans and stored them in her freezer for pies and candy making. Was something wrong with Belle? Sam had said so. Mildred felt a start of curiosity—a desire to talk with Belle and find out what was wrong and determine for herself if garlic was the cure. But in the meantime, there was this child in front of her: this girl wrapped up in her electric blanket who was going to have a baby and who was drinking cocoa as if she had never tasted it before.

"What does Al have to say?" Miss Budge asked. "If you don't mind telling me."

Janie's answer was immediate and eager. "He says that we are going to have to reconsider our future."

Good boy.

"A different work. A different place at least—not Bogotá?" Miss Budge encouraged.

Janie nodded yes. Her gray eyes glistened. And Miss Budge wondered if there would be time for her and the other Bereans to arrange a baby shower on the last day of the Missions Conference; and even as Mildred prayerfully wondered about it—holding the idea up to the Lord in that interior place where one tabernacled with Him--she felt herself stilled. Mildred laid down the idea.

"Perhaps you could serve in the mission field in some kind of supporting role rather than a primary one while you have a chance to adjust to the change in your immediate family," Miss Budge proposed.

"Oh, Miss Budge. I want to settle down." The young girl looked around the modest sun porch and then out at the other houses that bumped up against Cloverdale Road. "I want a house of my own for my baby. I don't want to travel anymore. I want a clean, warm house with schools nearby and to live in a proper city where pizza can be delivered."

Miss Budge understood how the young mother-to-be felt. But she was careful. It would not do to interfere between a husband and wife or to try and steer missionaries into a path not ordained by the Lord. Still, Janie was here in her house for a reason, and Miss Budge had an opinion after all. "There are many seasons for many different activities. It is not any more wrong to change directions than to change seasons."

Janie giggled. "You talk awfully funny sometimes, Miss Budge." And then the girl got up and hurried over to Miss Budge and threw her arms around her. She hugged her hard. "You remind me of..."

"Your mother. I know," Miss Budge said, receiving the hug. She reached up around the girl and patted her back.

Janie shook her head definitely. "No. Not my mother," Janie said, with a quick shake of her head. "Miss Budge, you remind me of all the people I have ever loved."

The words so shocked Miss Budge that she pressed one hand to her chest to store the words where she kept the deepest love of Jesus.

"I'm going to go wake up Al now and tell him I've told you, and he'll be glad because he didn't know how people would take it here. But people understand about babies," Janie declared. "And they won't mind if we ..."

Janie didn't finish the thought. Warmed by cocoa and the conversation, Janie skipped out of the sun porch, stopped long enough to place her used cup in the kitchen sink, and then scampered cheerfully off to the yellow room where Al was rousing. Talking ensued.

Miss Budge rocked. Her prayers that had been interrupted picked up where they had left off. "Sweet Jesus, Sweet Jesus, Sweet Jesus," Mildred said in between petitions, and asked God for mercy for everyone for most prayers boiled down to that basic request. Then, after saying "so-long," and whispering a "hello" to Belle who was still having her prayer time and not feeling well, Mildred wondered again what could be wrong with her friend; but when she did, her very spirit was not disturbed, not the way it could be disturbed when there was a sense of something physically wrong. Silently, one more time, she offered her friend to the Lord's care. Then, Mildred made herself get up to go cook her breakfast. The door to the yellow bedroom closed again, and Mildred didn't want to hurry the young people to eat because they had five full and very busy days ahead of them and many decisions to be made.

While she fried one egg for herself, Mildred repeated the words: "Everyone I have ever loved." She could not recall when anyone had ever said anything quite as wonderful to her before.

NINE

BUDGE AND COMPANY

"Miss Budge, do you want me to turn off this burner?" Al asked. His eyes teased her.

It was a joke to him, but not to Mildred. Among her circle of friends, the acknowledgement of forgetfulness—especially dangerous forgetfulness—was something you tried to hide. It was pure self-defense. Once the rumor of your "losing it" began, it was hard to stop it.

"Might as well not burn down the house today. We have so much to do," Mildred said, trying to match Al's light tone of voice.

Mildred hid what she was really thinking. This is one of the ways that *it* happens. You leave the burner on. Leave the house. Later on, the house burns down. But having your house burn down wasn't the worst of it. People started talking about how *it* happened and began to murmur, gently. *Isn't it about time you started thinking about moving into Assisted Living?*

One of the unspoken perks about living alone was that there were no witnesses when you saw for yourself that you had left the burner on, or the coffeepot, or the water running in the kitchen sink while you went to take a shower.

Al grinned, and it was a big loopy grin that allowed for Mildred to be human. She felt his warmth. Her mouth opened without permission, and she confessed, "Once I left the faucet running."

"Who doesn't do that?" Al asked, shrugging it off.

Al switched off the burner and then scratched his head in one smooth motion, while Miss Budge did what she usually did when she fought the fear of losing ground--her name for losing her wits. Trained to meet the situations of life with words of wisdom from the Bible, Mildred tried to remember the whole verse from Timothy about keeping a sound mind in order to partake of that incomparable peace, but all she could remember was that last part of the verse. Insecurity pierced her again. She steadied herself with one hand on the sink and held onto that small snippet of a verse, as if it were a life preserver.

"Sweet Jesus, help your Mildred to keep a sound mind."

"Easy, girlfriend," Al said, crossing over to her. And then as if he had done it every day of her life, Al squeezed Mildred's shoulders. "It's hard having strangers in the house." His right hand thumped her shoulder twice as his way of saying thanks.

"I hope you slept good. I sure did"

Miss Budge stiffened inside Al's friendly overture, and something in his gaze registered that tautness. Embarrassed, Al let her go and awkwardly backed away. Mildred wanted to say: 'It's not you. It's me. I'm not accustomed to such...' In her mind, she almost said, `nonsense.'

But affection wasn't nonsense unless you didn't experience it regularly, and so you trained yourself to categorize what you didn't have as a frivolous activity, making affection with others mean less so it could be less important to you.

The telephone rang, giving them both a reason to back away from one another as if nothing had been revealed or discovered.

Without asking for permission, Al walked over to the telephone and picked up the black receiver.

"Budge and Company." Al grinned again at his own joke, and Janie, who had joined them, giggled in what Mildred was beginning to learn was her wordless response to many kinds of stimulation. "The lady of the house is up to her elbows in soap suds right now. Can I help you?"

"He's so funny," Janie whispered, and her pale face blushed pink with affection for her husband. Miss Budge wished she would put on a robe. She might get another chill. Maybe the young girl didn't own a robe.

Then Al listened while the caller talked. "Uh-huh. I got you. Uh-huh. Makes sense. No reason not to. Come on over, and we'll work it all out," Al promised the other person on the phone, and hung up.

It was like he had been speaking in code. Miss Budge had no idea what Al was talking about. Further, he had invited someone to come over. Mildred had never seen anybody like him. But there Al Jones was: a complete stranger standing in her kitchen in blue striped pajamas, his dark hair mussed up and needing a shave and not self-conscious one bit.

After Al hung up the phone, he said as if he had done it a thousand times before, "That was Fran. She and her friend Winston are coming over to move some more furniture. Seems that The Emporium—I'm assuming you know what that is...."

Mildred nodded yes.

He shrugged. "The Emporium has decided to expand the back-loading dock and offer vendors more storage so that inventory can be moved in faster as pieces sell, and she's grabbed you girls a spot. Fran says she knows that you have company—that's us," Al said with a grin. He repeated his play on words, pleased with himself, "Budge and Company," and then continued. "I'm going to help Winston unload some more stuff out of your attic. You've got a lot going on, girlfriend," he told Mildred, who was wondering why Fran couldn't have waited until after the Missions Conference to start this new activity. It felt like too much.

Al read the expression on her face and said, "Everything will be all right." Then, he reached out to press Mildred's shoulders again, but stopped himself. Al thumped her on the back instead.

"Are they on their way right now?" Mildred asked, looking out the side window as if the truck might be already sitting there.

Al said, "I've got just enough time to eat a quick breakfast and get dressed. I'm going to help Winston tote and carry."

"You're going to help Winston tote and carry," Miss Budge repeated, and she couldn't keep the surprise out of her voice, for as many times as the church had tried to institute a shepherding plan, assigning one man (an elder or deacon) to be a help to the single or widowed members of the flock, no shepherd had ever offered to do any physical work for her or any of the other Berean women, unless you counted sending Forwards through the e-mail physical labor.

"It's too big a job for one man; and to tell you the truth, I get restless just sitting around. I'm glad there's something for me to do. Fran sounds like a first-class cutie pie. Aren't you gals hungry?" Al asked, looking around the kitchen.

"Janie isn't very hungry this morning, and I've eaten. I didn't know how long you would be or I would have waited to cook, and we could all have sat down together," Mildred explained unnecessarily. "Would you care for some eggs?" Mildred asked, moving toward the harvest gold refrigerator. Sometimes people made fun of the dated color of gold, but Mildred saw no practical reason to buy a new one: her old refrigerator had never stopped working, and the ice maker was a genius at producing cubes. Mountains of them!

"I'd care for about four eggs and all the fixings, but you aren't going to lift a finger, Ladybug. You, neither, Janie. Food's not your friend these days due to you know what," Al said with a wink. "I can get my own breakfast. Besides, you two gals need to get dressed because there's people coming over, and I'm pretty sure that you're the kind of woman who doesn't like to get caught in her jimmie-jams, Miss Mildred. Janie, you can get through in the bathroom while I make my breakfast," Al said, taking charge. "And by the time I'm finished eating, I can have the shower and be ready to help the Franster."

Mildred was temporarily immobilized.

"Why don't you just get used to having some help while I'm here?" Al asked. "We are grown up people after all."

Was that the problem? Was she so accustomed to tending to children that she didn't know how to get along with self-sufficient adults? The question surprised her. But perhaps she suffered from that condition deemed by pop psychologists as co-dependency: a fancy name for Martha's condition in the Bible before the Lord released her from it with his simple statement: "Mary has chosen the better way."

And then Jesus left finding out that better way up to you.

Church ladies spent a great deal of prayerful time trying to find and keep that better way and still get all the work done on their to-do lists.

"I mean it, now. You two gals go get dressed. I can take care of myself," Al assured them, moving about the kitchen with ease. He located another frying pan, found a spatula, then opened the refrigerator and saw the Hormel Black Label bacon.

It was a terrible shift in her thinking, but Miss Budge was torn between greeting Winston in her bathrobe or arguing with Al about cooking a breakfast for him—help the man did not seem to need. Mildred turned toward Janie, and the girl was watching Al. It was easy to see: Janie adored him. Miss Budge was beginning to understand why.

Miss Budge decided to do as Al directed. She performed her morning ablutions and was just getting dressed in her freshly laundered sage green corduroy two-piece pants set when she heard the sound of a truck moving down the street. Winston? Or the garbage truck? She had forgotten again.

She glanced at the clock. Only 9:45. Miss Budge hurried out of her bedroom, and was passing the guestroom when she heard Al whistling some happy tune. It was an Irish air that she could vaguely recall. The melody snagged her, and she forgot about racing with the garbage can to the street in time to meet the trash collector. In an instant, Mildred saw herself walking on a high green hill with a cool breeze catching at her hair, which felt long against her neck. She became a girl again, in an instant for an instant, and it was exhilarating. In that rush of sudden returned youth, Miss Budge shed twenty years, a thousand disappointments and another part of her heart which had felt heavy, since she had left her children.

Mildred reached the kitchen just as Fran tapped her signature double-rap knock on the back door before letting herself in. "Somebody's been cooking bacon," Fran surmised. "Winston's rolling your trash can to the street. The garbage truck was just behind us," Fran reported, as she sniffed approvingly, but was quick to explain that she was not hungry. "No, we're not here to eat. Did your company tell you we were coming? He did tell you, didn't he?" Fran's tone grew sharp. "Sounds like you've got quite a character. I don't know that I have ever spoken with a missionary who is as chipper as he is."

Mildred walked straight over to her friend and embraced Fran. The hug surprised Fran, but it didn't make her uncomfortable. Fran hugged Mildred. "It's not so bad having company, is it?" Fran asked. Her eyes glistened as if the hug had given her permission to ask questions and be happy too in an unabashed way. That morning, Fran's eyes brimmed with something Mildred had not seen since before Gritz died. Had it been eight years since that kind of joy had abided in her friend's gaze?

Mildred's brown eyes were sparkling, too, from the memory of a cool breeze that had blown in on Al's whistling and the unexpected glimpse of green hills in a foreign land that she wanted to see and from some tug of joy that had also been tapped into by Al's song. Mildred wanted to explain what she felt to Fran, but she didn't understand what was happening herself. All Mildred Budge could say was, "I think everything is going to be all right."

"See there," Fran said, going over to the coffee pot. She patted its base. The coffee was cold. She poured herself a sip in a cup with pink violets on it that was considered hers. Fran didn't mind cold coffee. Leaning against the counter, she announced simply, "I love Winston, Mildred."

"You didn't want to," Mildred replied, fighting the urge to hug her friend again. But a smile of rejoicing appeared on Mildred's face, and tears sprang to her eyes because her best friend was talking to her and telling her the truth that she had been keeping to herself.

"I was married to Gritz, Millie. I was really married to Gritz. And now I love Winston Holmes," Fran stated.

"You were really married to Cleveland," Mildred agreed. "And now you love Winston."

"You're the only one who remembers that Cleveland was his real name. Cleveland was my Gritz," Fran said because she needed to say it, and she needed someone to hear it just the way she meant it.

Mildred had the strangest feeling that Fran was saying farewell to her life with Gritz in a way she never had before. Mildred knew one more time that you could bury someone and go on living, but it could still take years to say all the good-byes your heart needed to say.

Fran collected herself and continued, telling Mildred what had happened to her. "At first, I felt unfaithful to Gritz. But now, with Winston it feels...."

"It feels. You feel." Mildred interrupted her, for she was feeling many emotions deeply herself. Mildred had almost forgotten what it was—to feel. She wanted to tell her, 'I felt something just seconds ago. Something mysterious and wonderful. And I don't want to cry about all my children!'

"Yes! I do feel," Fran admitted. "I didn't feel much of anything for a long time. And now I feel so many things," Fran said emphatically. "And I have a right to!" she declared.

"Or course you do," Mildred assured her. "Being sensible women, we train ourselves to forget how to feel so many things because it's easier to live an uncomplicated life than a complicated one. Emotions can be complicated."

Fran nodded succinctly. "And now I've told you."

"You've told me, and I am happy for you," Mildred said. "And Winston."

"Winston hasn't actually said anything formal, but I believe...." Fran said, and her voice dropped off as she watched Winston out the window. The boys were getting the truck ready and were about to come inside. She pointed towards them and discreetly changed the subject.

"So, you heard about the new deal at The Emporium. We can move more stuff out of our attics and keep it in the storage area. Then, when we sell something, we won't be delayed in restocking." Fran snapped her fingers three times. "We'll be bringing in more bucks because our merchandise will be right there, ready to go out on the floor. The money is going to pour in, and you and I are going to have to decide where we want to go on our travels."

"I would like to visit candy-making factories all over the United States beginning with the Hershey Company in Pennsylvania," Mildred revealed immediately.

"I'm ready to go!" Fran agreed instantly. "Why else would I have turned us into a couple of junk dealers?"

"I thought we sold antiques," Mildred said.

"Sure we do," Fran said, her eyes mischievous. "That's our story, and we're sticking with it. That doesn't mean we can't tell each other the truth."

Fran looked toward the living room as Al moved through it. They both heard the front door open and close. "Your Al makes himself at home. And he's not lazy," Fran added approvingly. "That's rare."

Fran did not need to say more, but the two friends had seen through the years that many times people who must learn to live on the contributions of others forget how to work for themselves, as if the act of working—physical labor for money--is a betrayal of faith.

"Al cooked his own breakfast. And he's never mentioned raising his financial support."

"He's going to have to bring it up sooner or later. That's why he's here," Fran said.

Mildred shook her head. "We had pizza last night for supper," Mildred revealed with a hint of pride. "With pineapple on it. And goat cheese."

Fran raised her eye brows. "You are living dangerously, Mildred Budge."

Mildred grinned. "My health insurance premiums are paid up to date."

"Speaking of cooking, what are we taking to the fellowship supper tonight?"

"I haven't had time to think about that," Mildred admitted.

Fran tossed the rest of the cold coffee in the sink and rinsed out her cup. "Oh, Mildred. Isn't it wonderful to be so busy that we don't have time to worry?"

Before Mildred could answer, the front door opened again, and the two men came in talking loudly. Al had control of the silver two-wheel truck, calling out to Mildred. "Don't worry, Ladybug. We won't scuff up your walls."

"Howdy, Mildred," Winston said, as he accompanied Al through the living room, speaking to the women as he passed the kitchen on the way to the pull-down ladder that led to the attic. Winston was wearing his blue Biscuits baseball cap, but it was pushed back. Mildred could see Winston's eyes. He looked as happy as Fran did.

"Your guest does make himself at home," Fran observed, but her tone was not disapproving.

"I like him," Mildred confessed suddenly. "And I like Janie. It is not common knowledge yet, but she's pregnant."

Fran's eyes narrowed in concern. "I always hate to think of a young woman in the mission field pregnant or with a new baby. It happens all the time though."

"She's a little queasy this morning. She drank some cocoa. Maybe she'll eat some toast in a little while. I don't think she slept well last night."

Fran looked around Mildred's kitchen and said, "I'll bet you she is so glad to be in a real home."

They heard the sound of the yellow bedroom's door open and waited expectantly. Janie appeared, freshly showered, her face void of makeup. Her red hair was still damp from the shower and curled by the steam.

"Janie, this is Fran Applewhite," Mildred said immediately. "She's a good friend of mine and on the Missions Committee," she added pointedly. Any missionary who knew how to raise support would understand the significance of Fran's position, for their church regularly adopted missionaries to support, but not all missionaries.

"Hello, Janie," Fran said.

Janie smiled sheepishly, and her pale skin pinked some more. She took a deep breath. "It's good to meet you. Where's Al?"

"The boys are cleaning out the attic," Mildred explained, watching the girl who was in a dreamy mood, not even focusing on being especially nice to a member of the Missions Committee who would vote on the allotment of church funds. The young woman would have to learn more about how to respond to the people who had authority over financial dispersions. Mildred almost hated for sweet Janie to learn that.

"I know. Al told me. He's going to work with Mr. Holmes. And I'm wondering if you would mind if I laid back down for a while. I am so sleepy. I don't understand it."

"Of course you're sleepy," Mildred said. "Do whatever you like. You're not hungry, then?"

Janie shook her head declaratively, and covered her belly by crossing both arms.

"Shall I wake you for lunch?" Mildred asked.

Janie smiled tentatively. "Maybe I could eat some Jell-O later."

Fran walked over and patted Janie on the shoulder. "We'll manage the boys."

"Okay," Janie said, sleepily, not arguing. They heard the door close again, and Mildred imagined Janie tugging the handmade quilt up around her—warm and snug, snug and warm--and she was glad.

"That still leaves the problem of two take-along desserts for the fellowship supper. And lunch first," Fran said.

Mildred faced her friend and began to plan their day. "You need to go with the boys, and tell them where to position the furniture. I can bake a couple of pecan pies for tonight. And I bought some deli meats. Why don't you bring the boys back here for cold cuts for lunch?"

"If it's meat, they'll love it," Fran agreed, as Winston called out, "You coming, Frannie?"

Fran's eyes lit up at the invitation. "Be right there, Winston," Fran replied. She looked around the room, as if searching for something. "I forgot. I left my purse in the truck."

It was a radical shift in a church lady's behavior. A church lady's purse was never very far away. It contained most of her tools for survival. People outside the faith teased church ladies about their purses, but Mildred understood. She had her own purse. It was as big as Fran's and packed just as full with the necessities: Chapstick, lipstick, Band-aids, safety pins, Tylenol, Kleenex, Honees (an imported hard candy from Italy that was especially good for a tickly throat in church), a fake wallet that a pickpocket could steal, and then the real wallet, stashed deep inside a zippered compartment with mad money for when the debit card won't register on a machine and rubbing the card with a plastic bag didn't solve the problem so you actually had to pay for gasoline with cash. If Fran Applewhite had left her church lady purse in Winston's truck, then she was besotted.

'She really, really loves him,' Mildred thought, and she smiled broadly for her friend.

"Go on," Mildred urged. "I'll see you in the noon o'clock range. Lunch will be ready," Mildred promised.

Fran nodded yes, as she hurried out the back door and followed the sound of Winston talking with Al.

After they were gone, Mildred got busy. She folded the blanket on the sun porch. Swept the small trail of crumbs from the morning's breakfasts. Ran the Hokie over the carpet where the men had trailed more debris from the attic. Then, she prepared two pie crusts and made two pecan pies from Belle's pecans. After that, she made some lime Jell-O in case Janie wanted it.

While the pies baked, Mildred brewed fresh iced tea for lunch. She considered whether to make the sandwiches ahead of time or lay the fixings out buffet style and let each person make his or her own. As Mildred went to check the bread, she saw with a shock that she had only a half loaf left. Al must have eaten a great deal of toast with those four eggs. It was too late to plug in the bread maker. And the small ladylike-sized yeast rolls made by Sister Schubert, and which every church woman kept in her freezer for emergencies, were too small for men to fool with and Al was a big eater. Concern rising inside her, Mildred stared off down the shadowy quiet hallway where the door to the guest room was still closed. She couldn't leave the pies or Janie to go buy some bread. She had about an hour before they would get back. Belle might have bread, but she had seen her and Sam drive off in the Old Girl, which is what Sam called his burgundy Buick

"Sweet Jesus. I don't know what to do," Mildred said, and it was an uncharacteristic response—part unceasing prayer, part talking to herself.

Almost immediately, she remembered how Liz Luckie had sounded, almost begging Mildred to call her to come help with the mission's closet. Without thinking more about it, Mildred retrieved the church directory, looked up Liz's number and dialed it.

The other woman answered instantly, her voice eager and lonely. "Mildred?" she asked.

"How did you know?"

"Caller I.D." Liz explained. "Are you working in the missions closet today? I can help you. What time?" Liz asked.

"No, no. It's not the mission's closet," Mildred explained. And then she hesitated. For in spite of the other woman's eagerness to work at the church, Liz was still a fresh widow, and she might not really feel like being social.

Too late to reconsider or change her mind, Mildred continued, sounding apologetic, "I have company for lunch. Two missionaries. And Fran and Winston, too. And I don't have enough bread for sandwiches, and I can't leave the house because the girl is asleep in the guest room."

"Oh, Mildred. I'm so glad you called," Liz breathed as if relieved. "I have a freezer full of casseroles. May I not bring a couple of them over? We could heat them up. Give the men a hot lunch instead of cold sandwiches?"

"A hot lunch," Mildred repeated. Wonderful. The cold meats had not been a happy thought to her from the beginning. "That would be better and very generous of you to share them," Mildred agreed cautiously. "If you are up to it."

Liz was enthusiastic. "I'll be over there in twenty minutes," Liz promised. "And Mildred...thanks for calling me. Really."

"Come on over, and Liz...." Before Mildred could say thank you, the other woman in her haste to escape her empty house had already hung up her phone.

Mildred paused then. Paused to catch her breath. Stopped to get her bearings. Stopped to ask Jesus was there anything else she needed to do? Her gaze focused on the house across the street where Chase lived with his mother and father. It was very dark inside, although occasionally something flickered, most likely the TV.

"Let's not lose the boy. Help me to do the good works appointed for me."

Then, the words came unbidden that she had searched for earlier:

"For God has not given us a spirit of fear, but of power and of love and of a sound mind."

Mildred felt renewed! She wasn't losing her mind; she was just taking longer to remember.

TEN

BREAKING BREAD

"What is she doing here?" Fran hissed in disbelief. Fran's cheeks were pink, and her red lipstick was smudged but in a different way. It wasn't on her front tooth, as usual. It was blurred on the left corner of her mouth.

"It just happened," Mildred explained in a hushed whisper to Fran in the kitchen.

Liz was still working on setting the table. Liz had insisted on doing that work. *"Just tell me where things are, and I'll do the rest. I want to,"* Liz assured her.

Mildred was having a hard time being a hostess because everybody who was coming to visit wanted to make themselves at home. Mildred had pointed to the buffet where her best daily dishes were stored, and said, "Everything we need is in there."

Liz had found a white cloth with butterflies made of white appliqué that Mildred had forgotten and some cloth napkins with her monogram sewn on by the mother of that student she had helped a long time ago. Mildred had forgotten about them.

"No, really, Mildred. Since when do you call Liz Luckie about anything?" Fran asked, leaning against the sink.

Mildred had not had time to explain to Fran about the mission's closet and how she had learned that Liz was one of those lonely people who doesn't enjoy her own company.

Mildred reported the facts. "Janie was asleep. The two pecan pies were already in the oven. I needed some bread for five people. I couldn't leave the house to go get it. And your lipstick is smudged," she whispered.

Fran blushed deeply. Then, she helped herself to a sheet from the roll of paper towels, and gently, not as if she were scrubbing, blotted her mouth, her memory distant for the moment.

Mildred turned away from Fran reliving a private moment toward the oven where the two pies were cooling on top of it. Big homemade yeast rolls were browning inside the oven now. "I couldn't leave the pies baking or a young girl alone. Janie would wake up and wonder where I was. She's very young."

"She's old enough to be pregnant, she's old enough to be a missionary, and she's old enough to be left alone in the house, Mildred Budge," Fran said. She tossed the soiled napkin, and patted her mouth as if to determine how much lipstick was left. She felt naked without her lipstick, but her purse was still out in the truck. She didn't want to go back outside to get it.

"I believe we have misjudged Liz," Mildred said. "I haven't had time to tell you about her. She's okay, really. Liz and I had a conversation the other day working the mission's closet...."

"Liz helped you with the mission's closet?" Fran asked, taken aback. She crossed her arms, and her blue eyes flashed. She forgot about needing her lipstick.

Mildred took a breath. "She is lonely. When I called her today, it was to borrow some bread. I thought she would just bring me a loaf of bread. It would have given her something to do."

Fran was looking at Mildred as if she were a stranger. Mildred dried her hands on a nearby towel, and implored, "Give her a chance, Fran. If I don't have anything against her, why should you?"

"I don't understand. I was gone a few hours....and this!" Fran declared, her voice incredulous. "Liz Luckie. The woman who stole Hugh Luckie right out from under your nose and who has put the white shower curtain on your dining room table as if it were a table cloth."

Mildred turned and looked at the dining room table that Liz was still working on, tugging on the cloth, moving the silverware so that it was laid just so. Liz obviously had the gift of hospitality—or something like it.

"That's what I use it for. That's why it was clean and stored in the buffet. You've seen me use that shower curtain as a table cloth. It makes a very pretty table cloth. And Liz did not steal Hugh. I let him go. Or, I think I let him go," Mildred replied truthfully. She didn't want to talk about Hugh, especially not with Liz in the other room. Mildred took the kitchen towel and began to wipe down the kitchen counter.

"Do you know she cleaned out Hugh's closet by herself?" Mildred asked as she worked. "Now, Fran, you know how hard that job is. You know one of us should have helped her do that. And here she is helping both of us. And Liz was glad to. Liz wanted to participate. We should really be ashamed of ourselves, Fran. We've been like school girls forming a clique that keeps the new girl out of the mix, and that's wrong, Fran. Deep down, you know it's wrong."

Fran made the same commiserating tsk- tsk-tsk sound that she used just before announcing that one of their friends had suffered a fall. "Your problem, Mildred, is that you always see the good in people. You really must watch out for that. I have warned you before about seeing the good in people. It always leads to trouble."

"I don't either. I see who people are a lot of the time," Mildred replied stoutly. "I think I see most people pretty clearly. Including myself." She did not add, 'and you,' but it was implied. Fran heard her.

Fran shook her head in denial. "No, you don't, Mildred. You see a good that does not always exist, and it's going to be the undoing of you. And speaking of seeing: I don't see sandwich fixings," Fran said. "Or a loaf of bread! So, what was that whole story about calling her for a loaf of bread?"

"That's right," Mildred said, draping the barely used towel over the edge of the sink. She elongated her speech, trying to keep the situation from escalating and her own exasperation which was building from showing. She had been enjoying a very good morning, and now Fran was causing trouble that didn't need to be caused.

"When I explained to Liz over the telephone that I planned to serve sandwiches, she thought about all these casseroles in the freezer that she could bring over. I didn't see any reason why that wouldn't be a good idea."

Fran looked at Mildred soulfully, shaking her head. "Tell me it isn't so, Mildred Budge. Tell me we're not eating funeral food."

"Hush. Don't call it that where the others can hear. Besides, it's not funeral food because we're not having a funeral." Hoping to pacify Fran, Mildred added, "She brought your chicken spaghetti."

"That makes me feel good. I may just take myself off the Fishes & Loaves committee. I made that bereavement casserole in good faith. It showing up here again today is a very bad sign. It's a bad sign, Millie—a very bad sign." Fran made the tsk-tsk-tsk sound again, shaking her head.

"I don't believe in bad signs, and you don't either," Mildred argued. "We're not superstitious. And my hot lunch is not funeral food. They were originally condolence casseroles, but now they are ordinary entrees for an ordinary lunch which we could enjoy if you would just make up your mind to do that."

"I smell rolls, too," Fran observed, her nose twitching. "And they don't smell like Sister Schubert's."

"Now, don't go crazy. You do smell rolls. But they are ordinary yeast rolls."

Fran's eyes widened. "I smell a rat," she said simply.

Mildred told her to hush again. "It is as simple as this. Liz brought some homemade rolls too. But that just proves she's generous. I don't know that I would share homemade yeast rolls with others. I'd hoard them, freeze them, and thaw them out two at a time when I had to eat a bowl of soup for supper because I get very tired of crackers, and you know you do, too."

"She's up to something. Serving homemade rolls is probably one of her tricks. Men love bread more than candy and sometimes beer, and that's saying a lot. You know how men can feel about beer." Fran studied the closed oven door with suspicion.

"Look, Fran. It's just lunch. I needed help. Liz was available. You were busy."

Fran took offense, as if the statement were an accusation rather than a fact.

"I was busy with *our* business," Fran hissed, as Liz left the dining table and came to the kitchen doorway, and asked, "Where are the dessert saucers? Hello, Fran."

Fran smiled with her mouth, but not her eyes.

"They are in the same place as the other things. The buffet," Mildred replied, and Liz turned back toward the big piece of furniture where Mildred stored her good dishes and better linens.

When Liz was busy again in the dining room, Fran said, "We sold those lamps, by the way."

Mildred was glad to drop the subject of Liz and talk about The Emporium. "What's our total now?"

"We've got over seven hundred dollars in our account," Fran reported.

"And The Emporium gets a third."

"They've already taken their third. They take it right off the top. Seven hundred is our net to date which we can split or use to increase our inventory."

"We're doing very well," Mildred affirmed, gratified.

"And we've gotten half your attic cleaned out today and maybe—just maybe—the boys will clear out the rest while Al is here. He's a worker. I'll give him that," Fran said.

"He really is," Mildred replied as the guys appeared. "You boys wash up, and then join us in the dining room. Al, do you want to call Janie?"

Al spun around and headed down the hallway toward the yellow room and the second bathroom while Winston washed up in the kitchen. He was so tall he had to drape himself over the sink. It was the first time Winston had ever made himself at home in Mildred's kitchen. Winston washed his hands thoroughly, using the liquid soap and then shook his hands over the sink, eyeing the kitchen towel skeptically. A real man didn't dry his hands on a woman's kitchen towel.

Mildred understood. She passed Winston a paper towel, and pointed toward her trash can to use when he wanted to get rid of it. Otherwise, he would have balled it up and put it in his pants pocket, and then washed the pair of pants with the wad of paper in it and ruined a whole load of laundry.

Liz reappeared in the doorway that separated the kitchen and dining room, and stood quietly waiting. She had been working as long as she had been there, but she still looked crisp in her white slacks and lavender blouse.

"I think we're ready to eat," Mildred said, reaching for the oven door. The rolls were browned and steaming when she whisked them into a bread basket.

Al reappeared, looking apologetic. "Janie says she can't face food right now."

Fran didn't wait to learn more. "Let's have a blessing and eat. We've got a big afternoon."

Mildred turned toward Al, but Fran stopped her. "Winston, will you do the honors?"

Winston appeared confused but faced the task head-on as they reached for one another's hands to create a circle around the table.

"Bless this food, oh Lord, to our bodies, and our bodies, oh, Lord, to your service. And bless the hands that prepared it, oh Lord."

They all said amen and sat down at the dining room table that Mildred had not used in months. Three hot casseroles in the standard disposable tin pans were arranged on trivets with serving spoons beside them. There was the chicken spaghetti, asparagus surprise (the surprise was almonds), and a third dish that was a version of the chicken spaghetti but had crumbled Ritz crackers on it.

No one who deposited a condolence casserole in the church freezer to have on hand to be delivered to the newly bereaved ever signed her name to her dish. But people knew who made what. People knew who used real cream and who was a fat-free cook. Everyone knew who skimped on the chicken and who used more broccoli florets to give people more to chew instead. When Mildred assessed the three entrees on the table, she mentally catalogued: Fran's, Connie's, and Anne's. They were the best cooks in the church, and their dishes were on her table.

Mildred offered another silent blessing as Liz looked around the table pleased, for it did appear to be a banquet. Each dish was steaming. Shaking her napkin out, Liz nodded her head to Mildred, signaling that she was waiting for her to begin, and Mildred stood back up. "These disposable tin dishes can be flimsy. Let's just serve ourselves from the center rather than try to pass them around."

It was a practical suggestion; and in her home, it was Mildred's preference that mattered.

Al helped himself easily. Fran picked up the basket of rolls and began to offer them to each person. Winston, who was directly in front of the dishes, was immobilized at the dangerous prospect of having to ladle drippy food that would get all over the clean tablecloth. Liz understood Winston's tension immediately and began to serve him. By the time she spooned the asparagus casserole with the almonds onto his plate, Winston was smiling foolishly and nodding yes to everything Liz suggested.

"He knows how use a spoon," Fran said, darkly.

Liz didn't pay any attention. "Of course he does, but men can be so clumsy with a butter knife." Still smiling—her mauve lipstick perfect-- Liz buttered two rolls for Winston, and watched appreciatively as he took a first bite.

"Good," Winston approved, tasting the chicken spaghetti, which he didn't know was Fran's. He only knew—because everyone knew—chicken spaghetti was the church signature condolence dish. It always had been. That casserole had been delivered to dozens of families through the years, and recipients had always responded with grateful thank-you notes to the Fishes & Loaves committee afterwards.

As she served it, Liz said, "If I am ever on the Fishes & Loaves committee, I'm going to suggest that we outlaw this chicken spaghetti casserole, and everyone learn how to make my beef tips over egg noodles. You can freeze the beef in its own bag and the cooked noodles in their bag. It works like a charm. They can both be microwaved, and voila—dinner is served!"

"Men don't like egg noodles any more than they like rice," Fran replied. "Isn't that right, Winston?" she demanded.

"I like egg noodles," Winston said, with a mouthful of roll. "Those big wide egg noodles with parmesan cheese on top. I like those. Why don't you ever make those, Fran?" And then before Fran could answer, this man of few words, said, "Fran doesn't cook much."

Fran's face registered surprise, and Mildred looked down, studying her meal.

"I like noodles, too," Al added, taking another roll. "This casserole is not so bad though. Somebody at your church can cook!"

"I'm glad you like it," Fran said, putting down her fork. She hadn't eaten much of the food on her plate, and the roll that she had taken to be polite had cooled and was untouched except for the big hole that had happened when Fran jabbed it five times hard with a forefinger to see if it was done.

Mildred ate, watching the others, listening for Janie (hoping she was all right), and wondering why Fran was behaving so irrationally and rudely.

Before the German chocolate cake, also brought by Liz and produced as an after-thought, was offered and served, Fran stood up, carried her plate of food to the kitchen, scraped the contents off into the trashcan, stacked her dirty plate in the sink, and said to Winston, "I'm ready to go. There's a lot left to do at The Emporium."

"I was planning on eating a piece of that chocolate cake, if we have time," Winston said, reluctantly preparing to stand up.

Al's voice stopped him. "Of course, we have time for a piece of cake. Liz here was kind enough to bring it, and I...." Al fumbled for what to say, and added, "I like chocolate cake."

"Me, too," Winston declared, settling back down in his chair. "That furniture isn't going anywhere."

Liz beamed, and she hurriedly sliced big pieces of cake and passed them around on dessert saucers.

While the dessert was being distributed, Janie appeared, standing groggily in the doorway and rubbing her eyes, like a child. "I'm sorry I didn't join you all. I couldn't wake up."

Al smiled at her, and stopped eating long enough to say, "Great cake! You missed out, Babe."

"There's plenty left to eat," Liz offered instantly. Her eyes grazed over the young girl whose lissome frame offered no hint of pregnancy yet.

Janie stared at the rest of the food on the table and spun away. They heard her coughing after the bathroom door closed.

Liz took Janie's response personally. "It appears that my lunch has not been all that everyone might have wanted," Liz apologized.

"Don't think that, Honeybun," Al said, and when he used that term of affection, Mildred looked over at him sharply. That was one of Al's special nicknames for her.

"I'm having a big hunk. And Winston's having a big hunk, too," Al said. "And it's been my experience," he confided conspiratorially, "that most women really just don't understand cake. But you do," Al said approvingly to Liz. "You're a different kind of woman, aren't you?"

Liz smiled. Really smiled. And her eyes glistened. She held up the cake cutter poised, ready to slice another piece.

"Can you handle the clean-up, Mildred?" Fran interrupted, while the men ate with a single-minded concentration.

"Where are you two going?" Liz asked, watching Winston who was making contented sounds over his cake. "Would you like a big slice of that wrapped up to take home?" Liz asked.

Winston nodded, and said, "I wouldn't say no to another piece right now." There was a trace of chocolate icing in the corner of his mouth. "That little one over there has got me moving furniture around at her booth at The Emporium," Winston explained. And while previously that kind of explanation might have spoken to a cozy familiarity, in the presence of Liz and in that moment, it very much sounded like a complaint.

Fran looked like she had been slapped. "You said you didn't mind helping me," she reminded him. Her hands went to her hips, and she frowned, first at Winston, and then revolving slowly, she stared hard at Liz who smiled disarmingly back.

"If you're tired, why not let me help?" Liz offered. "I'm good at arranging furniture, really," Liz said, adopting the role of mediator between Fran and Winston.

Fran's mouth clamped shut.

Before Mildred could answer, Winston did. "Well, sure," he said. "It might do you good to take your mind off of....things," Winston added awkwardly. "Be glad to have you."

Fran smiled tightly. There was an awkward silence before she finally said through clenched teeth. "Sure. Why not? It'll help to take your mind off.... things."

Liz brightened, and then clapped her hands together softly like a cheerleader. Her diamond rings caught the light. "I love antique stores. I have some fine pieces in my attic, too. Maybe you could sell them for me. A girl acquires so much treasure in a lifetime, and I do have kind of an eye for arranging furniture, really." Liz promised.

Mildred looked at the dirty dishes and took a deep breath. The food had been good, but the lunch had not gone well.

"Fran, your pecan pie for the fellowship supper is on the counter."

"Well, I can't take it with me right now," Fran snapped. Her blue eyes, which just that morning had sparkled with joy, flashed with annoyance.

"I didn't mean for you to take it now," Mildred said. "I was just telling you it is ready."

The two men looked uncomfortable listening to Fran and Mildred come close to having an argument. Liz sat back in her chair, her eyes downcast, as if she were embarrassed for them.

"Are you coming with us, Millie?" Fran asked, adding some dirty silverware to the pile of dishes growing in the sink. "You haven't seen our booth since the first day."

It was a ridiculous question. Mildred spoke slowly, hiding the growing exasperation she felt building inside her. "There's Janie. And all of this to do," she explained, pointing at the dishes.

The two old friends stared at each other.

"Okay, then. I'll see you tonight," Fran said tightly, her mouth clamped in resolve. "You'll bring my pie for me," Fran said. "Because I can't do everything."

"I believe I can get there from here with two pies," Mildred said.

Fran did not hear the implications of Mildred's tone of voice. Fran was staring hard at Winston now who was taking a long time finishing his second piece of cake.

"I'll help clean up," Janie offered, returning to the kitchen and sitting down in what was usually Fran's kitchen chair. She had done something to her face. She looked better. Pinker. Before, she had looked quite pale. "What are we going to do this afternoon, Miss Mildred?" Janie asked.

Mildred had not planned an afternoon activity to amuse her guests. She had managed a lunch, baked two pies, and somehow made her best friend angry by inviting a new widow to join them. She was tired.

And now there were dishes to wash and other chores around the house that required her attention.

"After we get the kitchen organized, we could do any number of things," Mildred said slowly, wishing she could take a nap. A nap sounded very good. Her brain rummaged around for some ideas that would amuse a girl in her mid-twenties and her husband.

Al's eyes darted from one person to the other and settled on Janie who shook her head gently. Her eyes sent him a message.

He cleared his throat, and said, "Since you good folks have got Liz to help arrange the furniture, I'll stay here with the two gals," Al said. "And do whatever they want to do."

Mildred wanted to take a nap. But now Janie looked like she was finally awake, and when Al volunteered to stay and keep them company, she brightened.

"The Fitzgerald Museum is in the neighborhood," Mildred suggested tentatively. No one ever said yes to wanting to go to the Fitzgerald museum, but she always offered it first.

Al's eyes darted longingly after Winston who would soon be leaving in a pick-up truck that he drove with the windows down and the radio station tuned to Country's best. Al stayed put, however. "Sounds fine to me," Al said with determination.

"Or there's Martin Luther King's Dexter Avenue Baptist church."

Janie wrinkled her nose. "Don't you think we're going to have enough church already this week?"

Mildred agreed, although it seemed imprudent for a visiting missionary who needed to raise financial support to say that out loud. Maybe the girl was subconsciously trying to sabotage their funding so she could quit, and her husband could find a paying job.

"There's the Alabama Shakespeare Festival, but it's clear across town. I always forget which exit to take," Mildred said, saying no for all of them. Al and Janie looked relieved.

After some more thought, Mildred hesitantly offered another option. "There's Hank Williams's grave," Mildred offered at last. "And we could get ice cream afterwards."

"Ice cream sounds good," Janie said quickly.

"Hank Williams?" Al asked, moving over to stand next to Janie. She patted the hand that he affectionately placed on her shoulder.

The top of his hand had a long scratch that hadn't been there that morning. Wounded in the line of duty.

"Your Cheatin' Heart?" Janie asked.

Mildred nodded.

"I love that song," Janie said. "My grandmother used to play that song all the time."

"The cemetery it is then," Mildred agreed, her mind registering that the funeral food had been funeral food after all.

"And ice cream," Al agreed, looking at Janie who nodded contentedly.

"A drive would be nice," Janie agreed. "If I can sit up front. I'm afraid of being motion sick in the back seat."

"You sure you don't want to go with them, Liz?" Fran asked, as Liz returned from freshening up.

Liz had freshened her mauve lipstick again. "No, I'd love to see what you and Winston are up to. And besides, I've had enough of cemeteries for a while, Fran," and her voice grew small.

"Do you want to follow us in your car?" Fran asked, as the two women went out the back door.

"Oh, no. I hate driving myself anywhere," Liz said. "I'll ride with you. You could just drop me back here afterwards. I'm parked at the curb. My car won't be in anyone's way."

Mildred didn't hear Fran's reply. She had turned on the faucet over the kitchen sink and was rinsing the dishes and preparing to stack them in the dishwasher.

"No, ma'am," Al said, moving to her side. He took the dish cloth out of her hands and said, "We have an arrangement. You are not going to do all the work. You go get yourself ready for an outing. You've been here all morning holding down the fort. I'll take care of this."

Mildred was about to argue, but Al shook his head. "I told you this morning I didn't want to see you waiting on all of us hand and foot and that includes doing all the washing up."

"You better do what Al says," Janie advised. "He thinks women work too hard."

Mildred relented, handing over the dish cloth. As she walked away, Mildred looked quickly out the front window and saw Winston drive off. Fran was wedged against the passenger door, and Liz was sitting in the middle between them.

Mildred thought about that while she was changing her clothes. Just when she was about to come out of her bedroom, she heard the doorbell. She couldn't remember when she had heard that front doorbell used more often.

"I've got it, Miss Mildred!" Janie called out.

"UPS at the wrong house?" Mildred asked, as she joined them, holding her hand bag.

"Not exactly," Janie replied. "But we do have a delivery."

Al chuckled, and Mildred followed the sound of his laughter. Al was standing in the foyer with Chase. The boy still looked like he needed a bath and a haircut. He appeared even smaller standing next to Al, who explained, "His mother said that she had an emergency and could you watch her boy? Before I could answer one way or the other, the woman took off."

Miss Budge's heart lurched. Chase looked lonely and uncertain, and she was afraid that he would be overwhelmed by so many new people.

"Chase?" Mildred said quietly. Her voice seemed to echo in the foyer.

Chase looked about, as if he weren't sure if he were in the same house as before.

Mildred walked over to him and ruffled his hair, placing her hand gently and comfortingly at his neck. He moved closer to her. She felt him breathe in and then breathe out. His small boyish frame was alive in the palm of her hand, and she felt an energy emanate from her and course through her hand and into the boy who absorbed it.

"Maybe I'd better drive, so Janie can sit up front, and you can sit next to the boy in the back," Al suggested.

Mildred nodded her agreement. "Ordinarily, I wouldn't take a child anywhere without checking with his mother, but..." She didn't finish the idea. She saw no reason to cancel their outing. The boy would be all right next to her, and she was glad Al would drive.

Mildred pointed toward the key ring resting on the counter. And then she said, "Would you mind fishing out some money from that envelope in the drawer there? We might need some money while we're out," she said suddenly.

"Sure thing," Al said.

He pocketed the cash and the keys and asked her if there was anything else she needed him to do.

"Janie never ate any Jell-O," Mildred recalled, looking around the house. There were a dozen chores she wanted to accomplish, but the list of housekeeping chores felt dead in that moment. There was a small boy beside her and a pregnant girl who wanted ice cream and an energetic man who was eager to get out of the house.

"Well, if Janie doesn't get around to eating it, I will. It won't go to waste," Al promised, and his eyes shone.

"Ice cream sounds good," Janie said, speaking up.

"Let's not worry about food anymore," Al said. "We won't starve before the fellowship supper tonight. Now tell me where I'm going," Al asked, as he held the door open, locking it with a quick twist of his hand before letting it close after them.

Once she was in the back seat, Mildred sat close to Chase while Janie took the passenger seat next to Al. Mildred gave Al directions, but her voice grew softer and softer as she gave herself over to being chauffeured. As they paused to pay their respects to Hank, Mildred had the strangest thought that she was not taking care of two missionaries; they were taking care of her.

When she realized that, Mildred's hand clasped Chase's and squeezed, and the little boy who just a few days ago had lived inside a shell, looked up at her and for the first time since Mildred Budge had met him, the boy smiled.

ELEVEN

ALL MY SINS AND GRIEFS TO BEAR

After the slow drive around the cemetery where they paid homage to Hank, Budge and Company stopped at the Dairy Queen for ice cream and Janie and Chase both ordered chocolate dipped cones. Janie approached hers tentatively, stopping between bites as if to test whether she could risk another bite. Midway through eating the ice cream, Janie gave herself over to it, trusting that she could eat it and keep it down.

Chase behaved as if he had never had an ice cream cone before. After first biting off the curlicue of his dipped cone, the small boy focused on eating his ice cream with the same concentration that he had taken to the computer screen. He didn't require a napkin. They had all sat together in a booth as if they had no place else to be and nothing else more important to do; and like a family, they talked about nothing and laughed while Mildred enjoyed a malt, and Al ate two 99 cent banana splits.

Upon the return home, just as she walked Chase back across the street to return him to his mother, Mildred casually told Al and Janie to help themselves to that envelope in the kitchen drawer if they needed more pocket money. She was pleased with the way she handled that. Discreetly. With finesse. Fran Applewhite couldn't have done better.

Then after a forty-five minute lay-down with no sleep, it had been time to get dressed for the first night of the Missions Conference. Later, when Fran and Mildred had time to discuss it, they would agree that attendance was light, but no one said anything negative during the conference itself. Instead, people bragged on the sincerity of the first missionary couple who had been introduced and how a love offering had been collected to help them with their living expenses while they worked to build long-term support. Mildred had thrown in her emergency fifty-dollar bill, thinking that she would have to write three- and one-half meditations to replace it. Then, she thought of the money owed her from The Emporium that would be direct deposited, and she smiled in relief. Even though no one in her circle of friends complained about not having enough money, most of the women she knew lived on what the government called a fixed income. That wasn't a hopeful name for the amount of money that was all you could expect to come in to cover bills that kept growing and the unexpected costs of events like missionaries needing traveling money and a young couple who liked pizza and, who, at the end of the first night of the conference didn't want to go back to the quiet house of a retired school teacher. They wanted to go out with the youth of the church, acting as chaperones.

"Miss Mildred, could we borrow your car? Some of the other folks are going bowling and on to Krispy Kreme for hot doughnuts," Al said, though Janie had already mentioned it to Mildred. His request was just a formality; Janie had prepared Mildred that the question was coming.

"They do have hot doughnuts this time of night," Mildred affirmed, recalling instantly the previous Christmas when she had gone into Krispy Kreme for hot doughnuts at twilight and walked out with three. Standing outside in the late chilly twilight holding a cup of steaming coffee that she had no business drinking so late in the day, Mildred had taken a bite of the warm doughnut that practically dissolved in her mouth. Almost at the same moment, it had begun to snow.

Snow in Montgomery, Alabama! It rarely snowed in Montgomery, and it had snowed. Mildred Budge had not eaten a doughnut since, for she did not believe that she would ever have another one that was better—or a moment so exquisitely sensual, cold and warm at the same time. Mildred closed her eyes inside the memory, coming to when Janie spoke again.

"We could drop you at your house, and we'd be really careful with your car, Miss Mildred," Janie offered anxiously. She was holding onto Al's arm, and Mildred softened. She loved her red and black Mini-Cooper, but she must not let it become an idol.

"One day maybe we'll have our own car," Al said, patting Janie's hand. The usual ready smile did not immediately materialize, Mildred noticed. The shadows offered a camouflage, and the girl, protected by the encroaching twilight, did not manufacture a ready smile of assent. Mildred saw the girl, felt the truth, and wondered how long it would take her to learn how to let her face tell the truth whether in the light or in the shadows.

"You two go have a good time with other young people. Eat lots of doughnuts. They are never better than when they are hot," Mildred preached. "I'll walk home."

Before they could argue, she added, "I'd like to walk." It worked. They headed off in their direction, and she turned toward home.

It was a lovely evening. The fragrances of the night flooded her senses, quickening in her a gratitude for both the company of her house guests and the time when she could be alone.

Al looked uncertain about leaving Mildred on her own, but then a crowd of the teenagers yelled to them. Janie's whole being gravitated toward the laughter and the calling, and Mildred saw that for the young woman the evening of bowling and hot doughnuts was a welcome romantic date—not a fund-raising opportunity, not spending a tiresome evening in front of the TV watching reruns of old television programs. Young wives—now mothers-to-be—didn't go on many dates in Bogotá, especially at night. The young woman's responsibilities would multiply soon enough; and if they went to Bogotá, the very real and imminent threat of being kidnapped and held for ransom would keep them home at night.

Before more conversation could ensue, Mildred waved good-bye, and headed off down the homey street in her neighborhood. She was glad to walk off by herself. Glad of the evening. Glad of the hum of activity at the houses along the way where people were milling around the flowerbeds close to their homes or sitting on their porches watching people like Mildred walk by and waving. She was glad of the memories that rose up in her. Glad of the fragrance of new grass and cool mint and tea olive. Glad that the day had grown warmer and that the next day promised to be warmer still. Soon, there would be honeysuckle and gardenias, and better, the smell of tomatoes growing luxuriously on vines in the yards. People plucked them like apples and sometimes ate them the same way. Juicy. Dripping. Tasting like sunshine.

"God be praised," Mildred moaned in gratitude for the hope of tomatoes and the presence of the unexpected gift of solitude.

The solar street lights began to pulse toward beaming, lighting her path through Cloverdale, and she felt as if some part of her interior self was waking up in the same way. Each step seemed to give rise to a refreshed wakefulness.

The neighborhood houses, built in a time when people wanted big yards, were mostly set back deeply on wide lots where old gardens and ancient trees had taken over. There was an occasional cottage that had previously been a carriage house—a place where once, long ago, in a different South the servants had lived. These smaller homes were like her own bungalow, intimate and warm and inviting with their well-tended coziness.

Mildred loved the variety of houses and old southern yards in Cloverdale as much as she recoiled from the cookie-cutter designs of planned communities that had been developed by real estate people around the heart of the city. On the periphery of Cloverdale were other neighborhoods with assigned names meant to establish atmosphere but did not achieve the other purpose of creating the character of the neighborhood.

Miss Budge preferred unsculptured bushes and casually kept hedges to mark loose boundaries. They fit the landscape of her mind better. She was taking a deep breath of this satisfaction, when she heard hurried footsteps surge up behind her.

"Miss Budge! Wait up." A man called out.

She stopped, searching her memory for the name that went with that voice, but it was only when she turned to see Mitch Harper coming after her that the connection was made.

Benjamin's daddy.

Sandra's husband.

One of Hugh's pallbearers.

Mitch Harper was a tall, good looking man with sandy hair, the lean look of a golfer, and the bearing of someone in authority. He was also an agent with the Alabama Bureau of Investigation.

Miss Budge's mind quickly assigned the descriptions that created Mitch Harper's identity for her, but those descriptors did not tell the real story of how Mildred was connected to the Harper family.

Miss Budge had been his son's teacher the year the boy was hit by a car while riding his bicycle on his way to a baseball game. The death of their only son had devastated Sandra and changed Mitch

Harper from an amiable relaxed man and neighbor into a man who kept to himself.

Mitch Harper wasn't a deacon or an elder. Her mind searched for the reason he was following her. Had they recruited him at church to be one of the shepherds who was supposed to follow up on how older single women were managing their lives? That must be it, she concluded. The elders must have reassigned the sheep to different shepherds, and she had been relegated to Mitch Harper. The boys did that sometimes when they reassessed the shepherding plan and tried to figure out one more time why it didn't work the way they hoped.

"Why are you on foot, Miss Mildred?" Mitch Harper asked, reaching her in three more broad strides. "I'll be happy to give you a lift home, Miss Mildred. My car is back there." Mitch pointed back toward the still illuminated church. The clean-up crew was in action, taking out the trash. Inside, the set-up crew was sweeping the floors and resetting the long tables for the next night's fellowship supper.

Mildred stared past Mitch to the church and shook her head. "I need my evening constitutional, but thank you for the offer," Miss Budge said in her school teacher tone that brooked no argument. As if to prove her point, Miss Budge began walking again briskly towards her house, where—if this eager shepherd would just let her go--she could have some time to herself.

"I'll make sure you get there safely," Mitch said, falling into step with her.

"I'm perfectly safe walking home, Mitch Harper. I don't need a watchdog," she declared. 'Or a shepherd,' she thought wearily. Then, feeling regret that she had sounded more abrupt than she meant to—but really, she would have enjoyed a few moments alone-- Mildred asked how his wife Sandra was doing.

"Sandra's all right," Mitch assured her, apparently unaware that Miss Budge had tried to brush him off. "She's stopped painting everything black, and that's a good sign."

Mildred remembered Sandra's grief and felt the heaviness of shared concern that she and the other women of the Berean Sunday school class had known when they had heard how their friend Sandra Harper had responded to the loss of her son. Sandra survived the initial loss of Ben by painting the grout in her living room floor black, then the face of the kitchen clock. The baseboards, too. Anyone who went to visit Sandra emerged with a hushed new report:

"She's painting the shutters black now."

"The window sills."

"The picture frames."

Mildred understood. Grief was real. It needed to be expressed. She was glad that Sandra's black phase had stopped, finally. Mildred had felt the loss of the boy, too. She recalled with a start that her own sudden downpours of tears had begun with the boy's death. Yes, her tears had arrived then, coming out later at inconvenient times so often that she had stopped trusting herself to lead a classroom. The tears had led her to her early retirement.

And now Ben's father was beside her, trying to shepherd her and all Mildred wanted to say was, `My heart broke over your son,' but she didn't.

"Did you enjoy the first meeting tonight?" Mitch asked, struggling to keep his longer stride slowed to match hers.

"It was fine," Mildred replied politely, though she thought the first service had been a lackluster beginning of the Missions Conference. She wondered if Sam was discouraged. He took these things to heart. He interpreted the church's lack of enthusiasm for missions not as disobedience but a rejection of his leadership.

"I'm just following up on how the missionaries are doing in the homes of hosts," Mitch explained, as the tree frogs began to make their early evening serenade. "How are you getting along with your house guests?"

Mildred considered the question. "Of course, it's different having strangers in the house...." she began as a preamble of reassurance.

"What do you mean by `strangers'?" Mitch asked.

"Strangers to me," Miss Budge amended. "I had never met the Joneses before, but they are easy to have in the house," she explained. "They are not overly religious, which is refreshing," she said simply.

Mildred felt Mitch nod in understanding. The shadows seemed to deepen to a violet grey, a color that enveloped Cloverdale at twilight. It was Mildred's second favorite time of the day. She preferred the sunrise, but sunset was lovely too.

"Like tonight, they wanted to go bowling and eat hot doughnuts with the younger people from the church, and I thought, young people should go bowling and eat doughnuts while they can."

"Krispy Kreme?" Mitch asked, solemnly, as they turned the corner that led to Mildred's street.

"Is there any other kind in town now?" Mildred replied.

Occasionally, new doughnut shops sprang up in odd places in town, but they didn't usually last long.

"I think the major grocery stores still make doughnuts," Mitch said.

"I don't eat those," Mildred said, her mind turning again to a consideration of the jelly cake she planned to make the next day for Thursday's fellowship. People liked cake, and Miss Budge liked to bake cakes.

"Al and Janie Jones seem like they're okay to you?" Mitch pressed as they passed through an ill-lit space under a bough of honeysuckle that was about to bloom. She slowed her walk and finally stopped altogether to breathe in the evening fragrance. There was nothing else like it. Mitch stopped walking, too, and he didn't question her. He seemed to understand, but his reaction to the honeysuckle was different. While she breathed slowly and appreciatively, he pivoted slowly in a circle, looking around for some encroaching enemy, like a sentry.

"They're fine," she said. It wasn't her place to mention Janie's pregnancy. The news would come out soon enough.

"Al Jones smiles more than any missionary I've ever met," Mitch commented.

"Yes," Miss Budge agreed. "Al appears to be a happy man, and Janie adores him. I think they're doing fine," she said.

"And you're all right?" Mitch confirmed as they reached Miss Budge's front lawn. It was a small yard compared to the back field that led to the Deerborns'. Miss Budge liked the size of her front yard. She could still keep it mowed with the old-fashioned rotary push mower when she felt like it. In the worst heat of the summer when she did not feel like it, she paid the extra five dollars to the teens who cut the backyard for her to cut the front grass, too.

"You can always call me if you need anything, Miss Mildred," Mitch assured her, as the light at Kenneth's house across the street was switched on and illuminated their living room.

Mildred had tried to call the family about the Missions Conference supper, but neither Linda nor Kenneth had answered the telephone. She had left a message, but they didn't return her call.

"You taught my son to read," Mitch announced suddenly. "I don't forget that, Miss Mildred."

"That's right," she concurred. Ben had been a slow reader and had been slowed down even more by the fear that he would never really become a strong reader. That fear had created a mistrust in himself that was the real problem behind Ben's slow reading. Fear had layered upon the boy through the years, tamped down under all the tricks and bravado that the children who are not strong readers learn to use to hide a deficiency. You have to peel all of that away delicately before you can begin the work of teaching a child to read.

She had tried a number of incentives before having the brainwave to buy Ben a magazine about cars. He was so interested in the subject he forgot to be afraid of the words that described the cars. That was the key to teaching Ben to read. There was always a key. One simply had to look for it and not stop until it was found.

Sitting together for a few minutes in the afternoons, Miss Budge and Benny had slowly read that first magazine aloud between them. And then, they read the next issue. And the next. It was while reading the car magazines that Mildred Budge had become smitten with the red and black Mini-Cooper she had subsequently bought. Early in her ownership of the car, it had felt to her like hers and Benny's car, and then she had dismissed that emotion as a lie. A woman had to be careful not to get mixed up and think that other women's children were her own in any way.

Miss Budge had pushed the limits of this philosophy. She had subscribed to the magazine for him and been initially tempted to sign the card that announced the gift subscription, "Zoom, Zoom, Miss Budge." Upon reflection, she thought better of the idea, believing that the words written like that might encourage the boy to become one day a driver who exceeded the speed limit. Instead, she had written: "Keep reading! Your friend, Miss Budge."

She wondered how long the magazine had shown up in the Harpers' mailbox after they had buried Ben.

"Ben was very good company," she said carefully, because grieving parents can't hear too much or too little.

"My son was a slow reader, but you stayed with him until he got the hang of it. No other teacher did that. They just passed him along because it was easier for them than solving the problem." Mitch pivoted and looked up at the night, as if considering what else he wanted to say. "I never knew what the problem was. Later, it didn't matter anymore," Mitch confessed unexpectedly.

Mildred saw then that Mitch wanted to talk about his boy with someone who had known Benjamin—someone other than his wife. Many couples divorce after a child dies. Mildred would not have been surprised if that had happened to Mitch and Sandra. Sandra was older than Mitch and had gotten more religious since her son's death. Mitch had gone the other way, retreating in his spirit while still showing up physically at church and going through the motions of being a shepherd, although, it seemed to her, lost himself. She prayed one day that would change.

Silently, for it appeared that Ben's father had said what he wanted to say, Mitch walked with Miss Budge up to the front door as she reached inside her purse for the house key. Like an old-fashioned escort, Mitch took the key and opened the lock for her.

When she was inside, Mitch handed her the key and looked her squarely in the eyes, and she didn't see Mitch Harper anymore. Miss Budge saw Benjamin Harper: the boy who lived on inside the man. And he was a wonderful boy, only grown up in his dad.

Eternity was standing in front of her.

Her face beamed with joy at the recognition, and Mitch automatically returned the smile.

"Lock up, and call me if you ever need anything," Mitch said, backing up two paces before turning back to retrace his steps in the early evening dusk. He disappeared into the shadows of Cloverdale in the same way that he had emerged out of them.

Miss Budge listened to the retreat of his footsteps and marveled again how people keep going with so much pain inside of them. She went inside her cozy home and laid down her Bible on the telephone table. She cleaned out her purse and rearranged the contents, lightening the load she would carry the next few days. She checked the clothes hamper in the guest bathroom and gathered the damp towels. She started a load of laundry, and changed into more comfortable clothes.

The young people would be gone at least a couple of hours. She could do anything she needed to do. Or, she could do nothing at all. She did nothing at first, and then had a sudden urge to write a meditation that popped up like the first star that suddenly shines in the night sky. She saw the devotional as a whole all at once, held it in her mind like a picture so she could remember it, then, fearing she would lose it before she could put it down on paper, she hurried to the telephone table, squeezed herself in, and pretending like what she was about to write wasn't a big idea, she testified that Jesus is in charge of life and death. She titled the meditation, "All my sins and griefs to bear."

By the time she was finished, gentle cleansing tears were streaming down her face. She was crying for Ben, for Mitch and Sandra, for Fran, for Hugh, for Liz, and Janie and AL, and when Mildred folded the pages and took them to her drawer to store until she could type them, she whispered, "That's the truest piece I've ever written."

At the last minute, she dedicated the short essay. She had never dedicated a devotional before, but the last line felt as right as the whole piece. She wrote: For Sandra and Mitch. I loved your boy, too.

And having said it out loud to herself and to Jesus, she felt another level of heavy grief dissolve and ease away.

TWELVE

DAY 2
DON'T MARTHA ME

There was no need for Mildred to hand over two five-dollar bills for Janie and herself at the ladies luncheon because all church ladies ate free during the Missions Conference. Children, too.

But the children ate by themselves in a separate room where the teens volunteered as babysitters and played games with them. Mildred wondered if Chase had ever played with other children. She doubted it.

Janie had seemed initially irritated to have Chase with them, but she got over it pretty quickly. In a way Mildred was flattered for she understood what it was: sibling rivalry. Mildred smiled at the thought that Janie was growing possessive of her and didn't want to share her with Chase. If Janie could only have realized how much Linda needed the help, the younger mother-to-be wouldn't have minded the boy being with them.

Mildred had a hard time leaving the boy with the teens.

But Chase didn't whimper.

Didn't cry.

Didn't sulk.

The little fellow just stood there watching, his eyes boring into Miss Budge's back as she walked off with Janie down the hallway that led to the smaller dining room where the ladies gathered for lunch.

"I used to tell mothers who dropped off their children with me to go on, as if it were a simple thing to do. It is not so simple," Mildred revealed, making herself keep walking.

Janie looked back though and waved good-bye happily. "The kid's all right," she assured Miss Budge. Then, Janie did the most amazing thing. She looped her arm through Miss Budge's and said, claiming her, "You must miss teaching, Miss Mildred."

"Sometimes," Mildred replied honestly. "But it was time for me to stop teaching. I know that," she said with conviction as they reached the doorway that led to the dining hall. She could smell the baked chicken with prunes and olives and brown rice immediately.

"Miss Fran says you stopped working too soon, and now you think of yourself as older than you are and that you are punishing yourself for retiring early because you have this work ethic that you didn't live up to and now you feel like a failure," Janie reported bluntly.

Mildred was surprised to hear that her best friend would talk about her behind her back. Very surprised. What else was Fran saying about her? With a start, Mildred realized that Fran probably talked about her with Winston. The idea made her wither inside.

Besides, what Fran had said to Janie about her retirement was not true. Not true at all.

Mildred Budge had retired because she felt led by God to retire. Church ladies didn't second-guess one another's leadings from the Lord. It just wasn't done, especially after the fact. "Fran is wrong," Miss Mildred replied flatly. Her eyes glinted with purpose in clarifying a misconception and a conviction that she would, when the time was right, make sure that Fran understood, too. "I most certainly do not feel guilty for retiring early. I did what I was supposed to do, and I am enjoying my daily life very much. While Christians are castigated and actually made fun of by people outside the faith for having a healthy fear of sin, Christians are truly the only people in the world who are entirely exempt from guilt because of what Jesus did for them," Mildred said, as they entered the large fellowship room and found themselves standing immediately by the buffet table. "I understand that, and I live it. Are you hungry?" she asked Janie.

The girl shook her head. "No, but I can stand it," Janie promised. Smiling ruefully, the left corner of her mouth turning up in what Mildred was discovering was the girl's true lopsided grin, Janie added, "I don't mean that the way it sounds. Sometimes I'm starving, and then other days—minutes, really—I can't stand the thought of food. It's like there are two of me," she said, and then hearing the implications of that, Janie looked brightly at Miss Budge and laughed.

Mildred nodded, her face broadening into a smile. "Let's take our places in the buffet line before the crowd gathers. When women are supposed to go down a buffet line, they all stand back because no one wants to be first. You can waste a lot of time being polite when the smart thing to do is just to get in line and fix your plate; then, you are in position to claim a good seat in the house where you can hear the speaker and slip out early if you need to," Miss Budge advised, leaning closer to the girl as she added the last tip. "It's not a sin to be a strategic thinker."

They picked up their dinner plates: extra-thick paper plates with compartments that didn't stop gravy and sauces from sloshing. Silverware and slices of thawing frozen pie were already on the individual tables. Ladies made their plates from the buffet dishes and found a chair at a round table that could accommodate six and sat down.

"Are these pecans in the salad?" Janie asked, craning forward to examine the large family-sized bowl of tossed salad. The greens were the kind that came in a big bag, and the description on the front of the bag promised that they had been tripled washed! Pre-washed lettuce leaves had been difficult for Miss Budge to get used to, but now she bought them for her own home.

"Yes," Mildred said. "And you'll find prunes in the chicken dish they are serving today. And big green olives."

"No chicken spaghetti today?" Janie asked, peering with more curiosity than appetite.

Mildred shook her head. "Chicken spaghetti is for condolences. This dish with the prunes and olives is for ladies' luncheons. I'm not very hungry either," Mildred said, as she ladled polite-sized portions on her plate. The big spoonful of the entrée fit tidily inside the larger compartment on the plate.

Mildred picked up a glass of watery unsweetened tea and looked about the room for a good table for herself and Janie and chairs enough for Fran, Belle, and two other friends if they arrived in time to snag them. She spied an empty round table near enough to the speaker to be able to hear and close enough to the door to be able to leave discreetly. As Janie followed her, the younger woman remarked to Mildred, "Al and the men have gone to some restaurant for barbecue. I just thought we might be eating barbecue, too. I think I could eat some barbecue with pickles. Lots of pickles."

"Not us. We get chicken, olives, and prunes," Mildred repeated, settling her plate down so that her back was to the window. It was too tempting to be able to look outside. Besides, sometimes the sunlight created a blinding glare. "The men will eat ribs and get sauce all over themselves, and it won't matter. Life as we know it on this planet would come to an end if church ladies did that." Mildred resigned herself to what could not be changed, and positioned her purse near the leg of her chair and waited for Janie to situate her plate. "When did you have time to talk to Fran last night?"

"While you were in the church kitchen cleaning up. I like this room better than last night's," Janie said, finally looking about. "I met Mr. Harper, too. He seemed nice. He asks a lot of questions," Janie said, as she studied the position of the silverware. She picked up a fork, looked at Mildred, who was sitting patiently with her food untouched in front of her, and laid down the fork again.

"Men ask questions when they don't know how to talk to women. Mr. Harper walked me home and did the same thing. He's trying to be a shepherd. It's a terrible burden on men in the church—this shepherding business."

A sudden influx of more women arrived, and the room grew much noisier. As soon as their table filled up, they could eat. But not until then. It wasn't polite.

Mildred Budge reached over and tapped the top of her wedge of lemon meringue pie. Still hard. Gummy. Moisture oozed from the crust that was thawing but not very fast.

Anne Henry, resplendent in her signature ensemble of a red skirt, white blouse, and blue jacket, tapped on the microphone and said, "Ladies, wherever you are, will you stop so we can offer grace?"

Not many ladies could hear the blessing that was uttered by Anne Henry. But somehow they all knew when she was finished; and if they had been a crowd that said amen, they would have.

More plates were then politely filled and chairs selected, but Belle and Fran did not arrive in time to sit with Mildred and Janie. Although Mildred was irritated with Fran, she counted on Fran to sit with her because Fran was better at making small talk than she was.

Four women appeared suddenly and with only polite nods to Mildred and Janie made themselves at home at the table and started to eat right away. Janie, who had been waiting on Mildred to begin eating, lifted her fork and speared a prune, studied it, and then, frowning, laid it aside.

Mildred ate three prunes and six bites of a tough, overcooked chicken breast. After that, Mildred and Janie picked at their plates, making their salads last so that they wouldn't be eating their desserts and finish too early before the others did. The women sitting across from them were chatting among themselves, and Mildred and Janie talked only to each other, settling into a rhythm that Mildred found comforting and which caused Janie to relax. Mildred felt Janie relaxing, and something inside of her exhaled deeply. It was as if Janie were her own daughter. The idea brought a tear to her eye, but it was not the kind of tear that threatened to become a downpour. Miss Budge looked over at Janie and then at the faces of the other young women at the table and thought: 'My Janie is prettier than all of you put together and sweeter, too.'

As one tear became two, Miss Budge blinked them both back, fiddling in her lap for her napkin in case she needed to blot her eyes surreptitiously. She reached, finally, for the frozen slice of lemon meringue pie. She forked off one small bite. The lemon filling was too yellow to be made from natural ingredients. The crust was soggy from thawing, and the meringue was not really meringue; it just looked like it.

"I'm going to help you bake your jelly cake when we get home, Miss Mildred," Janie said, and she frowned. "Will the men be eating pie like this?" she asked, grimacing before pushing it away.

"Banana pudding. That's what the men will be eating. Warm banana pudding with real meringue. Not like this stuff," Miss Budge explained. She slipped her knife under the topping, lifted it up and moved it to the side. Janie watched, and copied her actions.

Janie took a bite of the filling, and then laid down her fork. "I believe we're being discriminated against, Miss Budge."

Mildred agreed. "We are. It is completely unfair for men to have barbecue and pudding while we have prunes and imitation meringue. Let's make an extra jelly cake to have at our house and not share it with any men."

Janie grinned in return and reached over and patted Miss Budge's hand. Al and Janie were both very touchy people. Surprising herself, Mildred didn't mind. Instead, she turned her hand around and clasped the young girl's hand in return.

Anne Henry tapped on the microphone again and introduced the speaker. Darlene Hemmings took her place behind the podium. Lights dimmed partially, and images from a projector flashed onto the large screen hanging from the wall behind her.

Darlene was a tall woman dressed in a navy suit with a white blouse. She wore just the right amount of coral lipstick. Her salt-and pepper hair was short and perfectly groomed, shining under the lights of the chandeliers that cast reflections upon the amber walls.

"Has everyone here heard of Betty Crocker?" Darlene called out as her opening gambit to connect with a roomful of women. "Of course you have. Her likeness has been associated with bakery products since around 1936. She has been a help in our kitchens, but she has also been an on-going reflection of changing times and roles for women which began with her as a homemaker and changed during WW II when women left home to work at war jobs."

No one wondered why Darlene was talking about Betty Crocker. She was a woman, and at women's lunches the guest speaker didn't usually talk about a man, although Miss Budge didn't see why not. Women learned from men all the time; men could learn from women, if they were inclined or felt that the Bible gave them permission. Miss Budge had wrestled with gender issues in the church all of her life, and never more so than when she was in a woman's meeting where women established their own boundaries.

Darlene pressed a button, and pictures of Betty Crocker through the years appeared on the hanging screen behind her. "Originally, Betty Crocker was grandmotherly in appearance in the beginning of her career as America's top cook, but the longer Betty cooked and tested recipes and shared them on the radio and in mixes, the younger she became."

Mildred recognized the fashion styles of Betty Crocker. She was wearing a version of the white blouse that Betty wore decades ago. Mildred had selected her white blouse out of her closet this morning; it was the twin to the one she had donated to the mission's closet and that Liz had scorned. Mildred was wearing her good black slacks, too. Mildred had three pairs of these black slacks: one pair to be wearing, one pair to be in the wash, and one pair to hang in the closet.

"Betty had many outfits, but her creators—her handlers—never dressed her to be attractive to men," Darlene explained. "It was more profitable for Betty Crocker to always look like a homebody."

As Darlene made the statement, the women craned forward to study the pictures more closely. Each image reminded them of a certain kind of woman from different ages in American women's history. Betty Crocker could easily have been a church lady, if..." And Darlene leaned forward and dropped her bombshell, "If she had been real. But she wasn't."

Darlene let the news sink in. No Betty Crocker? No real Betty Crocker? But they had been cooking with Betty for years.

"Marketers of flour created Betty Crocker for their customers to identify with. They called her Betty because it is a friendly name. They found a woman who worked for the company who had a friendly signature, and she signed the letters with the name Betty Crocker. And they fashioned an image of her in their advertisements so that she would be attractive in a friendly way but not sexy. A sexy woman might have caused potential customers to feel competitive rather than identify with her image as the icon of homemaking that Betty Crocker was intended to represent. Whatever you think of her outfits, and we might disagree about whether they're pretty or not, Betty Crocker—or the company that invented her to be a communicator with their customers—could cook. And like so many of our real friends, she has helped us in our kitchens."

The women around the room mumbled in agreement. Everyone used Betty Crocker.

"There's always a lot of work to do in the kitchen or its equivalent: housekeeping work, playing the piano for the choir, or teaching VBS or Sunday school."

Heads nodded in agreement around the room.

Mildred sat up, listening. Janie, too. Around the room, other women were paying attention. Somebody muttered, "I don't like to cook."

"I just heard someone say that she didn't like to cook," Darlene acknowledged with a quick nod.

A voice in the back called out gaily, "My kitchen's been closed for years! Even on Sundays!" she added unashamedly. She did not have to say that she was breaking one of the rules that the preacher emphasized: she and her family were eating out on Sundays if her kitchen at home was closed.

"I hear you," Darlene said, and she grinned broadly and saluted her. "And whatever the hours of operation of your kitchen or how many tasks there are on your to-do list, I came here to remind you that you have inherited more from Martha in the Bible than the guilt we often foist on one another—or carry in ourselves—for being women who like housekeeping or other kinds of work. Most of the time when I hear Martha described, she is the one who is reported whining to Jesus that her sister is letting her do all the work. But in the very next few verses, we see her striding toward Jesus—not in the kitchen at all."

Darlene paused, and her face was lit with appreciative glee. She began to walk back and forth across the small stage of the fellowship room. "I see Martha striding away from the house and her to-do list. Striding away from being compared to her sister. Striding toward a powerful moment in her life when she greets Jesus, not out of a grief over losing her brother that could have immobilized her and obviously has not, but out of the kind of empowering vision that Jesus himself has imparted to her. That's Martha.

"After knowing Jesus, Martha has become a woman who sees her Savior and ours in a way that is instructive to us. Martha sees Jesus rightly as someone in charge of life and death. And she sees Jesus as someone who wants to hear from her and who wants to help her with what she needs. That's a very different Martha than the one we tend to associate ourselves with. We see ourselves in the Martha who is tied to her kitchen work; but, that condition was only a passing season in her life—a problem Jesus identified. He freed her to leave it behind. Jesus helps us to see ourselves clearly, and then Jesus sets us free from sin and ourselves. I've come here today to encourage you to let go of all of the old versions of you," Darlene said, waving at the images of Betty Crocker. "And be your authentic self. Close your kitchen, or keep it open, but be the woman Jesus wants to set you free to be. And being free means you are about to have an adventure."

The room fell into a deeper quiet then, listening.

"Let me read a letter to you from a single woman who wrote to the imaginary Betty Crocker when she was played by an actress on a cooking show that was very popular on the radio fifty years ago. The writer tells Betty Crocker, "I have so enjoyed your radio broadcasts. I consider you a real friend, and even though I do not have others at home to cook for, I enjoy good food, believing that I am one of those unclaimed blessings you described in your last broadcast."

Darlene laid the letter down and peered out at the audience of quiet women who were waiting and listening. "Now it might appear that this letter from a self-described unclaimed blessing is just the message of a single woman who is finding her consolation in being understood by a friendly woman who doesn't exist and whose creators and marketers want to sell her something. Nobody is selling us anything. Jesus is real, and he wants to give us himself and our very selves. Our identities are formed in Him."

And then Darlene snapped a button and the images of Betty Crocker through the years disappeared like vapor.

"Jesus is the better friend because he's real. He's a real Savior, too. There are people out there—both married and single—who are unclaimed blessings and don't know our Jesus. The Great Commission commands us to go and tell them the good news. In Christ there is no difference between the married woman and the single woman. This self-described unclaimed blessing is telling the truth not of her marital status but a truth about all of us: We are all unclaimed blessings until we have accepted the claim of Christ upon our lives, and when we do…."

Darlene leaned forward. "When we do, the recipe for our lives changes because we find out who we are. We're not Martha. We're not Mary. We are our very own selves—given life by Jesus and set free by Him, too. That is our calling, and it is our mission. We must go and tell others the good news that Jesus is, and He wants us to tell other unclaimed blessings about Him. Go do it."

Darlene paused then as if considering whether there was more to say, but she was speaking to a crowd of experienced listeners who had tasted the truth of her message for themselves, and they understood.

Darlene moved away then. And the applause that usually filled the space did not occur. A meditative silence happened instead. When the time for applause came and went without this exiting strategy for the speaker, Anne Henry got to her feet and called out, "Shall we sing?"

Before anyone could reply, Anne Henry signaled to Peggy, who slid onto the piano bench by the instrument in the corner, and began to trill some notes.

Mildred Budge admired Anne Henry, for she was not afraid to step up and lead in an arena where women sat back and waited for someone else to do something. Anne Henry stepped into leadership with joy on her face and a raised hand that beat the rhythm to the hymn established by Peggy at the piano, who made the hymn choice for them all by shifting from running octaves to: "People Need the Lord." It was Peggy's signature song in the same way that Mildred always baked some version of her jelly cake for the second night of the Missions Conference. The jelly cake was no Betty Crocker invention; it was a Mildred Budge concoction made with a simple yellow cake and the secret ingredient of homemade jelly produced by Mrs. Parsons, who grew her own fruit and then made her own preserves and jellies. Mildred Budge kept a pantry full of Mrs. Parsons's canned goods.

As the song began, Fran Applewhite appeared suddenly in the doorway. Looking around the room, her eyes searched until they found Mildred Budge.

Mildred felt Fran's energy before turning--felt her friend's need before Fran's eyes found Mildred. Before her best friend ever wended her way through the room, Mildred knew Fran was bringing bad news.

A terrible tension occurred instantly in Mildred's shoulders, and her body stiffened as she braced herself for whatever Fran was going to say.

"Miss Mildred, what's wrong?" Janie asked, as she felt the change happen in Mildred who had, just seconds before, been singing along and almost moving back and forth on her chair in a friendly accompaniment to the rhythm of the song.

Fran finally reached Mildred. She whispered hoarsely inside the singing that continued around them, "Winston's fallen and maybe broken his neck. Will you go with me to the hospital? I can't do this alone, Millie."

Fran leaned against Mildred's shoulder and ignored Janie altogether. The two old friends held one another's gaze as instant memories emerged of a lifetime of troubles they had faced and survived together.

Mildred folded her white napkin and laid it beside the plate. Pieces of white lint were on her good black slacks. She brushed at them absentmindedly as she reached for her handbag, still positioned at the base of her chair. As Mildred rose, she said what she was thinking, "Winston is a careful man."

Janie automatically stood up, too. Across the room, Anne Henry motioned for the next stanza to be sung. She nodded discreetly to Mildred Budge, who understood immediately. Anne Henry recognized what trouble looked like and was giving her two friends the time to slip out before a lot of women stopped singing and began to ask more questions than either of them was prepared to answer. Mildred would never have to thank Anne Henry for that gift of time to escape, but she would remember it.

Fran swallowed hard, fighting an hysteria that was close to the surface. Mildred had not seen Fran so close to losing control since Gritz had died.

"We've got to collect Chase first and take him home to his parents," Mildred remembered, as she pushed her chair back up close to the table. "Janie, I have got to leave now. Mr. Winston has been hurt, and we must go and see about him."

Janie interrupted. "I'll take care of Chase, Miss Mildred," Janie promised instantly. "I'll clean off our table, too," she said. "I can do whatever needs to be done. Really. Don't you worry about me or the house or the boy. You just go."

"Take my car," Fran said, handing over the keys to Janie. "I'll get it later. It's the green Honda parked in the handicapped space by the back door. I'll ride with Millie."

"We were going to bake a jelly cake together for tonight," Mildred apologized to Janie as she settled her handbag's strap in the crook of her elbow. It was a strange slowing down for just an instant—a strange hesitation—of releasing the tension, of collecting her wits, of double-checking whether Janie really could take care of Chase and find her way home—the way home to Mildred's house. Mildred looked into the eyes of the young mother-to-be and thought: 'Yes, my girl can do that. My girl will do that.' Miss Budge patted Janie's cheek in a rare move of affection that she did not ordinarily allow herself to express to other people's children.

Janie smiled tenderly at the touch. "You go and see about Mr. Winston, Miss Mildred. You, too, Miss Fran. I will take care of everything here."

Mildred hesitated. "The boy....Chase is shy."

Janie smiled softly, her gray eyes growing round and luminous. "I know, Miss Mildred. But I can talk to him, and I don't mind, really," Janie said, and it was her way of apologizing for minding the boy tagging along with them on ladies' day. "Besides, I am going to be a mother. This is a good chance for me to practice."

And Janie gripped Miss Budge by both shoulders and kissed her friend on the cheek good-bye. It was a quick, fierce kiss—the kind that 5th graders had often given Miss Budge right before running out the door and calling over their shoulders, "Luv ya!"

Only this time Miss Budge was the one who was leaving the safety of the protected domain to go out into the world where people got hurt and were alone, and where church ladies often made their pilgrimages of mercy.

THIRTEEN

CLEANING THE GUTTERS

"He was on a ladder over at Liz's house cleaning out the gutters," Fran explained, when they were settled in Mildred's Mini-Cooper. "Winston went over there to work this morning. I got that much out of Liz when she called me twenty minutes ago." Fran took a deep breath. It had cost her to say those words.

It hurt and confused Mildred to hear them. She postponed replying by looking carefully over her right shoulder before steering the car away from the street where she had parallel parked because she had found a place near the back door.

"Liz called you about Winston," Mildred repeated with disbelief, as she was almost immediately stopped by the first traffic light they encountered. It was not a dangerous intersection. If Mildred Budge had been a different kind of woman, she would have looked both ways and run the red light because they were experiencing an emergency, but she was not that kind of woman. She was the kind of woman who obeyed the rules no matter what the circumstances.

Fran looked out the window. "It didn't go well at The Emporium, Millie. It didn't go well at all."

Mildred did not know what Fran was talking about. Further, a dismal report on any aspect of life at The Emporium was completely uncharacteristic. Fran was insistently positive about The Emporium because she did not want Mildred to lose heart. Mildred considered the implications of that shift in Fran's perspective. Something awful must have happened, but Mildred couldn't hear *that* story until she had heard the rest of the story about Winston's fall.

"I am so sorry," Mildred said, as the traffic light changed to green. She tapped the accelerator with her foot, and the car lurched strangely and then picked up speed. A car always seemed to feel and react differently after someone else had driven it.

Fran shot Mildred a glance and asked, "When was the last time you got this car serviced?"

Mildred didn't answer—just pointed to the small cellophane sticker that was affixed to the upper left-hand corner of the windshield. "I don't remember when it was serviced, but I'm not due back for 2,000 more miles."

Fran stared out the window, willing herself not to panic. "You don't drive your car enough, Millie. Better take it back over there and get them to check the fuel line." She said the words *fuel line* easily, and Mildred did not ask how Fran knew about fuel lines. She just did.

Mildred nodded that she had heard Fran; and after taking a deep breath, asked the question, "What was Winston doing over at Liz's house exactly?" She studied the road carefully, holding her foot steady on the accelerator.

"It started at the lunch at your house. Got worse at The Emporium. And by the time we had sorted the inventory, Liz had Winston drooling behind her."

"Winston?" Mildred asked, incredulous.

"She got Hugh—why not Winston?" Fran asked, and her voice was tired. "I was right there. Liz played her game right in front of me. Winston had no problem shifting his affections, like that," Fran said, and she snapped her fingers to emphasize just how quickly it had happened.

"This is my fault, Fran. You were right about Liz obviously. I shouldn't have called her. I shouldn't have invited her to the house."

Fran dismissed the need for an apology from Mildred with a quick shake of her head. "No. I am glad to find that out about Winston. I thought he was a steady man. You know, dependable. But, he's not," Fran said, shaking her head. Her well-sprayed curls didn't move. White Rain hairspray made her Doris Day hairstyle sturdy. "That's the kind of information you need to know. But really, Mildred, a twinkle in her eye, a spoonful of casserole—that I made!—and he was hers. By the time I was offering her a tour of The Emporium, I was no longer with him. I was trailing along behind watching Liz tell Winston what to do with our furniture at our booth."

Fran let the news sink in. Mildred tried to absorb it, speaking slowly when she finally did need to say something. "There was no mistaking you were a couple at lunch yesterday," Mildred said, tightening her grip on the steering wheel. "And Liz twinkled anyway—twinkled this soon after Hugh?"

"You don't get married four times by letting grass grow under your feet," Fran declared. And then Fran twisted in the car and faced her friend, whose eyes were focused on the road. "But I'm not faulting only Liz. It takes two to tango...or, it seems, to clean out the gutters. That's what Liz had Winston doing at her house. She just ever so casually said that her gutters needed cleaning out, and Winston was all ears. Mine do, too. But I wasn't about to ask Winston to climb a ladder at my house. I was going to hire those two teenagers who do that kind of work and whose bodies are still so young and resilient that if they fell, they would bounce. I don't think my home owner's policy covers men Winston's age cleaning out gutters. I am almost certain there's a loophole in the policy that would cause them not to pay his hospital bills.

"Anyway, Liz said she was holding the ladder when Winston lost his grip and fell." Fran's mouth clamped when she thought of the sound of Winston hitting the ground.

"Liz was holding the ladder he was standing on," Mildred repeated thoughtfully.

"Winston is such a careful man, Mildred," Fran said, but she wasn't thinking about his care of furniture or even his truck. Fran meant that she thought Winston had better sense than to get mixed up with Liz Luckie, a woman who had only been a widow for three weeks. It had taken Winston six months to actually ask Fran to go on a date. Before that, he had simply loitered nearby wherever Fran was standing or sitting at church, trying to say something that would cause them to have a conversation.

Turning the corner on the street that led to the hospital, Mildred theorized softly, "So Winston was really only helping clean out Liz's gutters, which he might have been doing out of friendship for Hugh."

"Yeah, right," Fran said bitterly. "She twinkled, Mildred. Liz twinkled."

"No. No. Really. There could be that explanation. But I just don't see how Winston could fall off a ladder. But he did, and it was a bad enough fall that Liz had to call the ambulance."

Fran shook her head emphatically. "No, Millie. That's not how it happened. Liz did not call the ambulance right away. She left Winston out there on the ground—left Winston lying there alone--and went inside her house and called me and asked me what to do." Fran stopped to let the gravity of that announcement sink in. "Liz did not know my phone number, Mildred. She had to look it up. I bet she didn't even know my last name. I bet she took the time to study the pictures in the church directory and find me, and then find my phone number."

"Liz didn't call an ambulance right away?" Mildred was incredulous. "Why wouldn't she call an ambulance? A woman who has had four husbands with various ailments and needs for medical care did not know how to call an ambulance?" Mildred asked. Her hands gripped the steering wheel in confusion and a growing anger. Who was this woman who had slept while Hugh was dying and had now endangered their Winston? Only he wasn't their Winston any longer.

"I told her the number—9-1-1," Fran said, cutting her eyes at Mildred. "And then I told her I was coming to the hospital, and she didn't argue with me. But I went to get you, because I can't see Winston alone, and I know I can't face Liz alone because I don't know what I might say or do," Fran revealed. "I guess we need to call Winston's sister who lives in Florida. No one else has a legal right to speak for him. A patient needs an advocate in the hospital—someone who can legally make healthcare decisions for him," Fran said, and Mildred knew she was remembering Gritz.

Mildred moaned deeply inside her spirit. There had been many decisions that Fran had had to make for Gritz. Those had been hard days.

The two friends found a parking space close to the front entrance of the hospital and walked together as they had many times before through the sliding doors. Liz was standing inside in the lobby watching for Fran.

"You got here fast!" Liz said gratefully. "Thank you for coming. I didn't know who else to call," she confessed, and she began to wring her hands. Her nail polish was a deep glossy mauve that matched her lipstick, which was perfect.

Deeply distressed, her voice cracked when she explained, "Friends of the patient are supposed to be in the waiting room, but I don't like waiting rooms. I don't *do* waiting rooms," Liz added significantly, drawing herself back as if she expected to be judged for that.

"Which floor is Winston on?" Mildred asked immediately when Fran didn't.

Mildred understood. Fran was not going to ask Liz for any more information about Winston.

Liz pressed her hand around her mouth, cupping her lips. Even in her distress, she was careful not to smudge. "I think they said floor two or three. We could ask at the front desk," Liz suggested, turning toward the desk on the other side of the lobby, where volunteer seniors manned the information booth and fielded telephone calls.

The receptionist confirmed that Winston was on the third floor getting x-rays, and Fran muttered, "There are only three floors in the hospital. I think I could have remembered *three*."

"Oh, I know how upset you must be. I am upset. So upset," Liz said. "To have all that ambulance noise coming back so soon to remind me of....I miss Hugh desperately. I just couldn't think straight at first. I don't know why I didn't call the ambulance right away. Denial, I guess, and I didn't want to see the people next door coming out to watch. They are so rude and nosy. The only good thing that happened was when Winston fell, I was able to move out of the way before he landed on me." Liz stared solemnly at both women. "It could be me in the hospital. God spared me."

Neither Fran nor Mildred said a word as the elevator delivered them to the third floor, where the waiting room was just opposite. It was congested, with groups of people looking as if they were camping out. There were pillows and small blankets and a great deal of debris: empty cups and Styrofoam plates from the cafeteria and fast food restaurants.

Before Fran and Mildred could decide where to sit down, the heavy grey swinging doors that led to the examination rooms swung open, and a handsome young doctor emerged. Dr. Jody—that's what his name tag said--had that freshly-minted, just-out-of-med-school look. His clear, blue-eyed gaze was searching and fearless. His body had the leanness of youth—had not filled out as an older man's does. Dr. Jody smiled as he looked around the room and called out, "Which one of you is here for Winston Holmes?"

"She is," Mildred said, pointing unequivocally toward Fran.

"Is your name Liz?" the doctor asked, turning toward Fran. He quickly checked his clipboard. "Liz Luckie," the young doctor said, reading the name. "You can go back now," he said. "But only one of you at a time," he added without apology.

Fran spoke evenly, her voice calm and her gaze deadly. "I am not Liz Luckie." She stepped back and waited.

Liz said in a tremulous voice, "I simply can't do that. I simply cannot go back in another hospital room."

"Winston is asking for you," Fran said flatly. "You have to go. It's the least you can do, considering you had an opportunity to break his fall and moved."

Liz was startled. She was surprised that Fran was speaking so sharply. "This is no time to tease me. I have never liked teasing," Liz declared, and she almost stamped her sandaled foot. "Just because this accident happened at my house doesn't mean that Winston is my responsibility. No one can expect me to be responsible for him," Liz said, and she clutched her stylish expensive brown alligator purse to her chest. "I am never going to be anyone's caregiver again!" she declared.

She searched the doctor's clinical gaze for understanding with an imploring hope that Dr. Jody would sympathize, but he simply dismissed Liz as now irrelevant to the problem he needed to solve. Dr. Jody refocused his attention on Mildred, who was willing to speak and on Fran, who was still glaring at Liz silently.

When the doctor was not moved by Liz's plight, she announced in a self-pitying voice, "I really don't see any reason for me to be here. I'm going home. It's been an absolutely horrible day," she said, as the elevator doors conveniently opened. "I was only waiting here till you arrived, so that Winston wouldn't be alone."

She waited for the two friends to thank her, but neither did.

A woman carrying a canvas tote bag stepped off, and Liz hurriedly took her place inside. Liz still clutched her purse as if it were a security blanket; and as the elevator doors closed slowly, her gaze wore the look of a martyr.

When the elevator doors were finally closed, Fran spoke to the doctor. "How is Winston?"

The young doctor had to consider carefully how to answer her question. His patient had not asked for this woman, who appeared to be in a very bad mood and obviously wasn't a family member. Something in Fran's hard stare provoked him though. Dr. Jody answered with facts, carefully. "Mr. Holmes's x-rays show nothing broken, but he has some bruised ribs. We used a few stitches to fix a tear on his hand that occurred when he caught it on a metal gutter. We gave him a tetanus shot. He hit his head and was knocked out for a while, so we need to watch him overnight. He'll be all right in a couple of days. But he's going to need some looking after." The doctor waited for Mildred and Fran to digest the facts and then asked bluntly, "Is there someone else we need to call? A family member?"

"His sister lives out of town," Fran explained.

As the doctor stared at Fran, she said finally, "I'll go back there."

He nodded, looked around the room as if he were supposed to find someone else—didn't see the person he was looking for--and retreated the way he had come.

After the doctor had left, Fran said tightly, "Someone's going to have to go over to that woman's house and get Winston's ladder back. That's his good ladder. And his truck," she added with a frown. "I certainly don't want Winston's truck sitting at Liz Luckie's house all night. There will be enough talk as it is."

"We'll ask Sam to bring it home," Mildred suggested immediately. "Or Mitch Harper. He offered to help with anything I needed the other night. We'll get that truck and ladder home where it belongs if we have to load the ladder on the truck and then push it ourselves," Mildred promised her friend.

Fran stood still, staring at the heavy swinging doors that led to the room where Winston was waiting for Liz.

"You're going to have to go back there because we can't go home until you do," Mildred said finally. "Go on, Fran," Mildred urged. "You have to do it. It's just Winston. You know him."

Instantly, Mildred regretted saying those words because Fran looked at her soundlessly. Mildred read her friend's mind: *No, Winston is a stranger. I didn't know him, and he wasn't Gritz and I was unfaithful to Gritz after all.*

Ambivalent—her feelings hurt and memories of Gritz being in the room on the floor below anchoring her steps--Fran finally pushed through the swinging doors and disappeared behind them.

Worn out by the drama of the day and having company in her house, Mildred sat down in the nearest blue plastic chair by the lady who had arrived when Liz left and who was now sewing calmly, using materials from her crafty beige canvas tote bag decorated with a diminutive Confederate flag and the stenciled words underneath it: *Heart of Dixie.*

She smiled genially when Mildred sat down beside her.

"Y'all got a loved one in the back?" she asked, taking out some needle work. She held a small square of navy fabric and was working on some kind of design: a family crest with gold thread and some Kelly green woven through.

"Are you Scottish?" Mildred asked, letting the admiration of her gaze at the sewing do the work of paying a compliment. Mildred glanced at the clock. Half the afternoon was gone. She would miss baking the cake with Janie. It was likely that both she and Fran would miss the whole night at church and the missionary reports. Mildred had really wanted to be there. It was Al and Janie's turn to explain their calling and ask for financial support. As their hostess, she was supposed to be there.

"I don't think I'm Scottish," the woman eventually answered after thinking about it. "It does look like a family crest, I know. But it's not my family's crest. I just like it," she said, stretching out a long piece of shiny gold thread and running her fingertips across the embossed design. Then, she switched thread colors and rethreaded her needle easily. Mildred was envious that the other woman could see well enough to do that without glasses.

"Sewing calms me," the woman said, beginning in a new area. "I take my sewing with me everywhere I go."

Other people sewing calmed Mildred.

"My ex-husband is in the back getting a colonoscopy," she announced suddenly, looking at the doors. She didn't appear to be worried.

"That's always a good precaution—that test," Mildred replied, looking around for a magazine to read. She didn't really want to hear about a colonoscopy, but people really liked to talk about them. If Mildred could hold a magazine, perhaps she would not have to hear the whole story. But there wasn't a magazine within reach, and it would be too awkward to rise and go across the room and look under those dirty Styrofoam plates.

"If anyone deserves a colonoscopy, my ex-husband does. He is a real pain in the ass," the sewing lady added, pulling the thread taut. "The last time I was here with him—last year about this time in this very same room-- they carried me out on a stretcher." She smiled impishly, tugging at the thread that wanted to misbehave.

"Oh, my dear. You must have been very worried about him," Mildred said immediately.

"No," she said with a dismissive shake of her head. "I wasn't worried about him. He's the kind of person who drives other people crazy, but nothing bad ever happens to him. Do you know that type?"

"I think I do," Mildred said, thinking of Liz. She had not grouped people like Liz and this woman's ex-husband into a collection of people who were a type, but it seemed to be true. She would have to think about it later.

"So, what happened to you while you were waiting? Did you faint? Had you forgotten to eat? Or perhaps it was the smells of the hospital that caused you to wilt?" Mildred asked, although this waiting room didn't smell of anything antiseptic.

"Darlin', they don't carry you out on a stretcher for simply fainting. They wave some ammonia under your nose for that, give you a Coke, watch you drink that sugared water, and then roll you to the door in a wheel chair so that you won't trip on your way out and sue them for negligence."

"Is that right?" Mildred said, looking harder for a magazine. Any magazine. Any subject. Even *Sports Illustrated*. But there was no magazine. Mildred scanned the ceiling. Where was a TV hanging from the ceiling when you needed one?

"Nope. I didn't faint that time. I had one of my fits, is what happened. Sometimes I feel a little claustrophobic in hospitals," she confided, as her needle moved rhythmically in and out through the thick blue fabric, pulling the thread along.

The movement was hypnotic. And there was no escape. A disciplined waiting-room visitor, Mildred gave herself over to the inevitable. With nothing else to use as a distraction or as a barrier, Mildred watched the woman sew and prepared to hear her story.

"Don't you hate hospital waiting rooms?" she asked.

Mildred shook her head. "You get used to hospital waiting rooms if you live long enough," Mildred murmured, as Fran miraculously reappeared through the swinging doors. Mildred came to full attention then—was ready to stand up and join her, but Fran didn't look for Mildred. She went straight to the empty coffee pot on the visitors' station by the empty magazine rack.

Fran measured some coffee out from the big red metal can into the coffee basket and poured some water from the pitcher into the coffee's well. She pressed a button, and the red light came on. Then, Fran stood there preoccupied with her thoughts and her back to Mildred. Her right hand was poised on top of the coffeemaker's top, as if willing it to hurry.

Fran suddenly remembered Mildred and cast a glance over her shoulder, mouthing the words across the room, "Winston wants a cup of hot coffee!"

Mildred blinked rapidly—an S.O.S.—but Fran didn't read it. Fran was busy saving Winston; she didn't have time to rescue Mildred.

The sewing lady continued telling her story amiably, "It wasn't really me that had the fit and ended up on the stretcher, and it isn't exactly me who gets claustrophobic. It's all of us. I suffer from multiple personality disorder. It was one of the other girls who lives inside of me who has the fits," she explained.

The shiny silver needle continued to move in and out, in and out, as if nothing unusual had been said.

Mildred watched, watched, watched, when suddenly, the sewing stopped.

The sewing lady's hands went limp in her lap as she announced with some finality, "That other girl inside of me hates hospitals." She turned and said to Mildred very calmly, "I told her that she doesn't have to come out if she doesn't want to, but she doesn't have good sense sometimes."

Mildred nodded glassily and then stared hard at Fran, willing her to come back over and say that she needed Mildred to join her in Winston's room, but Fran didn't. There was enough coffee dripped for Fran to pour Winston a cup, and so she did, and swiftly went back through the swinging doors without a concern for Mildred.

"That was my best friend," Mildred explained wistfully. "Her boyfriend almost broke his neck."

"How exciting," she replied. "Your friend seems nice," the other woman said.

"She is very nice," Mildred replied quietly, wondering if there really was an ex-husband back there. It hit her that this woman might just drop by the waiting room to have a fit and that somehow, she, Mildred Budge, had ended up in this deranged woman's orbit.

The woman returned her attention to the denim square and her needle that she pushed in and out of the cloth. "I was married for a while like I said, but we were all of us miserable. I am so much happier living without my husband. He hated everybody."

"I'm sure he didn't hate everybody," Mildred replied diplomatically.

"Oh, he likes other people well enough. He hated all of me--us. All of the people inside of me. That's when we discovered fits. And in places like this...." She looked around the room. "When I'm feeling like I don't belong or I just want to get away, I let that other girl come out and have a fit, and then they load her on a stretcher and take her away until we all feel better."

The woman boasted of losing control as if it were a virtue. Mildred gave herself over to her curiosity and asked, "What kind of fit is it?"

Simultaneously, Mildred wondered, `What would that be like? To let go? Have some kind of fit that made other people step back and think, she's not who I thought she was at all?'

"First, my face screws up like this." The lady sucked in her cheeks and let her eyes cross in a way that reminded Mildred of her own fish face that she had entertained children with for years. "That face happens anyway when one of the other girls wants to come out. We pass on the face. I can't exactly show you really what it's like. It has to happen naturally."

"I see," Mildred replied, watching the swinging doors. Hard.

"And we've discovered if you will let your tongue hang out just a little bit—not a lot, because that looks forced—just a little bit, well, a peeping tongue really worries people. Getting to the floor without hitting your head can be tricky, but you'd be surprised how many people will try to catch you if you will give them enough clues that you are about to take a nose-dive."

"My friends and I work very hard at not falling down," Mildred replied woodenly. It was a common scenario among older ladies: they fell, broke a hip, ended up in a nursing home where they got a staph infection, and died.

The woman continued as if Mildred hadn't spoken.

"Once you're on the floor you have to let your legs shimmy. Sometimes a shoe falls off. Don't worry. Someone always remembers to pick that shoe up and put it on the gurney with you. I've never gotten home without both shoes, although sometimes my underwear goes missing."

She stopped in her sewing to ruminate. "Just between us, I have wondered if one of us is a nudist because sometimes I find myself standing naked in the laundry room, and I don't remember how I got there. And we're cold a lot."

Mildred made her face as composed as possible.

"You're one of the few people who has heard my story and not made an excuse to leave. You and the other lady are good friends?"

"Best friends," Mildred said, hoping the other woman didn't expect to learn her name. Or Fran's. To steer her away from asking that question, Mildred said, "So that other girl has a fit that you tell her to have?"

The woman made a small knot at the end of the thread by rubbing the thread's end between her forefinger and her thumb.

"That's right. Then, they give her some sleeping medicine; and when I wake up, she's gone, and I feel better. All of us do. Sometimes we sing together—harmony."

The coffeepot finished its work, and Mildred thought she would just ever so gently pick up her purse and rise without making any kind of sudden movements and go over to the coffee station and slowly pour a cup of coffee she didn't want to drink because caffeine kept her awake, and take her time adding the sugar and the cream, and maybe by then, Fran would come back and need her. But before Mildred could initiate her escape plan, the other visitors in the room lined up in front of the coffeepot and drained it dry.

Mildred sighed, and the hand that had reached for the handbag released its grip.

"Have you ever had a fit?" the woman asked bluntly.

The question surprised Mildred. She was about to say, no, of course not, when she told the truth instead. "I used to cry quite a lot. It's eased off since I retired."

"Crying is very good for you," the woman said. "My therapist says so. What makes you cry?"

It was the first time Mildred had ever told anyone other than Fran about the tears, and the admission felt good. She considered her answer.

"Right now this blouse I'm wearing makes me want to cry. I saw it just a few minutes ago. I was at a luncheon. Our speaker talked about Betty Crocker and showed pictures of her outfits through the years. There were a lot of Betty Crockers through the years."

"That's good to hear," the woman said. "Very reassuring. She looks so normal."

"She never really existed," Mildred tried to explain. "All those images of the different Betty Crockers are just images is all. Not a one of them was real."

The woman absorbed that news easily. "What did you have to eat for lunch?" the woman asked promptly. And when she did, Mildred thought of her mother. Mildred's mother always asked that question, too, whenever Mildred attended a luncheon. Her mother had not cared about speeches; she wanted to know what the menu was.

"Baked chicken with prunes on soupy brown rice," Mildred said.

"Sounds horrible," the woman replied.

"We have it all the time. It's our signature fellowship dish when it's only women. While we eat chicken and prunes, the men eat barbecue."

"Why do you keep eating that?" she asked. "I mean, really. It sounds horrible."

Mildred shrugged, then sighed. Her legs splayed in a way that she never let herself sit in public, slackly. Not on guard. Not held together by will, decorum, and modesty. "Why do I keep buying the same old-fashioned style of white blouse and the same type of black slacks year after year?" Mildred replied bluntly. "Because I always have."

"Yet another advantage to having multiple personalities," the woman bragged, and then chuckled. "I am not tied to traditions."

"I am," Mildred confessed, adding, "That woman who spoke at lunch gave us a lot to think about," she added. "She said Betty Crocker was dressed to be inoffensive, that her clothes were like a disguise that hid her...." Mildred leaned closer and confided, "Her sexuality. Sexual beings can be a threat to others and trigger a competitive urge that creates tensions."

"Like that other woman wearing that scarf who just left? She's just full of sexual tension, isn't she?"

Mildred stared at the elevator Liz had left in. "I wouldn't know about that," Mildred said, with wonder in her voice.

"She's the kind of woman other women think men like, but men get involved with her kind because she appears weak and needs a lot of help. It's a downward spiral from there. We've seen her kind before. Men think of her as sexy because she's needy—and kind of dangerous—yes, dangerous, that's what she is. Men are attracted to danger. They like to test themselves against it—like climbing a mountain because it's there. Like that."

"I almost know what you're talking about," Mildred said. "All kinds of people can get so lost, can't they?" Mildred asked, feeling like she wanted to cry. But it was a difficult impulse—a different emotion. She was tired and hungry, and she wanted her mother. She was always hungry after she left a ladies' luncheon. It was hard to get full on prunes and chicken. Her mother would have understood that. It had been a long time since anyone had understood Mildred as well as her own mother had; no one could replace a girl's mother. Mildred batted tears, and then got ahold of herself. The girl that still lived inside of her missed her mother; but the woman who was old enough to have retired was not allowed to show it.

"Lost where?" The woman asked frankly, stopping her sewing. The small square of fabric lay in her lap. The needle rested, too, the sharp end pointed at Mildred as if it were the end of a loaded gun.

"Not saved. They don't know Jesus," Mildred replied.

"Oh, that. You weren't planning to talk about Jesus, were you?" Before Mildred could answer, she said, "I have heard all about Jesus. I went to church when I was a girl, but I just never believed all that."

"Do any of the women inside of you know Jesus?" Mildred asked; and when she did, the woman turned fully to her and grinned.

"You believe me!" she announced, delighted. "Sometimes people don't believe there are so many of me. But really, it feels very crowded inside of me."

"Do you feel crowded and lonely all at the same time?" Mildred asked immediately.

"That's exactly how I feel," the woman said flatly, leaving her sewing at peace in her lap. "You are the only person outside of my therapist who understands that."

"Jesus understands, and a lot of church ladies would," Mildred replied. "We know who you are. You are an unclaimed blessing. That's what you are," Mildred stated firmly. "But Jesus wants to claim you."

"I do feel alone even though there are so many of me." She stopped sewing and said wistfully, "I have said Jesus's name before. A couple of us have, and nothing happened. It didn't work. I think there are just too many of us. We don't know who we all are. We don't know how to get to Jesus from here."

Mildred was discomfited. A multitude of theological problems arose inside of her that began with *maybe this poor woman isn't one of the elect* to *maybe this is some kind of demonic possession and an exorcism would be in order first.* As usual, when the question was bigger than the understanding she possessed, Mildred decided to simply rely on the truth of the Great Commission and repeat the promise that was meant for all:

"Jesus knows who you all are and where you all are. Ask Him to come get you," Mildred suggested.

"All of me?"

"All of you," Mildred assured her, as Fran returned. Seeing that Mildred was engaged in a serious conversation, Fran went still immediately and waited.

When there was a pause, Fran signaled Mildred to come with her.

Mildred nodded, and reached for her purse. She slipped her hand into the side pocket and extracted a small white and blue tract the size of a business card with the plan of salvation on one side and the meeting times of Christ Church on the other side.

"My therapist does say I am supposed to take care of us. That's my primary job."

"There's no better way to take care of all of you than to say the name of Jesus for all of you. He is a shepherd," Mildred said. "He can handle any size flock. My name is Mildred Budge. Come visit us sometime," she said, handing her the card. "If you're scared of crowds, come Sunday evening. It's quieter, and there are fewer people."

"A lot of people I meet won't tell me their names." She grew suddenly shy, and then said, like a child, "I'm Dixie." Her eyes cut involuntarily to the small Confederate flag, and Mildred wondered which kind of southern woman Dixie saw herself as being: Scarlett or Zelda or some other kind of woman with so many facets that a reference to a whole southeast region wasn't really big enough to provide enough history or space to tell her story.

"I am glad to meet you, Dixie. I really am Mildred Budge, and my best friend over there is Fran Applewhite."

"She seems nice," Dixie said, repeating herself. "She looks so normal," she approved, and there was longing in her voice. Dixie hesitated, looking at Fran and then at Mildred. "Where would I sit if I came to church?" she asked, looking up at Mildred. Her face showed some wear; but inside, she had the eyes of many children who had wanted to join a class but didn't know how or which chair was theirs. They always looked at Miss Budge to help them find a place to be.

"You can sit next to me," Mildred promised. She almost added, and Fran, but Mildred wasn't sure about that promise. Maybe Fran would not be sitting next to her in the evening anymore. In spite of the day's events, there was a strong possibility that Fran would be sitting next to Winston. "I am always there. Come anytime. It was nice talking to you, my dear."

The light changed in the woman's eyes. Her voice deepened to a gruff rasp, and she bellowed like a sailor, "Right back atcha."

Mildred kept walking.

Winston had two black eyes, but they were open when Mildred went into his room. He met her gaze at first and then looked away at his empty coffee cup.

"I was just helping Liz with her gutters," Winston explained lamely. "Hugh was a friend of mine," he added, and his chin went up defensively.

"What happened?" Mildred asked, moving to the window. It was still light outside, but a thunder cloud was approaching in the distance.

Winston closed his sore eyes, shutting out some memory he was afraid Fran could see if he kept his eyes open. His hand jerked involuntarily. Winston looked down at his disobedient hand, surprised at what his flesh was willing to do. Fran reached for his hand, and tucked her own inside it. His voice grew stronger.

"Ladies, I reached for a pine cone that was stuck in the corner of the drain pipe, and that's when it started," Winston said.

"Liz was holding the ladder?" Mildred confirmed. She liked facts, and she liked for them to be arranged in chronological order.

He opened his eyes and shook his head again. "I think her phone rang, and she let go of the ladder. She was in a hurry. When Liz let go of the ladder, there was a funny movement. Like instead of letting go, she accidentally pushed it. It jiggled. But maybe I imagined that. Maybe my weight shifted, and it just felt like that."

Fran and Mildred swapped knowing glances. Something deep and resolute settled inside Fran's eyes.

"Liz doesn't believe in...." Winston began awkwardly.

Fran leaned forward to hear. Mildred stood upright by the window. Lightning flashed on the horizon.

"Butter," Winston said finally.

"Butter? Did you say butter?" Fran asked, looking over to Mildred for confirmation. Mildred nodded.

Winston spoke clearly then, but kept his eyes closed. "Liz acts as if she likes butter. She puts it on food for other people," Winston revealed. "But she doesn't eat it herself. Or sugar. She puts that pink stuff in iced tea. I don't think she has real taste buds," Winston said, shaking his head as if to get rid of a bad taste in his own mouth. He looked at Fran and said, his eyes pleading, "I like your iced tea better."

Mildred pushed a chair closer to the bed, and Fran sat down without losing her hold on Winston's hand. Outside the dark clouds multiplied.

"I think I should go on," Mildred said, patting Fran's shoulder.

Fran nodded, her attention on Winston.

"Winston. Don't be climbing any more metal ladders when it's about to rain. They're natural lightning rods." She looked at Mildred and said, "This could have been a whole lot worse."

Winston peered out the window miserably. "I don't know what made me do it. I don't climb ladders that way anymore." Winston tried to shake his head, but the neck brace prevented it. "We were supposed to help chaperone the kids at the Water Ways Park tomorrow."

"We won't be doing that now," Fran said. "Sam will find replacements. You'll get better. The conference will be over Sunday. By Monday, all will be back to normal."

Winston studied Fran. His hand moved to his middle, where he felt the bandages over his bruised ribcage.

"Will it?" he asked her, and their eyes locked.

Fran's gaze dropped as she forced herself to sound optimistic.

"Sure. Everything will be back to normal after all the company has gone."

"I'll be helping you take your furniture over to The Emporium in no time," Winston said, but it was really more a question.

The memory of his complaint at lunch about helping them resurfaced. Fran tried to smile, but her voice failed her. "When you're ready," she agreed.

Mildred heard the ambivalence, but she didn't think Winston did. He smiled as if reassured. His other hand settled on top of the hospital blanket. He looked up at the blank TV.

Fran turned to see where he was looking, and read his mind. "Do you want me to turn that on?"

"I think you have to pay," Winston said. "I don't think it's free."

"Nothing in this world is," Fran said, and she didn't move. The television would stay dark for a while until they ran out of conversation.

Mildred wondered idly how long that would be, or if they would keep talking until they reached a place between them that felt like the agreed upon truth of who they were together now.

Mildred motioned to Fran that she was leaving. Fran nodded and stood up.

She walked over to Mildred and handed her Winston's set of keys. She let her eyes do her talking.

Mildred understood. "The truck and the ladder will be at Winston's house before he gets home," her best friend vowed. "Call when you need a ride," Mildred said from the doorway. "Janie has your car, and we'll come get you."

Fran brushed away the concern over transportation. The lines in her face had softened, and she was watching Winston for a sign that he needed anything. She was a natural caregiver. "Don't worry about me. You go on to the fellowship." Fran took a deep breath, settling in beside Winston. "I'll be here as long as Winston is," Fran replied.

It wasn't a promise. It was just the truth—one that emanated more from her own faithful nature than the new nature of their relationship.

FOURTEEN

TOO BUSY TO DUST

Mildred listened to her radio on the way home. The young people had it tuned to a station she didn't know, and she heard a song about a lost highway sung by Bon Jovi. She liked Bon Jovi—was pleased with herself for knowing the name.

Still replaying the lyrics in her mind, Mildred parked with relief in her own driveway and was heartened to see lights burning in the living room and the kitchen. The rain had started and stopped as it did many afternoons in the early spring. It was steamy, the air fragrant, the stars about to shine. She didn't need an umbrella to get inside.

"I'm home," Mildred said, calling out the greeting, as she stamped her feet on the front mat before stepping inside to the foyer. The pictures of the bridges needed dusting, she saw. She had been too busy to dust.

Life was good when you were too busy to dust.

The house was filled with cooking smells. Mildred couldn't remember a time since her mother had died when she had come home and been met with the smells of home-cooking. Mildred followed the warm aromas to the kitchen, where Janie was spooning green pepper jelly into a yellow Bundt cake.

Janie grinned, her red hair in curly disarray about her. Her clothes were wet in splotches, and flour had stuck to the dampness. The sink was full of dirty dishes. The mixing beaters were lying with dripping cream-colored batter on the counter. Cake flour was on the floor, and drops of batter speckled the kitchen cabinets from when the beaters had been lifted out before turning them off and flicked the yellow droplets everywhere. Mildred pressed her hand to her mouth.

Exhilarated by her cake baking efforts, Janie was oblivious to Mildred's reaction. She reported excitedly, "I didn't see about the layer pans until I had already used this one," Janie said, pointing toward the heavy metal Bundt cake pan that Mildred had forgotten she even owned.

Mildred hadn't used it in years—didn't know how Janie had found it.

"And then I realized that you needed to put the jelly between the layers of cake, and I thought, how can I do that, with only this one big layer? I found this," the young woman explained, holding up the melon baller. "And what I did was dig out small holes around the cake, which is not as easy as it sounds. Al ate the balls of cake."

"And now I'm filling the holes with the green jelly. You had all kinds of jelly, but I liked the color of this the best, and besides I think green is God's favorite color," Janie continued. "It won't look the same as yours, but it will be good, I'm pretty sure."

Mildred walked over and placed her arm around the girl's shoulders and hugged her lightly. "Of course your jelly cake will be good."

Janie affirmed this with a quick nod of her head. "I laid out the Cool Whip to thaw. It was still in your freezer, and the instructions said to put the Cool Whip in the refrigerator for a day if you are going to use it. But there wasn't time for that, so I set it there in the sunlight. I've checked it. I think it will be soft enough to use."

Mildred used Cool Whip for congealed salads. She had a pint of heavy cream in her refrigerator intended as the topping for her traditional annual raspberry jelly cake.

"Many people like Cool Whip," Mildred affirmed, as she studied the ragged holes in the cake, which now held small dripping pools of green pepper jelly made from bell peppers. Mildred and Fran often lunched on wheat crackers with pepper jelly and cream cheese. Pepper jelly had some kick to it.

"This would be a good cake for St. Patrick's Day," Janie observed. "I really like green."

"We could put some of this other jelly in the center for contrast," Mildred said, reaching for a small jar of Mrs. Parsons's mayhaw jelly, which was the color of plums and apple jelly combined. It tasted like that, too. Mayhaw jelly was not always appreciated by people outside the southern states.

Janie's head whipped around. "I was just going to sprinkle some confectioner's sugar on my cake. I saw how to do that in a cookbook over there," Janie explained, pointing to a shelf that housed Mildred's copy of the Betty Crocker cookbook. "And then we can place the Cool Whip beside it and let people help themselves if they want it." Janie eyed the small white plastic container with concern.

"It will be thawed by then," Mildred assured her. "It doesn't take long for Cool Whip to soften."

Suddenly, Janie reached over to the melon baller, where the last small piece of extracted cake had not been claimed by Al. "Taste this." She pressed the ball of cake up to Mildred's lips.

Mildred popped the cake bite into her mouth and chewed thoughtfully. It tasted like cake, except for the prominent flavor of vanilla extract. Cake mixes did not typically call for vanilla extract.

As if reading her mind, Janie confessed, "I used two teaspoons of that because some of the recipes in that book had it. Betty Crocker left it out, but what does she know? She isn't even a real person."

"People like vanilla," Mildred promised.

It might be just the contrast the cake would need to combat the tang of pepper jelly that had been spooned into the carefully dug-out holes, Mildred thought hopefully.

"Did you get Chase home safely? What did his parents have to say today?" Mildred asked.

"Yes, but he was here for a while because his mother wasn't home when I got back. He cooked with me until I saw her car pull up. He's really coming out of his shell. He had learned a song, and he sang it for me. We sang it all afternoon, over and over and over again," Janie said, and her remark was almost a complaint.

"Children do that," Mildred said, glancing at the clock. "We don't have much time to get to the church."

"I'm ready to go," Janie said. "Right after I change."

The girl was a mess, but she looked delighted about it.

"You go ahead, and I'll wrap up the cake," Mildred encouraged. She reached into her drawer and whipped out the tube of waxed paper, scrolled out a piece, and zipped it off.

"Is Mr. Winston okay?" Janie asked, hurrying off down the hallway. She talked loudly to Mildred while changing.

"Scared himself in more ways than one," Mildred said. "Where's Al?"

"Al is already at the church. They needed some help setting up some tables, and you know he doesn't like staying in one place for long." Janie reappeared wearing a denim dress with a white T-shirt underneath.

Mildred nodded her approval. She recognized the garment from the mission's closet. Janie picked up her cake.

"We've all been busy today," Mildred said as they left through the back door. "These days are flying by." She remembered her earlier fear of how to entertain her guests. They had not even turned on HBO or watched another episode of "Law & Order."

As they walked to the car, Janie reported on the afternoon's activities. "You wouldn't believe it. The telephone kept ringing. People wanted to know about Mr. Winston, and now they need two more people to help with the Water Ways Park tomorrow so I've signed us up to be chaperones," Janie said, as they got inside the Coop.

"I'm sure Sam is grateful for yours and Al's participation."

"Oh, sure. But I was talking about you and me. I told them you'd be glad to help." Janie leaned over in the car and lightly rested her cheek on Miss Budge's shoulder. She looked up at her and promised with a smile, "I'm not going to spend the whole day without you, Miss Mildred. Life is too short."

Sam handed the microphone to Al, who was uncomfortable in front of so many people. He stared out at the audience blankly. Mildred hadn't expected that. Al was so personable one on one; but in front of a group of people, he looked like a terrified fifth grader on book report day.

Before the discomfort could grow worse, Sam, who was standing beside him, tried to offer Al a cue.

"Just tell people why you're a missionary and where you believe the Lord is calling you and Janie to serve next."

Al visibly struggled to collect his thoughts. Squinting at the bright light focused on him, he reluctantly placed the microphone up to his mouth and started,

"I had a brain freeze there for a minute because I was trying to think of a way to say it. It's hard to talk about deep things. Things like this," Al said, pointing the microphone around the room to include the other people. "While I was thinking about it, I saw that it wasn't complicated. Not really. It's just kind of foreign. Strange, really, because we—Janie and I—we love people, and these days, that's strange," Al concluded, as he jammed his free hand deep into the pocket of his pants. He twisted back and forth nervously on one foot and let the words spill out, "We love people is what we're all about, and we plan to keep loving them. That's why we're missionaries."

Al waved to everyone as if he were running for office. He handed the microphone to Janie. She seemed small and too young to be in such a position, staring out at people wide-eyed, who, like Miss Budge, were nodding encouragingly that it would be all right.

At last, she saw Miss Budge across the room near the dessert table and was instantly relieved. Janie wiggled her fingers and blew Miss Budge a fingertip kiss.

Mildred nodded her head encouragingly.

"Well, first of all, Al and I are grateful for the welcome you have given us. Especially Miss Mildred, who has turned over her spare bedroom to a couple of strangers who eat pizza and like to watch TV. And she is the nicest woman in the world."

The crowd laughed and applauded Mildred. A former student in the back of the room who was now a deacon hollered out, "Budge rocks!"

As the warmth of the laughter and light applause settled down, Janie rotated slowly, attempting to meet the eyes of the people who were waiting patiently and ready to listen attentively.

"We've learned a lot this week. A lot," Janie added for emphasis. "I baked a cake. And helped take care of a little boy who couldn't talk until Miss Budge used her gift of healing on him."

The audience applauded again. Mildred Budge shook her head, no.

Janie continued. "That little boy who didn't talk much can now sing up a storm. He taught me a song that he learned here yesterday. You probably all know it the same way you know that you will eat chicken spaghetti for some occasions and chicken with prunes on others."

She waited for people to laugh, but they didn't. That surprised Janie. She shrugged and began again. "Anyways, this song maybe can explain what it is that Al and I want to do." Bravely, Janie held the microphone to her lips and began to sing without accompaniment:

"This little light of mine. I'm going to let it shine. This little light of mine. I'm going to let it shine. Let it shine. Let it shine. Let it shine."

Peggy slipped over to the piano and picked up the melody. Immediately, the congregation began to sing, too, as Janie led them in the song of missions for the church.

Grown-ups who hadn't used the hand signals that accompanied the child's song were suddenly holding up one finger, going through the motions that were generally evidenced by the children when they gave their recitals after Vacation Bible School. But adults and children alike were singing the song and pantomiming the lyrics, and inside the singing was a fresh joy that permeated in the room.

"Not going to let Satan blow it out," Janie sang, huffing on her extended forefinger. "I'm going to let it shine."

The congregation agreed, singing boisterously as the childhood song was sung over and over again, until Peggy on the keyboard shifted into another old mission conference hymn that the congregation loved and knew by heart. "Spread the light. The blessed gospel light. Let it shine from shore to shore."

The congregation sang and sang until hoarse. Mildred sang along too, watching Janie, who had gone quiet now. Al held her hand patiently; and when his eyes connected with Mildred's, he suddenly raised his other hand and began to beat the tempo of the song in the air. People laughed.

Peggy finally stopped playing when Sam took the microphone and described the Faith Promise cards as if no one had heard how the system worked before, but it was the same set of instructions every year: you made a monetary pledge for financial support of missions that you could not envision meeting, but you trusted in faith that God would supply the promised amount.

The ushers moved through and passed out the blue pledge cards. Some people filled them out instantly. Others took them home to pray over and bring back Sunday morning for the offering plate.

Mildred Budge wrote down the amount from last year increased by 10% on her blue card. That was how she computed her pledge amount every year.

While Janie and Al were being surrounded by well-wishers with questions about their ministry, Mildred went to the kitchen and found Janie's cake. Only about a third of it was gone. Maybe more of it would have been eaten if Belle hadn't borrowed the Cool Whip and used it for Thelma's Banana Pudding because it didn't have the meringue. There had been an uncomfortable moment during the dessert time when the Cool Whip had gotten on Belle's arm. She had flung some of it at Sam, who had not been amused. Quiet words had been spoken between them, but their friends had backed away, giving the couple a little space.

Mildred emptied the rest of Janie's now sad-looking pepper jelly cake into the kitchen trash can, so that when they were finally back in the car and Janie asked, 'What did people think of my cake?' Mildred could say, 'I don't know, but it is all gone.'

But Janie didn't ask about her cake.

And Jane wasn't worried about taking home Mildred's cake plate either.

Janie didn't ask Mildred how she had liked her short speech and Chase's song.

Janie greeted Mildred with a quick kiss on her cheek and explained, "Al's got something else to do. We are not to wait up for him." She was carrying the two blue Hawaiian shirts Liz had donated to the mission's closet and a pair of khaki shorts. "Here are our outfits for tomorrow."

"You and Al will look cute in those shirts tomorrow," Mildred said, hoping that Liz had not seen and would not be at the water park the next day. Surely not. She didn't think Liz was the water park type. "You can take them back to Seattle," Mildred encouraged.

Janie folded the shirts on her lap and held them carefully. "They're not for Al and me. They're for you and me. We're going to match, just like mother and daughter."

FIFTEEN

DAY 3 HEARTBREAK, HEARTBREAK

The phone started ringing early Friday morning.

Sam called Mildred from the church, and she could hear him scratching through items on his check list.

"We've got the truck and ladder back to Winston's house, and old Mitch Harper chauffeured Fran and Winston home. Has anybody checked on Liz?" Sam asked.

"Why would they?" Mildred asked. "She didn't fall off the ladder."

"You women are pretty hard on her," Sam said. "She's just trying to keep living, like the rest of us."

"Not exactly like the rest of us," Mildred asserted.

"Belle told me to tell you to wear sun block and some clothes that can get wet."

"I know about sun block..."

Before Mildred could finish her statement, Sam interrupted her. "You do own some casual clothes, don't you?"

The casual clothes he was referring to were what Mildred might have once called play clothes. And, no, she did not have any.

Her casual clothes were black slacks and any blouse hanging in her closet that was the color she felt like wearing.

"Janie has the clothes all figured out," Mildred admitted in a small voice. She was miserable at the idea of wearing Hugh's blue floral honeymoon shirt, but she couldn't figure out how to tell Janie, no. Besides, she had nothing else to wear.

"We take the kids skiing in the winter, Mildred, if you are interested. We can always use another chaperone, especially one who has a gift for healing children," Sam teased.

"Sam," Mildred said flatly.

"Just kidding," he said. "Although we really usually do need more chaperones for the winter trip."

"Sam."

"Okay. Not your good work. Got it. But you may hear from me again," Sam warned, and hung up.

Mildred's hand was still on the telephone while she prayed that God would rescue her from Sam's ideas that had been fueled by the recent success—as he saw it—of her hosting missionaries and all that had followed, when the phone rang again. Expecting to hear Fran on the other end, Mildred said, "Greetings to you and yours."

It wasn't Fran.

Belle coughed twice to clear her voice in the signature sound that meant, *heartbreak, heartbreak*.

Instant tears flooded Mildred's eyes, and she sat down at her telephone table and paid close attention. That's what a telephone table helped you to do.

"I'm here, Belle," Mildred promised. "What's wrong?"

Belle stifled a sob, then gathered her courage, and said what she needed to tell a friend.

"Millie....Sam does not think...." Belle faltered, for not only was she telling a painful truth, she was also breaking the bonds of a marriage's confidentiality that she had spent forty-plus years protecting. "Millie, Sam doesn't think I'm cute anymore."

Mildred was too good a friend to feign ignorance. Mildred had witnessed the event of Sam's suspected waning admiration for his wife's charms the previous night. While rearranging the dishes on the dessert table, Belle had accidentally grazed her forearm on Cool Whip and scraped the gooey white stuff off and flung some playfully at Sam. Sam had not laughed.

That was wrong.

Sam should have let his eyes grow warm when his wife flirted with him in public. But Sam did not. Instead, an unsmiling Sam had handed Belle a course white paper napkin and walked away, his carriage as straight as it had ever been when he was a colonel in the Air Force. Only last night it was rigid with disapproval—a coldness of spine and movement that declared to all who were watching: 'My wife is not cute anymore.'

For that is what it felt like to Belle obviously and had looked like to Mildred.

"What has happened, Belle?" Mildred asked carefully, expecting to hear a version of the event that had occurred the previous night. But it was something else.

Belle confessed recklessly, "I bought some new bloomers."

"Underpants," Mildred translated unnecessarily.

"And they were from a very pink store that puts winking eyes on their bloomers."

"Your bloomers winked at Sam...." Mildred's head began to shake involuntarily, no, no, for although a lifetime single lady, she could see what was coming.

"Sam didn't wink back," Belle whispered hoarsely.

A deadly silence followed.

Mildred could see her friend's face just as if she were standing in front of her. Belle's eyes wore the expression of funeral going.

Mildred moaned in her spirit, 'Jesus, Jesus! You've got a bride in trouble.'

Jesus cared.

When Mildred opened her mouth, unplanned words spilled out. "When Sam didn't wink back, it wasn't because he doesn't think you're cute, Belle, because everybody knows you're cute. It is simply that so many men still don't like pink. I mean, really. Do any men you and I know really like pink?"

Belle took a sharp intake of breath. "I had almost forgotten that many men don't like pink, although they are supposed to now."

"Some men pretend to like pink...." Mildred began, and then added bravely, "the way some people will pretend to like Cool Whip even though it really, really isn't whipped cream."

"Sam has never been one to pretend," Belle began.

A lull occurred. Belle added, and there was a kind of fresh joy that bubbled up when she remembered the previous night's fellowship supper, "Sam hates Cool Whip. I mean, he really hates it."

"Sam is a discerning man of taste and judgment," Mildred offered. "He married you, after all."

The two friends breathed in silence together on the telephone.

"If Sam doesn't like pink, I can let those bloomers go," Belle said, turning the other cheek. Her voice was stronger. "I don't know what I was thinking..." Belle said, and her voice trailed off. There was more to say.

Mildred gave Belle some time, then asked as quietly as she could, "What else, Belle?"

"I don't know where to start," Belle said.

She took two deep breaths and began to tell Mildred what was really worrying her. "You were at the Praise & Worship service last night," Belle began.

"I was," Mildred confirmed, unnecessarily.

That was Belle's cue to say something nice about Mildred's missionaries because Mildred's missionaries were the most popular missionaries at the conference. Mildred wanted that acknowledged, but Belle was too upset to be polite and say something like, 'You got the best missionaries of anyone!' Instead, Belle asked, "Did you notice how Liz was acting last night at the supper?"

"She is apparently recovering very well from her period of grief," Mildred commented.

"She buried our Hugh just three weeks ago."

"Liz doesn't like to be at home alone."

As if she hadn't heard her, Belle continued, almost feverishly, "Well, for a couple of days we all thought she was going after Winston. You don't know anything about that, do you?" Belle asked hopefully.

"I know Winston has been in the hospital. Fran has been with him. That's why they need extra helpers today at the Water Ways Park."

"Fran? That's good." Belle said. "I heard something about them, but I wasn't sure if there was anything, you know, settled."

"They are friends," Mildred said. She didn't have permission from Fran to say more, and reporting that 'Winston likes Fran's iced tea better than Liz's wasn't much of a boast.

"Sam drove Liz home last night after the Missions Conference because she said she didn't like to drive at night," Belle admitted suddenly.

"That sounds like Sam. Mitch Harper walked me home the other night. I didn't need him to, but he did it anyway. Do the guys have some kind of new shepherding plan? Have they decided to make an extra effort to be kind to widows and orphans?"

"I don't know," Belle said, dismissing the idea as unimportant. She cleared her throat again. "Liz has volunteered to chaperone the young people at the Water Ways Park today. They had enough chaperones, but Sam made a big deal out of her offering. He thinks she's a marvel—trying to get back into church life so fast. Sam says that Liz is a testimony to Hugh's good sense. I think Liz just wants to pretend to be younger than she is. How many face lifts do you think she has had?"

"I wouldn't know about that," Mildred said.

"I knew you wouldn't. And I knew you wouldn't repeat anything I have said, but I'm considering doing the whole church a favor and just killing Liz. I thought I would just sneak up behind her and hold her bottle-blond head under the water until the air bubbles stop floating to the top. I'll be happy to buy the coffin myself, and it will be a better model than the one she put poor Hugh in."

That hurt.

It hurt Mildred to hear Hugh referred to as poor Hugh. He would have hated that, and Mildred hated it for him. She thought about Winston and wondered how long if he hadn't fallen off that ladder it would have been before they would have started calling him poor Winston.

Belle laughed again, that brittle chortle that was empty of humor and filled with other incidents and stories of rejection by Sam that she had been living with for a long time and that had taken a toll on her. Mildred wondered then if maybe that was part of what was wrong with Belle, a malady that no doctor could or would ever be able to diagnose.

"I don't know what you expect me to do about Liz," Mildred replied. She heard Janie and Al in the other room and their sudden laughter. She wanted to hang up the phone and not be everyone's best friend or Miss Budge. She wanted to be Janie's pal. She smiled involuntarily. It had been good having young, happy people in the house. They had not mentioned leaving, and she didn't want to ask. She looked up at the ceiling and heaven and told Jesus: "I have changed. You have changed me."

"I heard you're helping at the Water Ways Park, too, and I want you to keep an eye on that Liz," Belle continued.

"Be a spy?" Mildred asked sharply. "I wouldn't be comfortable spying."

"A guard," Belle corrected.

"I thought you were going to be there so you could kill her," Mildred said.

"I'm so mad I don't trust myself. And I'm not having one of my good days. I didn't get much sleep last night." Belle didn't say more than that. The winking pink bloomer incident had cost her a night's rest.

"And I'm put out with Sam, so I'm staying home. Men can be so dumb about women. So, will you watch Liz and tell me if she gets up to any mischief?" Belle demanded.

The door to the guest room opened, and Janie gave a little wave to Mildred as she headed to the laundry room to use the iron and the ironing board.

"I'm not very good at this sort of thing," Mildred said, as she saw a black Mercedes pull into her driveway. "Speak of the devil," Mildred breathed into the phone.

"What is it?" Belle demanded.

"I've got company," Mildred explained.

"I was surprised to hear you let Sam talk you into having two missionaries at your house. They seem like nice folks. They're awfully happy to be missionaries," Belle added, mysteriously.

"I'm not talking about my missionaries." Mildred's voice dropped, and she wished with all of her might that it was Fran who was on the other end of the telephone, because Fran knew how to dial 9-1-1. "I've got to go," Mildred told Belle. "Liz is here."

SIXTEEN

MAN TROUBLE

"I don't try to steal other women's boyfriends. I walk by, and men just seem to follow me," Liz said, and her voice indicated that she was as confused by this predicament as the women whose lives it changed.

"You buttered Winston's roll," Mildred reminded her.

"But that's not flirting. All church ladies do that," Liz replied, as Janie came out holding Hugh's cast-off blue Hawaiian honeymoon shirt for Mildred and a pair of camper shorts.

"I ironed this for you to wear today, Miss Mildred," Janie announced before she saw Liz sitting on the sofa. "It's you," she said, her gray eyes narrowing. "What are you doing here?"

Mildred was surprised at the suspicious tone of Janie's voice, but Liz wasn't. Most women talked to Liz Luckie in that tone.

The expression on Liz's face revealed nothing. Mildred leaned forward. Did Botox do that to a woman's face? Enable her to hear that tone of a young woman's voice and not register any kind of emotion?

Janie was wearing the smaller Hawaiian shirt, the one that Liz had worn to match Hugh's on their honeymoon at The Grand Hotel in

Point Clear. The Hawaiian shirt still had the big silver heart-shaped pin on it that Liz had used to hold the orchid from her wedding ceremony.

"You can wear this shirt with these camper shorts," Janie said. "Hold out your arms."

Liz grew more still inside herself as Mildred obediently slipped on Hugh's honeymoon shirt. Mildred felt how wrong it was. "Janie, these two shirts," she began in an effort to explain and somehow spare both women's feelings at the same time.

Liz stood up abruptly. "Those two shirts are just right for the occasion. You made a good choice," she said. Her eyes signaled to Mildred: *it's all right.*

"Blue looks good on you, Miss Mildred," Janie observed. Her gray eyes sparkled with approval and anticipation. "We're going to have such a good time today. And I do love the water so."

Liz's mouth grew rigid as she reached over to Janie and removed the large pin. "Let's do this," she said, gripping the fabric of Mildred's shirt and tightening it at the waist with the pin from Janie's shirt. "You always hide your figure, Mildred. See how the pin here can give it more shape?" Liz asked, affixing the pin to Mildred's shirt.

Janie clapped her hands. "Miss Mildred, you could dance at a Luau."

"I have never imagined myself dancing at a Luau," Mildred replied, though she was instantly transported in her mind to swaying palm trees and an ocean breeze and a vista of water that made her salivate. She would go to Hawaii that afternoon if someone would just hand her the plane ticket, and that wasn't like her at all. Not at all.

Mildred held the camper shorts up to her waist. They hung past her knees. There were pockets everywhere. You wouldn't need to carry a purse with all these pockets. She thought they were the most sensible pair of pants she had ever seen. What would it feel like to be free of carrying her purse with all of its supplies?

"I'll see you at the water park," Liz said more loudly than she needed to. She picked up her alligator handbag. It wasn't big enough to carry the stuff that church ladies toted in order to be prepared for any emergency. She couldn't save anyone with the contents of that pocketbook.

Leaning closer to Mildred, Liz added, "I just wanted you to know that I didn't mean to cause any trouble." And then, pulling her shoulders back resolutely, she added, "Life is unfair."

Mildred couldn't remember when she had ever heard a woman their age mention unfairness in life. You reach a certain age, and you realize the futility of that observation.

"So, I guess I'll see you at the Water Ways Park," Liz said, and her voice held a question she was too proud to ask.

She asked, "Is that little boy coming with you?"

Things had happened too fast for Mildred to invite Chase. She felt badly about it, but she had her hands full. Besides, there would be time for the boy when the conference was over and the company was gone. The idea made her sad; life felt unfair. Very unfair.

"Not this time," Mildred said, as Liz waved, 'Ta' and walked off down the driveway.

When the car had backed out of the driveway, Mildred said, "I don't know if we misunderstand Liz or if she just leaves behind a trail of trouble, like a tornado."

"Don't you worry about her," Janie advised. "That's one woman who can take care of herself. Though she pretends otherwise," Janie said with a sniff, as she walked off down the hallway toward where Al was dressing.

Mildred heard Janie call out, "Al, did you get a pair of shorts? You're going to need 'em."

The entrance fee covered everything inside the Water Ways Park, and there was a lot to do inside. The church had paid for everyone, and Mildred wondered how many people would complain about that if they knew it. More than the ones who complained about the price of so many printed documents from the church and the postage to mail them.

Mildred Budge did not think it was her job or her good work to second-guess the way elders and deacons spent money, but really—paying everybody's way to a water park stretched her usual response of agreement with whatever the deacons decided about the budget. She repressed the impulse to compute the cost for what appeared to be over forty people and decided she would do her best to get the church's money's worth by having a good time and saving any child that might start to drown. All of the pools appeared to be shallow, and there were plenty of parents, other grown-ups and teens everywhere. Her lifeguard intentions were not needed.

Mildred looked around at the possibilities to have a good time instead.

There was a big slide that people reached by climbing up a narrow steep ladder. Once positioned, they whooshed down on what looked like knotted throw rugs in red, white, and blue. Mildred could almost see herself whooshing down the slide but not climbing up that ladder.

There was a large pool where an improbable wave kept coming in over and over again, and each time the children in the white froth screamed as if surprised.

There were too many children in one space screaming, and none of them looked like they were about to drown.

And there was the lazy manmade river that, the sign said, carried you around the circumference of the entire park and which required the use of an inner tube as a flotation device. The big black inner tubes were stacked like tires in a rack, and people were just helping themselves. They tossed them into the entrance pool, leapt on them stomach first or sat in them, pushed themselves off, and disappeared around a bend.

She saw more teenagers from her church, the dozen adults who were walking around like Mildred wondering just what kind of chaperoning was necessary, and, finally, Liz Luckie standing off by herself wearing a white shirt and black and white striped shorts, a floppy-brimmed white straw hat and the big black Audrey Hepburn sunglasses from the funeral. For color, Liz had tied an excessively long pink scarf around her neck, and it caught the breeze like a flag.

"We're going up there, Miss Mildred," Janie said, pointing toward the tall water slide. "Most of the teens are riding the slide. It won't take long to come down once you get to the top."

"That's about a hundred stairs. I'm not going up the slide," Mildred said. She took a second glance at Janie. "Are you sure you should be sliding in your condition?"

Janie laughed away the question as Al punched Janie. "Told you so," he said.

Al had not shaved that morning. His one-day beard was dark, and he was wearing aviator sun glasses, camper shorts, and flip-flops. "You can lead a horse to water but you can't make her drink."

"I would like a drink," Mildred said, wiping some perspiration from her upper lip. Her head was sweating, too, under the straw hat that she had found waiting for her on her bed next to her pair of new flip flops: all bargains from the Dollar Store bought by Janie with money from the kitchen drawer envelope.

"Stay put, girls," Al said, resurrecting his jovial voice with determination. "I'll get us some lemonades."

It was awfully hot to be so cheerful, Mildred thought, as Janie sprayed her arms once again with sun block.

"Did we cover your face well enough?" Janie asked with concern. "Because it is really hot. You look awfully flushed, Miss Mildred. I'm not sure we should have brought you. Do I need to send you home?" Janie asked, cocking her head to the side.

Mildred wasn't accustomed to being fussed over.

"I am fine," Mildred promised, scratching her left ear. Something had just bitten her.

Al returned from the quick trip to the Drink Hut, cradling three lemonades that he paid for with another twenty-dollar bill from Mildred's kitchen drawer dwindling cash envelope. Mildred had clipped a lot of coupons to build up her petty cash. Mildred decided that she didn't care. She could save it up again when her company was gone.

"Enjoy the day," she told herself.

Al grinned toothily as he avoided a trio of wet children running toward the wave pool. He handed Janie a drink and held onto Mildred's while leading the way to the entrance pool that launched people into the river.

"Come on over here," Al said, when Mildred was slow to follow.

She was walking as fast as she could in the flip-flops, which tended to stick on the concrete walkway.

Before Mildred knew what was happening, Al had positioned an inner tube with the likeness of a cartoon character—some woman wearing a red costume and gold bangles on her wrists, standing boldly with her arms out-- in the kick-off pool where floaters launched themselves along the river's winding path through the Water Ways Park.

"Sit there, Honeybun."

Mildred looked about wonderingly. She had never knowingly sat down on an inner tube in the water wearing clothes in her life. Perspiration pooled on her forehead. She felt it beginning to drip and brushed it away with the back of her hand.

Al grinned encouragingly. "The water will cool you off. We'll do the slide a while with the kids and join you at the finish line of the river. It circles the entire park and comes out right over there," Al said. He pointed to the opposite side of the river's entrance, where people were landing. They could pick up their tubes and come back over and start again, or the attendant collected the tubes and placed them at the starting point, like clean plates at a buffet.

Janie looked concerned. "Couldn't we just ride on the river with Miss Mildred?"

Al cast a silencing, no, in Janie's direction, and Mildred saw that he was growing restless. Men got restless. Mildred understood and wanted to make it as easy for Janie as possible. She instantly decided to follow Al's instructions and get out of their way for a while. Let them go play with the young people.

Determined, Mildred lowered herself gingerly, backside first onto the inner tube. The rubber tube was warm against the backs of her thighs. However, in spite of the warmth of the sun, the water was unexpectedly cool. Mildred's bottom sank further into the water than she had anticipated. She balanced herself with her elbows on the sides of the inner tube.

Al leaned forward and handed Mildred the large lemonade with a straw.

"Just let yourself float, doll. Let the cares of the world pass away. Feel the breeze. Let the sun shine on your face. Let go, Miss Mildred."

And with that, Janie and Al launched Mildred into the man-made river. As she drifted slowly away from them, she thought: 'I will miss them. I will miss my children.' But the idea didn't make her feel like crying.

As if they could tell her thoughts were affectionately about them, Al and Janie leaned in to each other and waved. But just before Mildred's tube turned the first curve, Al's hand slipped behind his wife's back, and Mildred had the distinct impression that he was patting his wife's bottom in public. There was something else, too: a hint of some kind of hidden laughter inside his eyes that Mildred could see because Al took off his sunglasses as he waved. When he did the expression on Al's face was different. And why shouldn't it be? Mildred thought. She had only known him three days. That wasn't enough time to learn a person's face very well. Look at Fran. Her best friend still had expressions that were rising up and appearing on her face, and Mildred didn't know them all.

As the sounds of voices receded, Mildred wondered what the expressions on her face told others. She drifted in the slow tempo of the first leg of the manmade river. Some artful groundskeeper had planted heavy, draping foliage on either side of the six- foot wide waterway, and Mildred found herself drifting along under swaying limbs that were fragrant with sun and water and that other fragrance that, at first, she couldn't place and quickly realized that it had to be chlorine.

The bridge of her nose felt warm, and she was glad she had slathered on sun screen. She couldn't remember how long it had been since she had gotten too much sun. Or walked in the rain. Or sang out loud outside where anyone could hear. She wished she could hear that song about the lost highway again that Bon Jovi sang.

Mildred took a sip of her lemonade and leaned her head back against the inner tube. The warmth of the sunbaked rubber float and the gentle sway of the water lulled her into a restful passivity. Her eyelids began to droop against the bright sun. Water lapped over the edge of the inner tube and dampened her shirt and shorts. It felt good. Soothing. The muscles in her arms relaxed, and her ankles and feet swayed purposelessly in the cool water. Mildred drifted, inhaling, her mind roaming as one sensation led to another. She felt like a kid again.

On either side of the water she could see young people moving in groups toward the slide, where whoops announced the newest launch of a daredevil. The motion of the river calmed Mildred. She was, ripple by ripple, letting herself sink into ever deepening relaxation when, suddenly, she felt a tiny stab against her hip. Tipping a hip up toward the sky, Mildred explored the region with her hand and found that the large silver pin that Liz and Janie had used to cinch the shirt had popped open and was in danger of stabbing her and her inner tube. She removed the pin, snapped it closed with one hand, and tucked it deeply into the side pocket of the camper shorts.

Mildred was attempting to regain that breath of easy peace known only briefly seconds before when an unexpected whirlpool of motion shifted her against the manmade shore. Eyes open now in surprise, Mildred found herself for a few moments whirling in an eddy, spinning like a top against something that looked like a boulder. Upon touching it, Mildred realized that it was only some kind of dense rubber—not a hard rock at all. How strange. And then she remembered Al's expression, and she could translate it: there would be startling surprises along the river, and he had known that and sent her off without warning her about what to expect. Al probably thought it was funny. Al would be laughing with Janie while Mildred was whirling around trying to hold onto the big cup of lemonade.

"He's like a big old kid," Mildred assessed as she placed her foot against the fake boulder. Before she could shove herself away and back into the river's more tranquil flow, Liz swirled by her on a Dora the Explorer tube.

Mildred tilted her lemonade toward Liz in greeting and was just about to tell her that her pink scarf was trailing in the water, when suddenly Sam appeared, perched on his own inner tube and paddling after Liz.

No. No. No.

'I walk by and men seem to just follow me.' Liz had said the very words herself.

Mildred wondered what her ethical response to this situation should be.

Unsure of what she was going to do, Mildred kicked off from the rubbery boulder, aiming her backside toward Sam and Liz. She wasn't moving fast enough, so she began to kick with her feet. Mildred could hear them ahead; and as she kicked harder, she heard Liz's lilting voice, "I miss Hugh so, so desperately. I don't know how I am going to get all the yard work done this summer."

"Baby...."

'Had Sam said baby?'

Then, Liz screamed like a baby.

"Hold on," Sam called out.

Mildred's tube bumped against another rubber rock, which gave her an additional opportunity to push with her feet. The flow of water changed, growing faster, and Mildred saw the foaming water meant to resemble rapids ahead that had already swallowed up Liz.

Sam was struggling to reach out to Liz and grab her hand, but she was flapping them in the air, trying to shield her make-up from getting wet, and crying,

"Mercy. Mercy me!"

Sam caught up to Liz and was holding onto her tube when Mildred heard him say,

"Hang in there, baby. It's not deep. We'll be at the end soon."

Baby.

Baby!

Not baby!

Mildred didn't think about what to do. As if she were riding in a bumper car, Mildred slammed into Sam's tube. Sam registered surprise. Having jarred him apart from Liz, Mildred took his place, hooking Liz's tube with her right foot as her hand with deadly surety, retrieved the big silver pin and snapped it open.

Without planning to, Mildred moved the hand with the pin and stabbed Liz's inner tube underneath. Then again. The poke made a whooshing sound, and the air began to bubble out and around her.

Liz didn't see. Sam didn't see.

Only God saw.

Only God knew that when the air began to leak out of Liz's inner tube, the fear that finally registered on Liz's face was real—more real than her feigned obtuseness about gutters or her need for Sam's hand in a man-made rapids.

It was honest-to-God fear: 'I'm about to have my makeup washed off and my hair soaked free of hairspray and curls. My clothes will be wet and cling to my body, which has grown older in so many ways that starch and foam cannot in this dripping moment disguise.'

Sam saw it happening, and laughed because men do laugh at such things.

Mildred didn't laugh. She asked, "Liz, can you swim?"

But before Liz could reply, she sank down into the water. All anyone saw then was the straw hat and the swirling pink scarf.

There it was: a real rock and a real hard place, and Mildred was in between them. As Mildred grabbed Liz's hand and pulled her up onto her own inner tube, Mildred prayed, "Forgive me my trespasses."

Liz was a drowned rat.

Really.

A man-stealing rat who had been surprised by an unexpected baptism that had not only destroyed her carefully contrived appearance, but also proved that Liz did not have a sense of humor.

Liz was the only person from church who didn't laugh. She was at Water Ways Park where these things happen. People got wet.

But when it happened to Liz Luckie, the woman did not laugh. There was one thing that Mildred knew about Sam that Liz did not know: Sam liked to laugh when he didn't know what to say. And Sam liked women who could laugh at themselves, because if he was laughing and they weren't, then Sam felt like they didn't see the world the same way and that made him not know what to say.

Mildred saw all of these dynamics happen as Liz stamped her feet at the end of the river ride where the tubes were left behind. Drenched, water squished from her clothes and shoes. She had lost her black Audrey Hepburn sunglasses. Her wilted wet straw hat clung around her, and the sheer pink scarf had sort of tied itself around her neck. Without her disguise, it was easy to see who she was. Mortal. Needy. And she didn't know how to laugh at herself.

Just that fast, the fascination with Liz was over-- for the day, at least. No bloodshed had occurred.

That didn't mean that Mildred didn't feel some guilt. Realizing that there was nothing to be said to anyone, Mildred palmed the jumbo safety pin and tossed it in the trash can the first chance she got.

Someone handed Mildred a cone of pink cotton candy as a tribute for saving someone's life (everyone knew the water wasn't that deep, but people wanted to glamorize it), and others who heard that Mildred had saved a woman from drowning-- sort of-- brought her other tributes: she was given a book of passes for three future trips to the Water Ways Park; she was granted a ten dollar gift card to be used at the Drink Hut because her lemonade got tossed aside somewhere on the river, and she was presented with an extra-large T-shirt that had a cartoon character and the words *Wonder Woman* on it.

Mildred graciously offered Liz the Wonder Woman shirt to wear.

At first Liz refused, but then Mildred leaned forward and whispered something in her ear.

Without even saying thanks, Liz grabbed the shirt and wrenched it down over her head. The shirt swallowed her up, making her look more like a drowned orphan than a serial widow who was all wet.

"Do they show now?" Liz demanded, pulling her shoulders back so that her chest could be surveyed.

Mildred glanced quickly and shook her head just as fast. "But you might want to wipe your nose."

She continued with that kind of good advice that real friends can say to one another when they have each other's interests—and the interests of other friends—at heart.

By three o'clock when the youth event was winding down, Mildred Budge was ready to go home. It was the first time she had ever been recruited as a chaperone and not been really needed by the young people.

"I think it's time for me to go home, too," Liz said, as she looked around for someone to drive her there. Sam couldn't leave until the event was finished. The other chaperones were scattered, moving about the park looking after the young people.

Al reappeared with Janie. His face was sunburned. He eyed Mildred's cotton candy. She handed it to him wordlessly. He really was just a big old boy.

"It's hot out here," Al said, taking a bite of candy. He scratched his beard. It itched in the heat. His eyes were freshly bloodshot from opening them in chlorinated water.

Janie looked exhausted. "Are you ready to go, Miss Mildred? We can leave, can't we? We don't have to get any kind of permission, do we?"

"We can go anytime we want to," Mildred assured her.

"Let's go home then," Janie asked, and Mildred was pleased.

"Yes. Let's go home," she agreed. Al already had the car keys.

When Mildred looked back at Liz she felt sorry for her. She was standing all alone. Even though she looked as helpless as ever, no man seemed to care. Not even Sam.

Mildred motioned to Liz to come on; and Liz hurried after them, awkwardly taking up the rear of what appeared to be a happy family on their way home after a fun day at the water park.

SEVENTEEN

WHO'S ON THE PHONE?

The church secretary called early Saturday morning and asked for Al or Janie.

Al was already dressed, so Mildred handed him the phone. Then, Mildred sat back down to continue eating her bowl of oatmeal.

Al's bowl was empty. He was eating toast now. That's how he ate breakfast: one course after another.

It was hard to fill up a man, Mildred realized.

After the phone call, Al's face wore an expression of irritated confusion, which he shook off, when he announced in wonder, "They want us to come over to the church this morning and talk about raising our financial support. I told them we'd come along later, and the woman on the other end of the phone got a little testy about it." Al sounded testy when he described her.

Mildred stopped. *Who had called from the church*? *The woman on the other end of the phone had not sounded like what's her name? Oh, what was that woman's name*?

While Mildred puzzled over the name of the church secretary, Janie and Al traded glances that Mildred could not translate.

When Al's gaze intersected with Mildred's, he said, "I guess you're wondering how long we plan to hang around." His broad smile had become a short bark of a laugh that was louder than it needed to be. It reminded her of Sam.

"You can stay as long as you need to," Mildred promised readily, looking at Janie. The girl was wearing another outfit from the mission's closet: an orange gingham shirt and a pair of green cotton Capri's. Fran had donated the pants, and Mildred wondered if Janie would mind that, knowing that they had belonged to someone so much older than she. But Fran always looked younger than she was, and Janie looked more like a teenager than a missionary.

Janie nodded to Mildred that she was ready for her cereal. Mildred spooned out the last cup of warm oatmeal and sprinkled on some brown sugar and raisins. She loved oatmeal. It was greatly undervalued as a comfort food—better than ice cream and better for you.

Janie sat down at the kitchen table on what had always been Fran's chair. Like Fran's cast-off Capri's, the place suited her, and Mildred knew another start of dismay that the girl would leave now. Life would leave her house, and she would be alone again, except for the boy from across the street. If she worked hard maybe Chase could start school in the fall.

"Orange is becoming on you," Mildred said. "Which is unusual because you have red hair. But it looks good," Mildred assessed, as she handed her the bowl.

Janie stared down at the cereal, avoiding Al. They must have had some kind of argument. Janie had been quiet, and Al had been in a black mood since after church last night.

When Mildred had asked why, Al had stared off into space and said,

"I thought they would take up one of those love offerings. Janie and I have pitched in. We both went to everything. She cooked a cake. Helped baby-sit that kid from across the street. I set up tables. I thought when it was all over, they would pass the plate around for us. But it was just those blue cards," Al said irritably. "Stupid blue cards. And why do they think we are going over to that church again this early on a Saturday morning when we've spent every night there and hours in between doing all kinds of stuff that's not a lot of fun? Probably want us to alphabetize those damn blue cards. Raise financial support as secretaries."

Janie stared down as Al complained.

"Do you know what they really want of us at the church?" Al asked bluntly.

He was looking at Mildred, and she didn't know what to say.

She answered as best she could. "They probably want to help you line up some appointments with other churches in the area to raise your funding," Mildred theorized.

"Is that all?" Al demanded, standing up, and Mildred felt the size of him.

`He needs to be outside,' she thought. He hadn't complained when he had had work to do. She wished that Winston wasn't in a neck brace. He and Al could go work over at The Emporium and unload some furniture. It was a big building, and Mildred's house was getting too small for him.

"What else could it be?" she asked.

Al scratched his beard and then his belly. "The secretary sounded funny is all. I heard some more people talking in the background."

"The regular secretary doesn't work on Saturday," Mildred said as the truth came to her. "Women of the church volunteer to answer the phone in the church office on Saturday because that's the regular secretary's day off. Those other people you heard are probably the clean-up crew for last night. We all take turns. There's always a lot of cleaning up to do after the Missions Conference."

Al didn't look as if he had understood a word Mildred had said. Janie spooned more sugar onto her oatmeal and began to eat it. But her appetite did not last. Three bites later, Janie pushed the bowl away from her and smiled apologetically at Mildred.

"Sorry," she said with a shrug. "I thought I could eat it."

"You'll settle down soon," Mildred promised, although she did not understand very much about the tempo of a pregnant woman's body adjusting to various stages of pregnancy. "When is the baby due?" Mildred asked.

Janie looked at Mildred and shook her head. "I don't know. I haven't been to the doctor yet."

Mildred shook her head in disbelief. "How do you know you are pregnant?"

"Oh, Miss Mildred. They have those kits you can buy at the drugstore. You pee on a stick, and it tells you in plain English."

Mildred winced at the crudeness of Janie's description, but the answer didn't satisfy her. "But you must see a doctor right away. If it weren't Saturday, I'd call and make an appointment for you right now. But there wouldn't be any point, would there? Because you're leaving." Mildred was surprised at the sadness in her voice, and hoped that Janie had not heard her regret. It was her own problem: losing Janie. And Al. Life would get back to normal.

It would be all right.

Janie shook her head. "No insurance. And Al says that women have been having babies for years without doctors. He thinks the medical profession is a money-making racket."

"It is a racket. Just like the drug pushers on TV. The pharmaceutical companies," Al interjected. "Legalized drug-selling. That's all it is. First, they make up a condition for you to have, convince you that you have it and that you need a fix; then, they sell the drugs to you." He looked out the kitchen window.

How quickly he had become discontented.

"Even so," Mildred said. "Pregnancy is not a condition that is fixed by drugs."

"It could be," Al said too quickly. Then, realizing that he had said something wrong, Al rubbed his whiskery chin and said, "I better get a shave before the day gets any older."

"Al gets tired of shaving," Janie explained quietly after Al had left the room. "I told him just to grow a beard, but he said people don't trust men with beards. I don't think that's true. Didn't Abraham Lincoln have a beard?"

Mildred nodded and decided to change the subject. Their situation was not one she could fix. "It was a good Missions Conference," Mildred said. "I mean, overall."

"I've never seen anything like it," Janie confessed, and her shoulders went limp. The girl was tired, too. Of course she was tired. She was pregnant and staying in a strange house and not able to eat in the mornings. Mildred wanted to wrap her in a big quilt and put her on the sun porch and let her rest. Keep her safe.

Janie ran her hand through her just-washed hair unselfconsciously. Her hair was drying with the mousse and caught the light. She had pretty hair, but it didn't look as red—it was more brown today. It occurred to Mildred then that Janie colored her hair and that she was using some kind of temporary rinse. That would explain why the orange color looked good on her. She wasn't a natural redhead.

"When you say that you have never seen anything like it, I believe you," Mildred said, slowly. "But....do you know the Lord?" The words surprised Mildred, coming out of her mouth unplanned.

"Jesus?" Janie clarified, not uncomfortable with the question.

Mildred nodded seriously, as she abandoned the dirty dishes and settled down into her chair next to the girl, who seemed ready to talk.

"Of course," Janie said. "Praise the Lord and all that. I know who Jesus is."

"Mercy me," Mildred said, unconsciously imitating Liz from yesterday.

"Jesus is not just an expression, Janie dear, though people use his name like that all the time. And Jesus is not just an idea—some kind of piece that you move about in an intellectual puzzle and call it theology. He is alive. And His Spirit lives...can live inside of you, if you'll let Him. And when you do, you become the person you are meant to be," Mildred promised.

"Jesus lives inside of you and the other ladies, doesn't He?" Janie asked thoughtfully. "I think I see Him in you," Janie said, studying Mildred.

"Thank you," Mildred replied, deflecting the praise. "He wants to live in you, if you want Him to," she pressed.

Janie took a square of Al's cold toast and nibbled tentatively. Thinking hard, she sat back in her chair and said the most amazing words, "I think I do. I think I do want Jesus," she said. "It's so nice here. So clean and orderly. Is that what you mean?"

"That's a start," Mildred said, as someone chose that most inconvenient moment to knock loudly on her front door. "We will come back to this, Janie. But before I answer that door, will you say the words—say His name?" Mildred felt an urgency in that question.

"Jesus?" Janie asked, crossing her arms across her stomach in the way that pregnant women did when they wanted to remind themselves: 'I am not alone in my body anymore.'

The knocking continued, soft and constant.

"Jesus!" Janie said with a light laugh, and then she hollered through the open kitchen door toward the living room. "Al, get the door!"

They heard the front door open.

It was Chase again. Alone. Carrying another Ziploc bag.

This time Mildred didn't even ask where his parents were.

Al followed the boy in; and for a second, Al allowed them to see that he was irritated. His voice proved it.

"Miss B. I don't want to tell you your business, but your neighbors think you are the unpaid babysitter. How long you gonna let this go on?"

Mildred was startled by the tone of Al's voice and the exasperation. Janie attempted to cover for him.

"Al, you go finish getting cleaned up. Maybe we can go out while the boy's here. We can take the car, can't we, Miss Mildred?"

Before Mildred could say yes, Al shot Janie an infuriated look. "I don't want to go to the church and talk to anybody until something is decided."

"I didn't mean that. I meant we could go for a drive—look around some," Janie explained.

Feeling the tension from Al, Chase came over and stood close to Mildred. He handed her another bag of organic cereal—payment for babysitting. Mildred didn't open it. A stillness came over her. An authoritative stillness. She recognized it from her quiet time when she was reading the Bible and the Holy Spirit wanted to get her attention. He did it like that: with that authoritative stillness that translated: Watch. See. Pay attention.

Mildred placed the bag of cereal on the table and looped her arm around the boy's shoulders. "Have you had breakfast, Chase?" Miss Budge asked brightly, and her voice was different. Different enough that Al looked at her thoughtfully, quizzically.

"I've got to get away from this food," Janie announced suddenly, pushing her chair back. It scraped on the floor, and the boy looked down and pointed at the marks. Mildred shook her head gently, pulling the boy closer to herself.

"We can go into the den," Mildred offered. "I'll do the dishes later."

"I'll do the dishes," Janie said as the telephone rang.

Mildred discreetly steered Chase into the next room near the telephone table.

"Greetings to you and yours," Mildred said brightly, holding the boy as she answered the phone. But before anyone could reply, Al wrenched the receiver out of Mildred's hand. Startled by his abruptness, Mildred stared at Al in disbelief as he pressed the receiver to his ear.

Mildred couldn't hear who had called or what they had to say, but she watched Al's face; and intermittently, Mildred turned toward Janie, whose expression went from relaxed to guarded. Finally, there was a look in Janie's eyes that Mildred had never seen before. Al's, too.

Mildred pulled Chase close to her.

"I told you so," Al said to Janie, and there was a small trace of blood on his jaw line where he had nicked himself shaving in a hurry.

"Who was that?" Janie asked, brow wrinkling. She pressed one hand onto her midriff, the way that Winston had tried to test his bruised ribs after his fall.

"Someone who thought that they was talking to the old lady. You want to know what the message of the day is?" he asked Mildred sarcastically, and there was an anger in him that surfaced, replacing the jovial voice that had grown too loud just minutes before.

"What message?" Mildred asked quietly as she nudged Chase more toward the front door. She wanted to reach for Janie, too, as Al's anger filled up the room.

"You are supposed to leave right away, Miss Ma'am. Get out of your own house."

"Why would I do that?" Mildred asked carefully, her voice fading as she saw a cold hardness show in Al's eyes. The grin was gone. Holding her gaze, Al jammed a hand down into Mildred's purse on the table and found her car keys and her wallet. "I'm going to take us a love offering, considering we got stiffed last night."

Mildred understood everything then, but her expression did not change. It was the one she had always worn that covered the grief she felt for the students in her class who tried to cheat on tests.

"Get whatever you want, girl. We're getting out of here now," Al ordered Janie.

Janie seemed to slump. She didn't move fast enough. Al walked over and slapped Janie hard across the face. "Get moving," he told her.

Janie wouldn't meet his gaze. "You said you'd never do that again," Janie replied in a wounded voice.

Chase grabbed hold of Miss Budge's left leg, and the former school teacher patted him on the head, running her hand down his neck to the small of his back. She pressed him hard with a hand that said, *Stay close. I've got you.*

"Take all the money she's got in the house," Al said. When Janie didn't move immediately, Al barked, "Get moving! I don't know how much time we've got."

Janie was too slow. Al flung his hand out, the back of it slapping against Janie's arm and chest. She recoiled, then steeled herself.

It had happened before.

"Leave her alone," Mildred commanded. "This instant."

Al walked over and slapped Miss Budge hard across the face.

"You shut up," he said. "I am worn out with hearing you yammer on and on," he said.

The boy clung to Miss Budge.

Janie hurried to the bedroom and returned with one packed suitcase. It had been readied for a quick getaway. She carried some of the embroidered towels bunched in one hand. Her eyes would not meet Mildred's. The boy was trembling against Mildred's leg, hanging on.

"Did you get that diamond brooch?" Al asked sharply.

"It wasn't there," Janie said, not meeting his gaze or Mildred's either.

"What do you mean—it wasn't there?" Al demanded. "It's either there, or that one knows where it is," he said, jabbing a thumb in Mildred's direction.

"Ask her yourself because I don't know where it is," Janie explained with a flash of self-assertion.

Al revolved slowly toward Mildred. A small smile showed up on his lips but not in his eyes. They were dark and angry. He was a stranger.

"You think you're smart, don't you?" Al demanded. "Where did you hide it?"

Miss Budge did not answer him. He moved as if to slap her again, but Mildred did not budge. She stood her ground, her gaze covering Janie, her right hand on the boy's head. In response to the strong tensions in the room, Chase wrapped himself more tightly around Mildred's leg.

"Get the kid," Al told Janie. "We're going. I don't have time to make her talk."

"I don't want to fool with him anymore," Janie whined. "Really."

Al smacked Janie again on the rump. "Do what I tell you. The little creep is our insurance policy. We're going to need it. We don't have much time," he said, going to the front window. He looked out. There was no traffic.

Janie reluctantly reached out to grab the boy's shoulder.

At the same time, Mildred reached down and tilted Chase's head up, and began to sing softly, "London bridge is falling down. Falling down. Falling down."

Her eyes crossed suddenly, and her cheeks were sucked in. Chase's grip tightened on her hand, and a small quizzical glow grew in his eyes as she sang just before falling, "My fair laddie." Miss

Budge plopped to the floor, and Chase dropped down immediately by her, holding onto her hand.

"What the hell? What's going on with her?" Al asked. "Get the damn kid."

"Something's wrong with her," Janie said. "You hit her, and now she's having some kind of fit," Janie declared as she half-heartedly reached for Chase, who clung to Miss Budge as she drooped, and then fell backwards onto the floor. A shoe fell off as her legs shimmied. Flat on her back, her tongue peeped out of her mouth and lolled, while her eyes rolled back in her head. Chase sat down firmly beside Miss Mildred, holding tightly to her hand.

"She's having some kind of fit," Janie said. "We've got to call an ambulance."

"You call an ambulance. I'm leaving," Al said, moving toward the front door.

"We can't leave her like this," Janie objected, falling to her knees beside Chase as he held onto Miss Budge.

"People will be here in a minute. They can call the ambulance."

Janie shook her head.

Al walked back to her, his eyes locked on hers. He took her wrist and yanked it. Janie pulled away. "I won't leave her like this," Janie said.

Al leaned down and kissed her violently on the mouth and then ran out the front door with Miss Budge's car keys and the wallet that he had taken from her purse.

In the distance, they heard the first sounds of a police siren.

Miss Budge heard the tires of her precious red Mini-Cooper peel out of the driveway as the sounds of a police siren drew closer. Janie reached for the phone and was dialing 9-1-1, when Miss Budge sat suddenly upright on the floor and felt around with her foot for her missing shoe.

Chase grinned and tried to make his eyes go crossed. He reached out with both hands and pressed the sides of Miss Budge's cheeks to make them go in again, like a fish. She took both of the child's hands in hers and kissed the palms reassuringly.

"Miss Mildred! Are you all right? You must have fainted. You gave me a scare, I'll tell you," Janie exclaimed, as if nothing had changed between them.

Mildred stood up, brushing off the back of her clothes.

"You didn't have a fit," Janie concluded, looking at the front door. Al was gone. The police car was in the driveway with the blue light still rotating. The siren died.

"I met a woman the other day who described how to do that when she wanted to leave a room and couldn't," Mildred explained standing up, as car doors slammed outside.

"What's going to happen to me?" Janie asked plaintively, as the reality of her situation began to dawn.

Mildred didn't answer the young woman. She held on tightly to Chase as the front door was pushed open and two officers came inside, trailed by Sam Deerborn and Mitch Harper.

Sam stopped when he saw Janie. His eyes moved from her to the boy and then past them both to the spare bedroom.

"Al's gone," Mildred reported. "He left alone in my car. He stole a wallet from my purse."

"No biggie, as long as you're all right," Sam said, studying Mildred's face. She nodded that she was fine. "We'll call the credit companies and cancel the credit cards," Sam promised instantly. "I'm so sorry, Mildred. But you're all right," Sam confirmed.

"He doesn't have my credit cards," Mildred said. "And I only have two anyway." She did not add that she used them judiciously and paid off any charged balance immediately the next time a bill came due. She was uncomfortable with debt—always had been.

Mitch Harper stepped closer. He eyed her with great concern, his gaze moving steadily like a camera that pans a scene before coming to rest on a focal point. His gaze found its resting point on her face.

"The man hit you," Mitch said, observing the red hand print that had not faded entirely from her face. He stopped himself from reaching out to erase the redness—stopped himself the way men impose a discipline on themselves that will keep them from being misunderstood. Miss Budge smiled at Mitch the way she had once upon a time smiled at his son.

"Just the once," Mildred admitted, changing the subject. Physical pain wasn't always important. When you live long enough, you learn that. She leaned closer to Mitch and confided, "What Al took wasn't my real wallet. I changed that out. I put the dummy wallet in my purse—the one that I use when I leave town. One encounters pickpockets when one travels," Miss Budge explained.

"When did you do that?" Sam asked. "When exactly did you change out your wallet, Mildred Budge?"

Without thinking, she pressed her left hand to her cheek, rubbing the redness, and the rubbing made it worse. A bruise was coming.

"The second day they were here I knew something was off, but I didn't know what it was," Mildred Budge said, turning to Mitch Harper. "You were right in your suspicions, and I'm sorry I didn't answer your questions better that night you walked me home. You will forgive me, I hope."

Mitch didn't reply. That was also true of men. She couldn't remember when she had ever apologized to a man who acknowledged that he had heard her. To accept an apology must mean that one had been hurt in the first place, and men weren't willing to admit to that.

"Why didn't you tell me you had suspicions?" Sam asked, as Mitch passed Janie off to a uniformed policewoman.

"About the time I realized that they weren't missionaries, I knew that they were my good work to do. And of course I had to do it," she explained simply. "The harvest is white."

Janie turned in the doorway, her eyes searching for Mildred's.

"Save me," she pleaded as Mildred Budge walked over to the shredder and pushed her hand down deep in to the shredded pieces of other bills and documents that thieves might have used to steal her identity. She brought out her real wallet and the rhinestone brooch her Aunt Eileen had left her.

"It's only glass, but it is an Eisenberg Original," Mildred explained, almost apologized. "And it's not worth very much—except to me. Otherwise, I would have just let you steal it." And then holding Janie's gaze, she said what had taken her twenty-five years of teaching in the public schools to learn herself:

"I can't save anybody. Only Jesus can do that."

EIGHTEEN

THE PROBLEM

"The problem with you, Mildred Budge, is that you insist on seeing the good in people. It will be the death of you," Fran said, slapping the tops of her thighs with both hands, a mannerism she used when she truly meant what she said. It also meant she was emotional about what she was saying, although nothing in the tone of her voice revealed that. "We have had this conversation before. When are you going to hear me?" Fran demanded.

"I do not always see the good in people," Mildred argued immediately. In fact, just the opposite was often true, it had seemed to her. Often she had seen that people were not good—not good at all.

"You saw the good in Janie, and she turned out to be no better than a common criminal," Fran declared. She eyed her friend with an angry compassion, and Mildred Budge understood that emotion. It made Fran angry when her friends did not live more self-protective lives.

"Now, Fran, you know that's not entirely true," Mildred replied. "The girl had fallen in with bad company. She could change."

Everyone could change who accepted Jesus and then counted on Him to remake them to become the person that He intended.

Mildred did not have to remind Fran of how sanctification worked. Fran, like every church lady Mildred knew, was working out her own salvation with fear and trembling. Sometimes when Fran was lecturing Mildred, she was really preaching to herself. Both women did that. Such was the state of their sisterhood that they understood the loop of repentance.

"Al hit you—struck you on the face!--on his way out the door. You should have told someone right away that they were imposters. I mean, really, Mildred. What were you thinking?"

"Thinking something and knowing something are two different things, and the man did hit me," Mildred said, and she marveled once again that violence existed and had come into her quiet home on Cloverdale Road.

"People are basically bad," Fran said emphatically. "The sooner you accept that, the better off you will be. And you will be theologically correct, I might add."

"You did add it," Mildred replied.

"That's because you seem to need to hear it again and again, Mildred Budge." Whenever Fran Applewhite was very serious, she used both of Mildred's names.

Steel polished steel in the friendship between Fran Applewhite and Mildred Budge.

"Christianity is based on it. Sin is. Accept that, Mildred Budge."

"I accept the reality of sin. It is just easier for me to see the planks in my own eyes than the specs in other people's." She looked at Fran, and the two women's eyes met, and simultaneously they laughed. They knew each other's specs very well.

"It is not so very hard to see the specs in other people's eyes," Fran said, stretching out the words in the way that Southern women did. "Janie and Al lied to you. They impersonated real missionaries. They stole their identities. They took your money. He drove off in your car. Those are a list of their specs that I see very, very clearly."

"But he didn't get my real wallet or even come close to stealing my eternal identity," Mildred argued, though she was not defending them. She was trying to tell the truth.

"Big deal," Fran said, dismissing Mildred's implied distinction. "He couldn't do that anyway. We all know who you are. What we don't know is why you let those strangers stay in your house. Al could have been an ax murderer, for all you know."

"Ax murderers are not as common as people think. Al was with Janie, and she could never be an ax murderer. I gave the man credit for Janie--Amanda."

She needed to remember that. Janie's real name was Amanda Fleming. It was taking Mildred some time to get used to it. In her heart, she knew the problem: she preferred the girl called Janie to the criminal named Amanda.

"What about the real missionaries? Do they know that a couple of conmen were impersonating them down here?" Fran asked, looking around the kitchen. Was it time to make iced tea? Lunch?

"Mitch Harper figured that out. He sensed something was wrong when Al couldn't say the blessing at the men's luncheon. Agent Harper went sleuthing. Finally, he called the real missionaries in Seattle. They answered their own telephone. That's how he knew for sure."

Fran waited while Mildred caught her breath.

"Al was stealing their mail and putting back the pieces that didn't interest him. They never knew. He intercepted the invitation to come to the Missions Conference, set up a new e-mail address, and worked the rest of it out online with Sam. The internet may be the devil's workshop," Mildred mused.

"A virtual world," Fran agreed mournfully. "I like the real world better."

"How is your real world?" Mildred asked discreetly. She had not seen Winston since The Incident. Winston was hiding out at home, still embarrassed to have fallen off a ladder at Hugh's widow's house.

"The man has gone crazy since he hit his head. Winston proposed," Fran said. Shaking her head, she added ruefully, "He's asked me to marry him. I wish he could have just kept his mouth shut."

The news did not surprise Mildred. It didn't surprise anyone but Fran, who had declared when the friendship began, "We're just keeping each other company."

"When's the wedding?" Mildred asked. "Just tell me the date, and I'll bake the cake."

The to-do list was created instantly in her mind: The hostess chain would have to be activated. A reception would need to be planned. And it would be a big reception because Fran and Winston were long-time members of Christ Church and very popular.

"I said, no, and it wasn't hard to do," Fran said, staring off at the neighbors' house, where the UPS truck had just arrived. "Their business must be doing pretty well," she commented, squinting. It was the same look she got in her eyes when she talked about their booth at The Emporium. Fran was a natural-born businesswoman.

"I don't know about that," Mildred said, following Fran's lead. Conversations with her did not usually run in a straight line. "Chase is coming along. I'm going to start on his numbers next. I'll have him reading first-grade level by the fall. I think I can, Lord willing," she added, not wanting to get ahead of the Lord and his plan for Chase and for her.

"They're using you, Mildred," Fran stated flatly. "You're a natural-born teacher, and they are using you."

"I know that," Mildred said. "But sometimes, that's what happens to Christians—and teachers—and mothers—and neighbors."

"It does," Fran agreed. And she hesitated. "I didn't mean to use you, Mildred. You never really wanted to open a booth at The Emporium."

Mildred looked up. "I did not initially. But I like it. The change has been good for me. I like having all that stuff gone from my attic. I never have to dust any of that furniture again. And, the money is welcome. Maybe we can take a cruise one day and see the world," she said, watching Fran.

The question of a cruise had come up many times, and Fran had declared, "I'm not the cruising kind. I get claustrophobic."

Mildred didn't know how one could get claustrophobic on a ship with the sea to watch, but Fran was afraid she would.

"Can you cut down on writing those meditations now?" Fran asked.

Automatically, Mildred looked past her friend to the den where her books and legal pads rested near her stack of different translations of the Bible. Writing meditations had transformed her quiet time into labor.

Somehow Fran had known that they were becoming harder and harder to write but not because Mildred was burning out with nothing to say; she had too much to say.

She was having a hard time fitting the stories of God into such small sizes. The truth of God kept filling up and overflowing the allowed word count. She had a new meditation in mind though: it was about Moses and how his mother placed him in that basket and laid it in the river and watched the river take her child away toward the plan God had for Moses, and mothers can trust their babies to God....something like that. Mildred was still thinking about it. But she could feel it growing inside of her. Would it be the last one she ever wrote? It might be. What a strange idea it was to leave behind an activity that was supposed to be a type of stewardship of a spiritual gift. But it happened. Had happened. Would happen again. To receive a good gift from heaven—and then let it go.

Mildred nodded, shifting her focus back to Fran. "Yes," she said. "And it may be time for me to change about writing the meditations." Her spiritual antenna went up, tuning into God's leading, but all Mildred Budge detected was the slight nudge that she budge toward finding a publisher who liked longer pieces rather than the short ones that were becoming harder to write. She would have to pray about that.

In the meantime, she asked Fran, "What's going to happen when we've sold everything out of our attics?"

"I've got a plan," Fran explained. "And it's a beautiful plan."

"I thought you might," Mildred said, taking note that Fran had switched back to pronouncing the word beautiful the way she had before Winston had infiltrated her life and affected her vocabulary.

"Mildred, we're going to start reading the classified ads and attending estate sales. People like us die all the time with their attics full. The relatives will need help cleaning them out. We aim to serve at our business, which we have not named yet. That was your job."

Mildred hesitated. The idea surfaced that had been lurking in the background of her attention. "Do you remember the speaker at the ladies' luncheon?"

Fran nodded politely, but she hadn't been in the room long enough to be able to pick Darlene out of a police line-up if she were called.

"In her speech she mentioned a lady who wrote to Betty Crocker and signed herself as an Unclaimed Blessing. What do you think of that name for our booth?"

A smile dawned Fran's face. "That will do. That will do just fine as a name for our booth."

Mildred nodded agreeably as the issue was settled and said, thoughtfully, as much to herself as to Fran, "But you'll get married one day."

"I don't know about that; and if I don't know, then nobody knows but Jesus," Fran said, snapping open the morning newspaper. She began to scan the classified ads, circling notices that interested her. "Our rhythm got disturbed, Millie."

"Liz broke up the rhythm but not you and Winston," Mildred said. "I'll keep practicing my song."

Mildred had long ago pledged to sing at Fran's next wedding. Fran promised to dance at Mildred's.

"I think I've changed my mind about "Walkin' My Baby Back Home." I think I'm going to want 'The Long and Winding Road' if I ever need one," Fran said, as she began to make notes of addresses of just-announced estate sales.

"That's not a very happy wedding tune," Mildred observed, reaching behind her for the spoon that she used to poke around in her flower boxes. People said she had a green thumb when what she really had was an old spoon. She poked the soil around her potted mint plants on the kitchen windowsill. Keep the soil aerated. That was the key to growing plants.

"You get older—the tunes of real love aren't so very cheerful," Fran declared, cocking an eyebrow. Mildred was surprised by that sudden movement of Fran's eyebrow. She hadn't seen that expression in years. And here it was: back again. Mildred grinned, and wished she could make her own eyebrow do that. Was it wrong to covet such a thing as another woman's expression?

"You do not sound like a woman happily in love, Frannie."

Fran laid down the newspaper and her pencil. "Winston surprised me. I thought I knew him. Thought I knew who we were together. I was wrong. But when I got over that—and got over being grateful that he hadn't been killed by that serial widow—I started wondering if I really wanted to live with him. You know? Day in, day out?"

"That is different," Mildred agreed, as the UPS truck chugged away from the neighbors' house across the street. It wasn't a very loud sound, but something about the rumbling forward motion of it caused both women to wait for it to leave their street before speaking again.

"And people often want what they cannot have, and when they can have it..."

"They don't always want it," Mildred agreed. There were days when they could read each other's minds and complete each other's sentences, and then there were the days when each woman was a stranger to the other. Each woman was under the divine cultivation of a Creator who was universal and personal and unceasing in His labor to perfect the church He considered was his bride.

"But mainly Winston proposed for the wrong reason and too soon. It would have been too soon before Liz, and it is certainly too soon now just because the old goat scared himself and feels guilty about how he acted. He was unfaithful to me, Mildred," Fran said, and her chin went up, because even though she could say the words, they hurt her. "He was unfaithful to me and unfaithful to himself," she declared, closing the newspaper emphatically.

"Did he ever explain or really apologize?" Mildred asked, feeling her friend's pain. There wasn't anything to be done about it except acknowledge it.

"Nope. Just proposed," Fran said. "I guess marrying me was supposed to cover it."

"An apology would have been smarter," Mildred surmised, wondering if Fran could hear the red flag that went up with that assessment.

"It would have been. You can't live with someone who can't apologize. I mean—what would he do after we were married and he made a mistake and he couldn't apologize? He can't keep proposing," Fran said, and laid the newspaper aside.

"You want something to eat?" Mildred asked, opening the pantry door. She stood in front of it, shopping.

"Do you ever just get tired of eating?" Fran asked. She rose and put on a pan of water to boil for iced tea.

"I do," Mildred said. "And tired of planning what the next meal will be and getting the food in the house and of feeling like a pack mule. I've got some cold cuts, but for the life of me I can't stand the idea of eating them."

Fran nodded in agreement, as Mildred unscrewed the jar of peanut butter and opened a fresh tube of crackers. When Fran saw what Mildred was doing, she got them each a paper towel to use as a plate and a butter knife to spread the peanut butter. "Do we want iced tea—again?" Fran asked.

"There are two small Coca-Colas in my fridge, if you want to risk it," Mildred said.

"You've been risking it for years. Do you think I don't know that?" Fran asked, reaching inside the refrigerator. "You keep a stash of Cokes and jar of bacon grease that you think no one knows about. We all know why your black-eyed peas taste better than anyone else's. Bacon grease! God bless you for living dangerously, Mildred Budge."

"You're supposed to throw that jar away if I die before you do," Mildred said flatly.

"Not any point in it. Everybody knows about you and bacon grease," Fran said She snapped off the Coke caps. "Have you ever really thought about that? Everybody really knows everything about everybody else. Really."

Mildred took a bite of cracker. The peanut butter stuck to the roof of her mouth. She swallowed, and then asked, "If that's true, what's the answer to your question about Liz? Does she kill them? Or do they just die—coincidentally?" Mildred asked archly.

Fran sat back in the chair that Janie had just left, and Mildred felt a sharp start of loss.

How was the girl doing in jail? Would she qualify for bail? If so, would Mildred be able to raise it? Would the church help a girl who had posed as a missionary?

"Liz doesn't kill her husbands. She just doesn't save them." Fran says. "She saves herself first, and when she does...."

"Men fall off the ladders she's supposed to be holding steady."

Fran nodded abruptly. "It's her modus operandi. We all have one. Hers happens to result in the deaths of her spouses."

"Mine was teaching. But it isn't anymore. At least, not the same way. You told Janie that I felt guilty for retiring. But I don't."

Fran made herself another cracker and listened, for she recognized the moments when Mildred was ready to see the truth and tell it. Fran was a good listener.

"I felt compelled to retire," Mildred confessed. "I wasn't burned out exactly. I felt led to retire. As if God had something else for me to do."

Fran smeared more peanut butter on another cracker and took a bite. Crumbs fell. She didn't brush them off. She listened.

"But I haven't agreed with the plan though I knew it was true," she confessed with wonder. When she did, a light flooded Mildred's face and eyes and Fran thought: 'My friend is so lovely. Everyone thinks I am the beauty, but Mildred! Look at her beautiful face.'

"That's what you saw in me, Fran. I left the school children behind, but I didn't let go of them. I've been holding onto them—all of them...." Mildred confessed with surprise. "But finally, I see. I can't save them. I have to let them go, because I cannot save them. I never could save them. I can only pray for them."

Fran finished her cracker, took a sip of Coke, and then rose and took the small bottle to the sink.

"As much as I like Coke, I just can't drink it. I'll wait for the iced tea," she explained, sitting back down. She waited another five seconds in case Mildred had something to add, and then she spoke.

"Millie, you're just like all mothers, except you have never been a biological mother, so you don't know that about yourself. You've always thought that you loved children like an aunt. But you haven't. You have loved them like a mother. And you have always wrestled with letting them go. But Millie, all mothers have to learn that—to let go of their children. It always hurts, and then you reach that point where you have to let go of yourself, too. Let go of yourself as a mother. That part is a surprise," Fran said.

Fran had three grown children, and she rarely mentioned them.

Mildred nodded, wiping her hands on the yellow-striped kitchen towel. She rose and went to her living room, leaving behind the left-overs from their lunch without cleaning off the table. Fran followed her, surprised at the change in her friend's routine of not tidying up after herself.

Mildred walked over to the pictures of the bridges that connected one shore to another and took them off her wall. She stacked them on the sofa.

"Do you want me to have Winston take those to The Emporium?" Fran asked. She studied them to see if they had any resale value.

They were charming pictures. Nostalgic pictures. She had liked them once upon a time, but they did not charm her anymore. They were too tied to one place in the now irrelevant past, and she wanted to live in the present—fully in the present. Mildred didn't want to see these pictures of bridges hanging any place she might see them again. They were a definite part of her past, and the past was behind her. It took great discipline to leave the past behind.

Sometimes it was harder than repenting of sins and accepting forgiveness.

Mildred went back to the kitchen, and Fran followed her once more.

"Yes, please. Tell Winston that he would be doing me a great service just to take them where I will never have to see them again."

Fran didn't ask questions about that. Something in Mildred's manner communicated that the truth behind it was too deep, too connected to the past for her friend to talk about what she meant easily. Besides, there was a good chance that there weren't precise words that could be used to say exactly what she meant. There were sorrows too deep for words. Fran respected that, so the only question she asked was,

"What's for dessert?"

NINETEEN

COME AND SEE

Sam came out of the prayer parlor and walked past the pulpit through the front of the sanctuary to reach the second pew where Mildred was reading her scripture before the evening vespers. She liked to be quiet before worship began. She liked to be quiet most of the time. Sam's voice jarred her, calling her from a reverie that was part prayer, part musing, part resting.

"Mildred, would you come with me?" Sam asked, leaning over. He offered his hand as if he thought Mildred was older than he was. She wasn't. One more time, Mildred took note of Sam's Old Spice and the fragrance of a bath soap that Belle bought and the detergent that she used to wash his clothes. All the fragrances blended together to become the aroma of Sam. Mildred smiled softly, coming to life out of her quiet time.

Sam's eyes glinted with purpose. In his drive to use his gift of administration, Sam sometimes overstepped the boundaries and tried to tell other people what their stewardship roles were.

Mildred wanted to say, stop for a moment, Sam. Stop fruitifying—was that a word?-- and be still with me. I would like a friend to be still with me. This impulse pulsed gently within Mildred; but like many words, she kept the notion to herself.

If a man asks for your shirt, give it to him. If he asks you to go a mile, go two.

Mildred Budge rose, and her body felt lighter, springier, more trustworthy. Her youth had been renewed like the eagle's; and even though she believed the scripture, Mildred was surprised one more time when the Word happened inside of her again.

Mildred Budge felt younger than she had before she retired from teaching school. And less heavy. And in that moment, another layer of worry that she had been bearing fell away. Mildred was not afraid she was going to cry.

Taking note of this encroachment of peace and assurance, she left behind her open Bible and her purse to hold her place on the pew that everyone knew was hers on Sunday night.

Sam stepped back and waited for Mildred to precede him, and she did, wondering only then why she was being summoned to the prayer parlor.

As she felt the curious stares of other people waiting for worship to begin watch her leave, she smiled to herself. She recalled the hundreds of children who had been summoned to her desk for a reprimand or sent to the principal's office because their infractions were greater than a teacher could handle.

Miss Budge, the fifth-grade teacher, had rarely sent a student of hers to the principal; she had always felt disloyal to a student if she had not been able to establish the boundaries for that student and then help that student see the wisdom in maintaining them. She felt the movement of those students in her own legs, and wondered where they all were—where they had walked in their journeys.

Her steps slowed as she approached the prayer parlor. She stood framed in the doorway, her feet ensconced in low-heel black shoes stolidly placed on the ground with enough space between her feet to achieve the balance and perpetuate her reputation that was often characterized, "She's got her feet on solid ground—that Mildred Budge."

Inside the prayer room were all the deacons and the elders and Brother Joe. Mildred suddenly realized how tired he looked. How had he gotten so tired and no one had noticed? Were they all so busy being fruitful that they had been unable to see that their pastor was tired, the way Joe was tired? Deeply. Why the poor boy was barely hanging on, and there was Sam coming up with another meeting for him to attend. For all the boys to attend. She looked at Sam and thought if he had been her student she would have sent him to the principal, not because she could not tell him what the boundaries were but because boys like Sam needed to be in time out occasionally to remind them how to be still.

She made a mental note to pray for Joe and pray for Belle who had lived with Sam all these years—and who knew what that was like?--and then Mildred closed her eyes briefly, for it seemed that there was no end to the items one added to the prayer list even on days when God commanded them all to rest. Even as she chided herself for working, Mildred thought with determination that was very like Sam's: *We need to get busy and find the new minister before Joe ends up in the hospital!*

'Help Joe. Help us. Help me, Jesus,' she prayed silently, as all the men rose, every one of them. She smiled her universal hello, nodding as she made eye contact with each man; and then as the men nodded in return, they waited for her to lower herself onto the green velvet high back chair before taking their seats again.

The chair was uncomfortable. But it was too expensive to give away or put in a rummage sale to raise money for missions. The hard-backed chair had been moved around the church building for years and had finally landed here. It was a memorial gift from some woman long ago in honor of her husband upon the occasion of his passing. The man had been an elder whose name was not said anymore, but the record of his membership and service to the church was inscribed on a small bronze plaque on the back of the chair. Mildred Budge searched her memory for that name, but she couldn't remember it. *Perhaps that wasn't a sign that she was older than she felt. Perhaps it wasn't a sign of anything. Perhaps she just couldn't remember.*

Accustomed to women making small talk easier, the men waited uncomfortably for Mildred to speak. When she didn't, Brother Joe leaned forward and said unexpectedly, looking right at her, "Mildred, we have disturbed your quiet time before evening worship."

"You have," Mildred agreed, but her tone was not a chastisement; she was simply acknowledging the truth.

The light in Joe's eyes faded for a moment, and she thought: he's going to die right here, right in front of us, and everyone will say, "He died serving the Lord."

In the back of her mind, she heard her father warn her: "People will work a good horse to death. Mildred, you are a good horse."

She sent a quick prayer to Jesus that Joe would not be overworked and then turned her attention to Sam, who cleared his throat, announcing in this way that he was taking over the conversation.

"We were going to come see you at your home, but there you were just sitting there all quiet and by yourself in the sanctuary, and it's best not to let the sun go down on one's duties," Sam said too loudly.

His voice carried, and the sound of it pleased him. Sam looked around the room to confirm that all had heard him, and the other men—team players all—nodded that they agreed.

But that wasn't how the scripture read, Mildred thought. She cast a quick glance at Joe to see if he would sharpen the interpretation of that referenced verse, and then watched as the misuse of it was left behind so that the men could fulfill their mission.

Men are so funny, Mildred thought. And so serious. It was too bad that there wasn't an incident in the Bible of a male equivalent of Martha, so men could be set free from their duties to find that better way that Mildred and her female friends were learning each day of their God-given lives. Too bad that the boys couldn't see themselves in Martha, just because she was female. She had never heard Martha referenced as a sermon point for any group that had men in it.

She saw Winston on the far end and offered him a smile. He looked miserable. He couldn't meet her gaze. She tried to send him an 'It will be all right' smile, but he was staring at the table top. Fran was saying "beautiful" the regular way, and Winston must have heard that by now.

Sensing her wandering thoughts, Sam's voice grew louder, commanding attention. She had an idea where he was going. Sam was never louder than when he was trying to demonstrate that he could be humble.

"We owe you an apology, Mildred. We asked you to host missionaries who turned out to be criminals, and if we had been doing our jobs better—if we had been better shepherds--we wouldn't have been so easily fooled."

Mildred smiled again, benignly. What had happened was nobody's fault. Something in her instant forgiveness made Sam want to apologize more.

"You could have been in danger. You were in danger. We deeply, deeply apologize, Mildred." Sam was sincere. Loud and clear, Sam was very sincere.

Mildred waited a few seconds though she could have answered immediately. Forgiveness was a tricky business. If you were too quick to forgive, Sam didn't think you had really heard him. In order to keep the meeting short, she appeared to weigh his confession before offering her reply. Then, she did speak, and her voice contained a rich timbre of teacherly authority.

"You are absolutely forgiven," Mildred said, trying to tell the truth.

"After all is said and done, you are the woman of the hour, no doubt about that," Sam added, opening a grey folder that his hands had been fidgeting with while he spoke. He removed a document from the folder and held it up for all to see. Mildred leaned forward but still couldn't read it. Sam summarized the contents:

"Scott Ridley and Amanda Fleming are wanted by law enforcement nationwide, and there was a reward for information leading to the capture of Scott Ridley. They haven't caught him yet."

"They're not even married?" Mildred asked. Part of her wasn't surprised. Part of her was grieved. She sat back deeply in the chair that had been given in honor of....*what was that man's name*? Did it matter? But that was the whole purpose of a memorial gift—to remind members of the church of the people who had been there before.

When women in the church died, the ladies' group went together and took up a collection and bought memorial flowers for the day of her next birthday, and that was it. Her name was in the bulletin. The flowers are given today in honor of our sister (add name) who passed away on (add date). Mildred had often added the names and dates herself, leaving the standard Bible verse that accompanied the memorial flowers announcement: Precious in the sight of the Lord is the death of his saints.

Sam, the saint, leaned forward on the table, using his pen to tap the surface the way a judge holds a gavel. The demeanor of a judge suited him.

"Nothing about them was legal." Sam paused, and then told Mildred what he really wanted her and the boys to understand: "I have applied for that reward on your behalf."

It was a shocking announcement. Mildred watched as Joe sat back tiredly in some state of defeat that he could not even explain. But Mildred understood. Nothing about applying for a financial reward fit Mildred's sensibilities. *How could Sam know her and not understand that*?

But Sam didn't understand. His expression was earnest. As Mildred looked around the room, she saw the faces of the other men so pleased with how they were attempting to take care of her now that Mildred couldn't tell them: *Don't load me down with that kind of money. I don't want anything else that I have to guard or take care of or manage*.

But she didn't. Instead, she said very simply but with the kind of authority that had always communicated well with school children, "I will not accept any bounty money."

Sam had expected that reply. It was the kind of dumb statement that women made because they didn't know any better, and that's why a man like him had to help Mildred see the light. He pressed forward immediately. It was his way. He had a plan. Even though Sam had just apologized to Mildred for trespassing against her, he did it again.

"I don't think you need to worry about that. They haven't caught that slippery fellow yet. I think we can all agree that he was a pretty slick customer."

Mildred had liked Al. In her deepest self, Mildred still liked Al—felt something warm for him, as if he had been one of her former students who had not lived up to his potential. The men in front of her would have liked to have been sworn in as a posse, gotten on horses, and gone after the bad guy, she saw. Al was a sinner in need of the saving grace of Jesus. That's who Al was—whatever his real name happened to be.

Part of Mildred hoped he got away. She knew who Al was—what Al was—but he had lived under her roof. Her hand went to her cheek where Al had struck her.

"He's a dangerous man, Mildred. They'll catch him. Don't worry," Sam advised, and the other men nodded, as if they could protect her from the evil ones of the world who went about seeing whom they could devour.

"What are we going to do about Janie—Amanda?" Mildred asked.

"Are the ladies going to tend to her, or do you want the shepherds to go see after her?" Sam asked. "I hear they frisk you at the jail house, Mildred. How do you think you and the ladies would handle being frisked?"

Mildred had not thought of that question. And was it true? Did they frisk visitors, or was that Sam's way of trying to control her comings and goings by creating fear? Mildred looked at Sam again. She had known Sam a very long time, but he was a stranger to her in some ways still.

"Fran and I will tend to the girl," Mildred announced, and she stood up. Her rising surprised Sam. The other men rose immediately, and Sam followed suit, looking around the room as if he were temporarily disoriented. It was harder for him to get up than it used to be, Mildred saw.

She added firmly. "I don't want that money, if it comes. Not a penny." Mildred couldn't see tending to Janie and taking money for Al, too. No, she just couldn't see it. Her head shook involuntarily.

"You can be proud later, Mildred. You live on a fixed income. A retired teacher's income," Sam added significantly. "And you need a car. Yours has not yet come home."

"I know what my income is," Mildred replied tartly. She didn't mention the missing car. She had been praying about the car since Al had stolen it. Jesus would help her figure it out.

"Mildred," Sam said, taking a tone.

"Sam," she replied.

"Now, Mildred."

"Now, Sam."

"Don't be so ornery, Mildred. You have to budge in your stubborn ways sometimes."

"Don't call me in here to apologize and call me ornery," Mildred replied as the organ music began calling the people in the sanctuary to that place of quiet expectation. It was time to meet with the Lord. There were always ten minutes of instrumental music before the announcements of the day were read, and then before anyone knew what was happening, worship began.

"Glory," Mildred whispered almost to herself. But to Jesus. And to thousands of students she had known that lived inside of her. That's how it felt. Until recently, it had felt so crowded inside and lonely, too. She wondered where all her former students were—every one. And if they were happy and safe. Saved, that is. Miss Budge resolved that one more time when she got home she would pull out her old roll books and run her fingertips down their names and pray for them in the Spirit wherever they were. Their families. Their children now, too. There were so many people who needed the Lord, and God knew all their names. His book of life was much bigger than all of her old roll books.

"What did you say, Mildred?" Sam asked as his hands began to fuss with the folder.

"I'm going to leave you fellows to your to-do lists. It's time to go to church," Mildred announced, turning toward the sanctuary, where she could be still and find the quiet that brought her a rest she knew only in Jesus. *Only in Jesus. Only in Jesus.* Why wasn't there a hymn with that refrain? Maybe she would write one, she thought, and the idea surprised her. She had never written music before. But as she turned toward the light of the sanctuary, she considered the adventure of it, and inside, deep inside where the potential to live abided as living water, she thought, maybe I will write a song. A love song. Imagine that.

"Five thousand dollars, Mildred," Sam called after her.

She waved his words away. "Glory," she whispered. "Glory to Jesus."

Music was beginning out there where worshipping God happened: it was an event, not an idea. She stepped on the threshold and looked out at the pews that were filling up. She knew the evening people. A lot of the morning people didn't come. And then, sometimes evening people came for a while and stopped, and months later started up again. She didn't look up. No one sat in the balcony at night. It wasn't necessary. There was plenty of room below in the main sanctuary on Sunday evenings.

The door at the front of the church opened. The air in the room changed. Starlight came in as a woman stepped through.

The visitor stood there, looking around. Looking for something. Looking for a place where she could feel at home. Mildred recognized the visitor immediately.

Mildred walked past her pew and her purse and her hymnal all the way to the back where the woman stood uncertainly, looking around for a place where she could sit down and belong.

The evening light eased the lines around the visitor's face, softened the fierce expression inside her eyes. Mildred touched the woman's shoulder in greeting.

"Dixie? Is that you?" Mildred asked. "That is you," she declared with certitude.

The other woman eyed her quizzically, staring intently, holding tightly to the small white card with the plan of salvation on one side and the times of the church service on the other that Mildred had given her in the hospital. It was an old-fashioned tool, like the telephone table at Mildred's home.

"Dixie, I'm so glad you've come. I've got a place just for you down front on that second pew right beside me."

Dixie's eyes widened as she looked around the cozy sanctuary, trying to get her bearings. She looked down at Mildred's hand, which was now resting on her forearm.

"You're in the right place," her hostess assured her. "Do you remember me?" the church lady asked, as she began to lead the lost woman nearer to the altar at the front of the sanctuary.

"Don't *you* know who you are?" Dixie asked, drawing back. She looked around the room for an escape or for some help. Mildred wasn't sure which. She patted Dixie's arm reassuringly, and replied with assurance.

"I do know. I am Mildred Budge. And Jesus—the man who came to fix what Adam broke—will help you learn who you are."

BONUS EXCERPT

FROM *MILDRED BUDGE IN EMBANKMENT*

As Sam's burgundy Buick broke through the lightweight road guard and crashed downward through heavy brush, church lady Mildred Budge knew she was not going to die.

Her life story did not pass before her eyes. She felt no panic.

Later, Miss Budge would wonder about that--wonder if she had missed some kind of heightened insight into the meaning of her life. And as a thoughtful person does as she ages, the retired public school teacher would almost regret that she had not been more deeply touched by a near-death experience. What would she have learned that might have informed the rest of her life and made it better?

But in that moment, Mildred Budge thought first only of the inconvenience of being stranded in a kudzu-filled ravine nowhere near the interstate because Sam Deerborn, the chairman of the pulpit committee, had wanted to take this narrow two-lane back road to their destination on a quiet Sunday morning when there weren't other travelers about.

The church lady thought, too, of missing the sermon hour of the young preacher who was the third candidate under consideration to replace their previous pastor and next on the list for the pulpit committee to visit. Finally, she grieved that the elastic in her left knee-high stocking had failed entirely. The stocking was now rolled down around her ankle fully, and it was going to be a nuisance all day long. Oddly, reaching toward that irritation of a collapsed stocking was the impulse Miss Budge fought against---not death.

When Sam's Buick finally smashed into the ground, Miss Budge did not see the big picture of life and how death informs the understanding of it. She saw a rabbit that woke up when the car slammed into the earth, and her eyes were open long enough for her to see it sprint away.

After the rabbit, Miss Budge saw that the three other people in the car were remarkably passive to have sailed over an embankment. They chugged through brush as the Buick's tires tried to find some traction to counteract the powerful pull of gravity.

When the nine-year old Buick crashed against a trio of drought-parched pine trees, bunching up the sun-faded hood and triggering the front seat airbags to expand while dried brown pine needles showered them, Mildred, perfectly peaceful inside of herself, shouted jubilantly, "Jesus saves!"

"We're all right, Budge," Jake Diamond said in response to Mildred's excited testimony.

Budge is what Jake called Mildred. Just Budge. Mildred liked it. It felt like a nickname, a term of real affection, rather than a misuse of her last name, which happened frequently. Mildred looked down at Jake's brown hand holding hers. She marveled that someone was holding her hand at all, and she knew a start of embarrassment at being caught holding hands with anyone in public. As the car gasped, belched, and the panel of lights on the blood-red dashboard blinked out totally, Budge squeezed Jake's hand and asked, "What in the world?"

It was an open-ended question with broader implications that would later require prayer for an answer. Like the use of her last name as a shorthand method of address, Mildred Budge's question, "What in the world?" expressed stupefaction and concern. It was one of her signature prayers to God when he moved in his famous mysterious ways and was a companion plea to her other frequently uttered prayers of "Have mercy," "Help me, Jesus," and the universal cry of unequivocal helplessness, "Lord, Lord, Lord."

"Sam?" Jake said. "Lizzy? You two okay up front?"

Sam's head and torso were covered by the white billowy airbag which had automatically inflated. He was snuffling. That is, Sam was breathing. Mildred thought the slow rise and fall of his shoulders represented more a sigh of relief than the deep inhalations of breath that come after a big surprise when adrenaline surges and then recedes.

In the passenger seat beside him, Liz's airbag had also inflated, and the serial widow was fighting it, punching it with her small, prissy fists.

Jake let go of Mildred's hand and reached out and solidly gripped Liz's left shoulder. "Steady, Elizabeth."

That was Jake Diamond.

When his door opened and Jake stepped out, the car shifted, not dramatically, but enough to indicate that not all four tires were firmly on the ground.

Mildred went very still as she waited for Sam to become himself again, because he was just breathing deeply there in the front seat, held in by his shoulder strap and the airbag. The passenger door creaked clumsily open, and Jake's brown hand navigated the surprisingly resilient airbag and unsnapped Liz's gray seatbelt. Unlike Liz's hands that were balled up in little fists ready to pummel an enemy, Jake's hand was outstretched and peaceful. His hand seemed to quiet the troubled atmosphere inside the car that was charged with residual fear and surprise. Jake eased the airbag away with his gentling hands and coaxed the pugilistic Liz to a place of stillness.

He has praying hands, Mildred observed. *Hands that speak to God of us.* The odd idea faded away as her senses took hold and brought her more and more to the moment inside the car where they were now altogether in a new way. They were survivors.

Mildred saw Liz's face captured in the mirror on the down-turned visor. The aging beauty queen's expression was one of torment and fear--not at all the perky, starry blue gaze she was famous for at church and which had successfully induced four different men to marry her, all of whom she had buried.

"Come on out of there, Lizzy," Jake said. He helped Liz to shift her legs out of the car.

While the other woman made her escape from the front seat and as her first foot touched the earth, Mildred could almost feel the ground beneath her own feet, and that feeling of imminent connection drew her more and more out of that heightened place where she was living, breathing, and still saying inside herself now: *Jesus saves. Jesus saves. Jesus saves.*

Mildred released her own seat belt, felt around for her brown leather Grace Kelly handbag on the floorboard, opened her own car door, and let herself out. Jake's eyes met Mildred's as he continued to prop up the pale Elizabeth. Liz had raccoon eyes from where the fresh mascara she had been applying in the car had smeared. The collapsed white airbag, so like a crumpled pillowcase that now needed to be washed, bore traces of Liz's mascara, too.

"Let's get her over there," Jake said quietly to Mildred, who was now listening to that interior voice that had stopped testifying and was now quietly narrating the story of her life to her while she lived it. It was a very comforting still small voice that sometimes she thought was only her inner Miss Budge, and sometimes she believed it was the eternal voice of Truth just keeping an accurate record of history being lived out in her: *You have been in an accident. Sam is hurt and seems to be out of it. Jake is helping Liz and has called her Lizzy and she hates that. You are still standing, although the elastic band in your hosiery has failed entirely, so don't buy that cheap brand again. You need to see about Sam because Jake is busy.*

"Budge, get a move on," Jake commanded. He caught Mildred's eyes, and she felt the word 'steady' though he did not say it to her, and Mildred was gratified, for Elizabeth Luckie was the type of woman who needed to hear that word of reassurance from a strong man, but Mildred Budge was not.

Retired fifth-grade school teacher Mildred Budge was a common-sense, faith-created church lady who could rise to any occasion. She looked at Jake wonderingly, her left hand gripping her brown handbag that she used year-round. She had given up changing out seasonal handbags years ago as a waste of energy. Now, she used one well-made handbag until it wore out; then, she threw it away. *Who cared if the color of her purse matched whatever outfit she was wearing*? Chin up and ready to march to safety, Budge said forthrightly in a voice that was unfamiliar to her own ears, "There was a deer."

"There was," Jake agreed, finally scooping up the wobbly Liz. "Budge, you need to get over there by that tree in case this car is going to blow up or catch on fire."

Mildred looked around while Jake shuttled Liz quickly to a place underneath a red tree. Mildred Budge had often felt the need to learn the names of trees, but she was tired; and when she was fatigued, proper nouns—and that included the names of trees—escaped her. When that happened, Mildred only identified trees by adjectives and colors. She stopped, a faint smile on her face as she listed the trees she now identified that way. There were weeping trees, and Christmas trees, and good-smelling trees, and dead trees, and unkempt trees that needed to be pruned, and today, there was this red tree toward which she needed to move. Budge looked down at her root-bound feet and tried to walk. She blinked at her feet hard as if they were separate entities that could be telepathically commanded to move.

Jake reappeared, put a strong arm around Mildred's waist, and said, "Come on, darlin'."

Mildred could not remember when anyone had last put an arm around her waist or held her hand, though many people in Montgomery, her hometown, call everyone darlin' because they couldn't remember proper names either. She wanted to tell Jake that he was not remembering the rules about how people treated an older church lady. Even church ladies didn't properly hug or kiss each other; they gave those lipstick-saving air kisses to which Miss Budge had not accustomed herself. Mildred thought air kisses—a pantomime of affection that church ladies inflicted on one another—when unavoidable, were one of the great humiliations of being alive. Air kisses told a terrible story of no one quite making a connection with you—just sort of pretending to while passing through your life. When Mildred Budge thought of air kisses, tears occasionally filled her brown eyes.

"You got out of the car, so your legs can work, and they will work. Move that left foot, Budge. Now move the right foot, Budge."

"Left. Right. Left. Right. Left. Right." And then Jake's arm was no longer around her, and Budge was standing beside the woozy Liz.

"Thank you," Mildred tried to tell Jake, but the words came out all rattled because in spite of the fact that she was the inimitable Miss Mildred Budge and truly believed that Jesus saved, her teeth were now chattering from shock.

Just before the airbag inflated, keeping him from breaking his nose on the steering wheel, Sam thought dismally: 'I have killed them. It's my fault. Belle has been telling me that my driving's not so good, and maybe she is right. Maybe I should have given up driving last month when I ran that "Stop" sign.'

And then, even though the airbag did its job, something in the moment that was akin to impact made Sam black out.

The other passengers assumed that Sam's blackout was due to the accident, but that was not true. Losing consciousness was an impulse that Sam had been fighting for some time. Going over the embankment simply gave the retired Air Force colonel an excuse to allow himself to slip finally into a state of not-knowing that had been attracting him for months, maybe years.

All the responsibilities that he had chosen to bear and all the work that made up Sam's to-do list reached a breaking point at the embankment, and Sam simply allowed whatever inner force there was that managed a man's consciousness to say, "Lights out, good buddy."

Sam blanked out. But not completely. There was a part of his consciousness that hovered inside of him, taking note of what was going on while his eyes were closed and his face was learning the contours of the airbag. It was taut and flexible at the same time. There were other people in the car, but the chairman of the pulpit committee was all alone up against the airbag, and he surrendered--no fight left in him.

It seemed perfectly natural to surrender to inertia while the car was airborne and turning the steering wheel a fruitless endeavor. Then, the car slammed against the ground, and Sam exulted in that moment of impact. Would liked to have relived it over and over again in the same way that when you're a kid on a roller coaster and a fast dip on the track makes you swallow your heart, you want to do it again. Sam wanted to hit the ground again and again, and surrender over and over again to the experience of smashing into the earth. The collision satisfied Sam, and he hid that satisfaction inside the airbag as the car rollicked hard. They came to a harsh stop against the trio of pines.

Sam felt Liz's fingernails claw his right thigh, but her hand departed quickly when the grabbing onto him did not stop the car from lurching or coming to that final neck-jerking slam against the pine trees that were so young that they really shouldn't have withstood the impact of the heavy car, but they did. Dry needles dusted the top of the car, and Sam thought for a second, *I just washed the Old Girl and now she's a mess.* He saw instantly that she was going to be past ever cleaning up again. Inside the airbag, a smile too big to emerge on his face showed up inside of him, deep, deep inside of Sam where he kept his grit and his will and the determination to keep going. The Old Girl was stopped, and now Sam could take a time-out from cleaning her up, keeping her up, and assorted other chores that were his daily lot. The smile inside of him yawned as his memory began to do the job of recording the story, but he was not taking note of the story he would tell; he was identifying those parts of the story that he would never tell anyone ever. Not even God. For inside himself in the deep well of his soul, Sam kept a separate book about himself, and it was the story of what he was really like that no one else knew and which he didn't pay much attention to because what's the point? Life was a mystery, and in many ways, Sam Deerborn, who presented himself as an open book to others, was a mystery to himself.

For Sam had experienced a deep satisfaction in crashing into the pine trees—as if a part of him had wanted to do it all his life. And it reminded him of the mailboxes that lined the sides of the streets in his quiet Southern neighborhood, and how often, when driving down a street, his hand had wanted to steer the car over and knock the mailboxes down like bowling pins one after another, only he never had. *Why would a man even think that?* Today, Sam had hurt his Old Girl, a car which had been a faithful vehicle and which was now, most certainly, going to be called *totaled*. The man others knew as Sam Deerborn, Belle's husband, was sobered by the event. Inside of himself, the other Sam was bemused and curious about what he might do next.

He would have to say good-bye to his Old Girl that had been dependable, and they did not make this shade of burgundy for automobiles any longer. It was such a respectable hue of red, and Sam thought it was so much more reliable a color than the cherry reds of cars painted for younger drivers and which seemed to fade faster in the sunlight. No, the burgundy resembled the deep resonating hue of a good leather rather than a painted tin can, and the Old Girl had mostly retained the depth of her color except for the hood, which had faded some. If Sam had believed in naming cars, he would have called her Ginny after a girl he had gone to school with and whom he had thought of marrying before he had met his Belle.

"Sam?"

Face buried against the airbag, Sam heard his name called. Heard the deep assuring tones of Jake Diamond and then Mildred Budge getting out of the car, and Sam had a vague sense of being sorry earlier that morning that he had been rude to Millie for bringing along that blue Igloo cooler that he had reluctantly stowed in the Old Girl's trunk.

He didn't understand why he had been so cross, for Sam loved Mildred Budge. He loved her in the way that people who are growing older together learn to love each other at church, where one's home life expands so that you are not only residing at your residence, you share a larger sense of family. The reminder of the size of this heaven-bound family was the local church on the corner. Sam and Mildred had been members of their church for years.

Sam decided in that first moment after the crash that he needed to apologize to Mildred about the blue Igloo. Make things right. He would just have to find the right moment.

Before Sam could plan what to say in his head and add it to the always present to-do list that was much longer than the stuff he wrote down on a sheet of lined yellow paper on a legal pad each morning, he heard Liz Luckie whimpering. That was good, because Sam had heard her cry like that at her husbands' funerals, and that meant she would be okay. All three other passengers were going to be all right, and he hadn't killed any of them except the Old Girl he had been driving. Sam inhaled, and listened to his breath come and go, come and go. One day it would go altogether, but until then, breathing was like walking. Take one more breath. Let it out. Put one foot in front of the other. That was life. One more step. One more breath. Over and over again. And now he had lost the Old Girl. Well, it was his personal loss, and Sam would handle it. He was a man, and he could handle whatever he had to face. Sam's hands still gripped the wheel hard. Needing to let go, Sam held on and it felt to him like his hands were fixed to everything, and he couldn't get loose.

That is how it felt to him at church, too. At Christ Church, Sam Deerborn was the go-to guy. The senior elder. When no one else could get a job done, good old Sam could. When no one else wanted to do a job, good old Sam would. And he hadn't really wanted to chair the pulpit committee, because he had learned from experience that the grief you got from the congregation for whoever you hired simply wasn't worth it. You couldn't please everybody no matter how hard you tried and no matter how many informal polls you took on fellowship night or how carefully worded the questionnaires were that got mailed out to the congregation to find out what they wanted their next preacher to be. It didn't matter how hard you worked or how smart you were or if there were fifty great guys applying for the job and you chose the very best man for the job, that man would not be good enough for everybody in a church as big as Christ Church. No, Sam Deerborn had not wanted to chair the pulpit committee again. Three times was enough already!

Still, as much as Sam said that he did not want to do it—be the go-to guy this time--he did not want to see the process fouled up and the church end up with a man they would have to keep at least three years (That was the decent time to keep someone if he wasn't working out). So, reluctantly, against his own better judgment, Sam agreed to form the pulpit search committee and chair it.

He placed the job advertisements in the right periodicals and then logged in the resumes by date, read them, identified the top three candidates in order to save everyone some time, and passed out copies of the resumes to the committee members. All he had left to do was take the committee members to hear the three men preach before they—the committee--voted to invite the right one to come and preach to the congregation, which would then collectively vote yea or nay. However, once a candidate was brought in for the show-and-tell Sunday morning service, it was considered a done deal. The congregation usually just rubber stamped the hiring selection by voting yea. If anyone disagreed or took that other bothersome position of abstaining from voting either way (Sam despised fence-sitters), Sam would call them up and explain that it was so much better if they could tell the chosen candidate who would be offered the job and who would always ask, "How strong was the vote?" that "We're behind you one hundred percent!"

The four-member pulpit committee had recently visited the churches of the other two men and heard them preach. Today they had been on their way to scout the third and final preacher.

So far, the committee was split two and two in favor of candidates one and two. Sam knew reasonably that there should have been a fifth committee member to break any tie, but carting five people around was awkward even in a big Buick. So Sam had settled on having only four members to comprise the committee, believing that his powers of persuasion would ultimately mitigate not having a tie-breaking fifth person on board. The two girls would vote with him at least.

There was still this last and youngest preacher who had made the cut and who could, if selected, be the right guy for the younger members of the congregation; but looking ahead, Sam couldn't see how the whole congregation would be able to get along with such a young man or keep up with Steev, who spelled his name with the two e's in the middle, and what was his last name? If Steev, with two e's in the middle, was half the guy he was described as being by his references, he could walk on water, and no man was that light on his feet. You had to read between the lines when you read references. Too much praise of a candidate from a current employer could mean that they were trying to run him off and getting him another job was their way to do it.

Sam Deerborn had lived a long time, and preachers were only human, like the people they were called to serve. He had tried to mentor as many of the preachers as he could, even old Joe, who was supposed to have retired years ago but kept coming back to fill in every time a preacher left. Sam believed he could have been more help to old Joe if that old preacher had been the kind of old dog who could learn a new trick, but Joe wasn't teachable. He had no ambition in him either. That was the biggest problem with Joe—no forward motion in him. That is what Sam had tried to explain to him, but Joe had just smiled and excused himself—said he could hear his mother calling--which was a funny thing for that old preacher to say. It was only a while after that when Sam realized that Joe's mother could not possibly have been alive, so the old guy was losing his marbles, too. Sam hoped that this last time was the very last time they would have to call Joe in to pinch-hit while a new preacher was being identified and called to lead Christ Church.

"Sam?"

He heard his name again, and there was no ignoring it this time.

"Sam?"

Jake opened the door and pushed the airbag away from Sam's face. Against his deepest will, Sam's eyes fluttered open, and he was surprised to see some blood on the airbag.

"Sam, snap to. We've got to take care of the ladies," Jake said.

A hand was placed on the back of his neck. The grip of Jake's hand steadied Sam, calling him to attention. Sam felt his seat belt unsnapped, and Jake tugged on his left arm.

"No reason to panic. Everyone's okay. And no gasoline is leaking," Jake reported. "I don't think she'll blow up. The car is sitting fine."

Sam wanted to say something, but there was blood running down his face and into his mouth; and when Sam opened his lips, he found that he didn't like the coppery taste at all.

Jake saw it all happening from the backseat where he was sitting with Mildred Budge. They had tried to put him in the back with that woman who had killed four husbands; but thank God, Lizzy had announced that she got motion sick in the back seat, so she was up front with Sam and away from him. Boy, Lizzy had beaten the tar out of the inflated airbag with those little hands of hers, and Jake couldn't help wondering what else she had done with them. A woman just didn't become a serial widow without having done something with her hands. Jake Diamond did not have to think twice about it. He had decided to keep his distance from that one.

Yet, there she was—Liz Luckie--sitting in the front passenger seat, and here he was in the same car with the woman he had decided to avoid, and Sam and Budge and he might all be in harm's way just because the Lady of Death was on board. Hadn't they just flown off an embankment?

How in the world did Liz, a professional beneficiary of men's estates, get put on this real live search committee to find a pastor for real live people who believed in a real live God and a real live Jesus?

Already the Black Widow was a problem. Queen Elizabeth had liked that first guy that preached on grace, and Sam had agreed with her because Old Sam didn't want the rich widow to have an opinion by herself. Obviously, the second preacher was the better choice for their congregation, and Mildred Budge saw that right off, too. At present, it was two against two. Jake Diamond and Mildred Budge were new allies.

Jake had been on enough search committees at the local university where he worked to know how to assess the viability of candidates and to read between the lines of what they put on their resumes and what they didn't and what they emphasized about their missions and what they didn't see as part of their job description. But when you cut to the chase, that first guy preached grace, which meant he wasn't willing to preach Jesus front and center, and fifty-six-year-old Jake was too old not to want to hear Jesus preached front and center.

The second guy had mentioned Jesus seven times in his sermon. He had chosen John the Baptist for his focus. But if John the Baptist was the first sermon—could a sermon on Jesus be far behind? And so, automatically, ipso facto, Jake Diamond voted for John the Baptist—the second preacher, hoping for more of Jesus down the road, and Budge had agreed with Jake's choice, though she had not explained why. Jake had meant to ask her why, but he had not been able to talk alone with Mildred yet. Lizzy was always around, and Sam ran a tight meeting. Sam did not allow any time for just sitting and talking, which was a shame because sitting and talking was what people really needed to do.

You would have thought there might have been some time during the ride in the car for just talking about the candidates, but Sam had gotten them off to a bad start this morning by being irritated with Budge for bringing a cooler on a simple day trip. Sam would not allow the cooler in the car or any kind of eating, and Budge was a church lady that way. She couldn't help taking provisions with her. It was what some old-fashioned church ladies did.

But not what a church lady like Liz Luckie did.

When Sam said that about Budge's cooler, Lizzy had let her icy-blue eyes smile as if seeing Budge put down made her happy. Then, after Sam reluctantly stowed the cooler in his trunk and they had been assigned their places in the car, Budge had pretended to go to sleep in the back seat, but she wasn't really. It was just her way of tuning out Lizzy who was talking ninety miles to nothing in the front seat, and Sam was going, uh-huh, uh-huh, and then the deer leapt right in front of the car and, a split second later, they were sailing over the embankment.

It was strange being in the air. It felt like one of those dreams where you think you can fly, and Jake had thrilled to the weightlessness. Budge had, too, for her eyes had popped opened, and rather than fear death, Mildred Budge had worn an expression of a kind of surprised delight—you just never know with women.

Being a sensible man, Jake did wonder if they were going to die as the ground came at them, but he had a funny peace about the whole thing. He remembered the strangest bliss--that he didn't blame the deer or Sam, who had chosen this dumb route instead of taking the interstate. Jake didn't even mind so much that Lizzy was on the pulpit committee and was putting on eye make-up while they were about to crash. She wasn't much of a mystery to Jake. He knew her type. Liz was one of those women you had to pay attention to; and when you did, you would not see a deer before it was too late. She would cause you to lose your focus about so many other things. Only there were too many things that a man had to keep track of. Jake didn't see how any man with a real life would have the kind of time to give Liz what she needed. Her type would drain a real man dry. Steal his thoughts. Feed on his complete attention. Demand his life as proof of his love, if he let her. Knowing that, Jake resolved as they sailed over the embankment: `Don't court death, but you don't have to fear it. Remember this. Remember life. Remember what it feels like to sail out without holding any grudges against anyone. This is what living is supposed to be.'

It felt like flying did in a dream. It felt like heaven.

Over the embankment they all went, while Liz was applying extra mascara using the mirror in the dashboard visor and attempting to make eye contact with Jake in the backseat, as if he, a black man who had made a comfortable life for himself in a white man's world at the university and at the mostly white church near downtown Montgomery, would mess up his life or, more probably, shorten it, by swapping meaningful glances with not only a white woman but also with a white woman who had buried all her loving husbands.

Jake almost laughed out loud when Liz attempted to twinkle at him. Jake Diamond didn't have a death wish. If he had been sitting closer to Budge, he would have elbowed her, and said, 'Look there. Do you see that? Do you see The Liz making eyes at me? I don't want to die.'

But Budge was hugging her door, doing that 'I'm asleep thing' and fighting the urge to scratch some itch on her ankle. Her hand kept stretching almost involuntarily that way. And then the deer leapt, Sam swerved, they smacked the railing, a limb dragged across the car's roof, and as they sailed out over the embankment, Budge opened her eyes and her mouth made an O, and then, just as a rabbit leapt out of harm's way, she started testifying that Jesus saves! As the car arced groundwards, it was like there was no sense of danger for her, and that's one of the chief reasons Jake stayed calm. Everyone knew that Mildred Budge had common sense; and when she didn't panic, Jake Diamond didn't either.

They weren't the same angels that circled overhead at the last funeral when they had buried Hugh Luckie, her fourth husband. They were a different group of angels, much smaller than angels were generally thought to be, and they were circling so fast overhead that at first Liz thought they were spokes in some kind of celestial wheel. As the car went over the embankment and then rocketed downward, the movement of the angels slowed to the point that Liz could make out their shapes, and the same question that had haunted her for the last four funerals arose out of a deep well of grief that no one who had not buried all of her husbands could understand: 'What in the world is happening to me?'

Almost as soon as she asked that question, she heard FussBudget say "Jesus saves" and then the same question she lived with when she saw the angels: "What in the world?" Liz was relieved by the idea that plain-as-vanilla Mildred Budge might be able to see what Liz had begun to see years ago after her first husband died. For Liz Luckie saw bunches of angels. And when the angels started showing up like that, usually somebody died. Or just had.

Then, people blamed her.

People didn't say those words out loud. They just made faces about her behind her back. Liz saw those faces the same way she saw those crazy angels out of the corner of her eye. She hated those angels that swirled as flashes of light and hovered and haunted and dared her to try and build a life that they would tear down by simply taking away the one she loved every single time. She had been aware of the angels for a long time, but it wasn't until the death of Hugh Luckie that she put two and two together and got the answer that produced her newest question: 'Why are angels of death trailing me around?'

And having finally figured out what the angels were up to—coming to take away someone who loved her--Liz Luckie had decided that when she saw the angels again, she was going to fight them.

Liz pummeled the airbag, trying to get at the angels of death that had stolen her husbands from her, leaving her alone without a soul to help her fasten a simple necklace or tell her when she needed to touch up the roots of her hair. She couldn't see as well as she used to; and when you have been a beauty all your life and age robs you of your beauty in terrible stages, you don't want to look so closely at your face or the roots of your hair or your poor hands that even wearing plastic gloves while dishwashing couldn't stop from looking older.

Liz punched the airbag. Then, she reached over and clawed Sam on the leg for getting them all into this fix. Then, she caught a glimpse of herself in the visor's mirror and screamed because she had gotten so old, though she was still only sixty (she planned to stay only sixty for as long as she could pull it off). Liz missed being beautiful desperately.

She missed all of her husbands desperately.

And she desperately hated to see the flurry of angels, because that meant only one thing: Death.

But who was going to die this time?

One of them? All of them?

Did Mildred Budge know? That woman knew more than she usually told. Liz had tried to get Mildred to be a friend—had almost succeeded—but then there had been that unfortunate accident with Winston, Fran's sort-of boyfriend. Because Fran Applewhite was Mildred's best friend, FussBudget had chosen Fran over Liz, and Winston's falling off the ladder had not been her fault, but Liz was blamed for it anyway, like always. Right when they were about to become friends, Mildred Budge had pulled away from knowing Liz better. Later, when Liz had tried to talk to Mildred about what had happened, Liz didn't get much out of Mildred except that frank brown-eyed stare that would make an honest judge start confessing his trespasses. Mildred Budge was famous for that cow-eyed stare.

Feeling misunderstood and panicked, Liz prayed in the car just before it smashed into the ground and then crashed through bramble until the pine trees stopped them altogether: "God, don't let one of the men die today."

For the famous widow knew her reputation. She knew how other men and women saw her.

But her reputation had not been built solely upon her husbands all dying. Since her last funeral, Liz Luckie had been unlucky in Sunday school classes, too.

No Sunday school class could keep her.

Liz had gone from class to class at church trying to find a place where she could sit and listen to stories about God without causing a commotion, but she no sooner sat down than the man in charge began to talk directly to her in front of everyone. If there was a cross-referenced Bible verse to look up, any man in charge in any Sunday school class asked Liz to look it up. If there was a name to add to the prayer list on the white board, the man in charge handed Liz the marker and asked her to write that name on the white board. If the leader in charge told a joke, he turned to Liz and waited to see if she laughed. Liz was always extremely polite about laughing at men's jokes. When Liz exercised common courtesy, the women scowled, and the other men felt competition for her attention take root and begin to grow.

During the coffee hour, another man would try to tell her a different joke that was better than the one the teacher had told because men were competitive that way. There had been times when Liz Luckie tried to be rude instead—had not even smiled and even let her gaze go a little frosty (and that could actually backfire because sometimes a frosty woman can make a man's love grow hotter), but it was hard to act cold when a man was trying to please you. Before too long in any Sunday school class or during the fellowship coffee time, Liz Luckie was the center of the men's attention and the object of other women's contempt.

Liz Luckie was a man magnet. And she didn't want to be. She just wanted to go to Sunday school, sit down, and not feel lonely for as long as the class period lasted.

For Liz was not one of those women who could get used to being alone. Many women could. Liz saw the women who could live alone. They all sat together on the pews that had become known as the widows' pews, but Liz would not join them there. FussBudget sat there, although she had never been married. There were women like that who appeared to be widows, but really, they were mostly old-maid school teachers or retired librarians or government workers. Whatever their marital status, they were women who were content to be each other's company. Not Liz. Never Liz. She would never consent to that. Never.

Just thinking about it made Liz feel anxious and in a hurry. Life was going by pretty fast, and she couldn't take hold of it or catch up to it. She wondered how other people managed. Did they ever have that feeling of either running or being pushed by unknown forces? As the car hit the ground and the airbag slammed against her face and mashed wet mascara around her eyes, Liz Luckie repressed the question that slithered up in her consciousness from time to time:

'Was there a real devil other than one's own fearful nature, and if so, how could one get away from him? Maybe the devil's real name was Time.'

Liz was haunted by bands of misery-producing angels and tormenting questions that seemed to come from the devil. She was scared.

Liz felt pursued by death, and she wanted to feel at peace with life in Jesus. Even last week she had been chased into church by old Mr. Peavy who had called out to her to slow down as she climbed the steps of the church. Only he didn't say those words, "Slow down." Mr. Peavy said, "Don't you look pretty?"

Liz had always been able to translate men's language, and she had known that Lem Peavy was asking her to slow down and walk into the church with him. And if they had walked into the church together, they would naturally sit together during the service. Then, he would hold the red hymnal for the both of them, and once she was singing the same song with him off of his page, well, she was done for.

That is how a courtship could begin—as simple as that. But this time, the question, "Don't you look pretty?' did not trap her. Because Mr. Peavy walked slowly and with a cane, she had been able to scoot away, moving right to the threshold of the church where the two deacons handed out the order of service. On the threshold that led to the sanctuary Liz had looked to her right where the widows' pews were and knew she would be safe there. It was a no-man zone, and Mr. Peavy wouldn't follow her there and sit down beside her. Still, as safe as it appeared to be in one respect, it felt dangerous in another. Liz simply could not join the other single ladies in the unofficial widows' section who announced their aloneness like that. She never had been able to join women who seemed resigned to being alone or old.

They were the type who wore those red and purple hats as if bright colors made up for living alone. Liz had a great deal to say about the ways that others duped women into wearing uniforms that made them all alike--even that purple and red combo meant to suggest independence and flair and which was just another uniform after all. Liz Luckie was herself. She was herself, alone now, and determined to be herself, alone now.

With that purpose in her heart, Liz had used her charms to inveigle her way onto the pulpit committee so that other people would see her as someone who didn't just get married and bury the poor man who had found her desirable. She was someone who had a job to do at church. She was going to prove it. She was going to help them find the right man for the job and not marry the man or later ask him to perform a marriage ceremony for her!

Liz was working on her reputation all right. She had been making progress, but there were those angels of death circling overhead again like buzzards in white, and she knew what they meant. God help her and the people who were in the car with her whose lives were in danger now.

`My Lord,' she began. Almost as soon as she thought the prayer, Jake's strong arms scooped her up, and like a groom carrying his bride, that man delivered her to safety, leaving FussBudget Budge to fend for herself.

Liz automatically closed her eyes to absorb Jake's strength. It was the same way she had always been carried by each one of her grooms except Hugh, her last husband. As a low humming sound began inside of her sounding like an echo of the wedding march, Liz forgot her intentions to be herself alone and allowed the smile of delight to surface that so many men had found irresistible.

But when Jake lowered her to the ground, he did not stop to receive the glow of her feminine approval. As her hero walked back to get FussBudget, she whimpered in a new assault of grief. Tears rolled down Liz's face, for Jake Diamond was immune to her femininity.

"See there?" she called out to the angels of death; and to her surprise, they zipped away.

ACKNOWLEDGEMENTS

My deepest thanks to my friends, sisters and family members who love me and understand the nature of what I do and encourage me in this activity: Guin Nance, who embraces the creative process in her own life and who teaches others how to do it, too; Patty DeBortoli, who lives creatively day by day as she reaches out to others as a counselor, mother and sister; Julie Helms, who likes doughnuts, falling snow and sharing the view of her mountains where she lives with Jody Helms, her husband and my steadfast brother-in-law; Mary Ellen McCord, who, like Mildred, teaches young students to read while her husband Steve coaches his students in good sportsmanship; my beautiful niece Lola Leigh McCord and her husband Jon Linna, who are my neighbors and the parents of Jon who likes to play the piano with me and has hair that catches the sunlight; my niece Jan Hrivnak, who has a pure heart, is a wonderful mother, and is married to the handiest guy in the family, Garrick, who is always ready to help me; Sarah, the luminous young wife of my nephew Ben Helms; Rhonda Helms, who has a very special place in my heart and not just because she is married to my nephew Jody Helms; and Katie Simpkins DeBortoli, who is presently in beauty school where she shares the beautiful love of Christ with others. Keep doing that, Katie. Everyone needs Jesus.

Friends who daily enrich the lives of others and certainly mine are Sue Luckey, who loves to read and encourages so many Alabama teachers to nurture this discipline in their students all over our state;

Ron Luckey who knows how to smile and when he does, the world grins back; Jennie and Bill Polk, who are the often unseen laborers at church but I see you (Thank you for all that you do.); Lori Tennimon, who understands the need for fellowship and sensitively gives it, and her husband Dan Tennimon, who is one of the good guys.

Mildred Budge and I would be very lonely without our friends at church: Carol Henry, who is a skilled and talented artist and graciously consented to becoming the likeness for Mildred Budge; Anne Henry Tidmore, the current Regent of The First White House of the Confederacy and my good friend; Betty Little, who knows the secret of contentment and can share it with a glance; and Fran Howland, whose zest for living inspires me. I am grateful to the members of my Lunch Bunch and the Bereans Sunday school class for including me.

As ever, I send my gratitude to Jack Cates of Cates Optical for keeping my glasses well-adjusted so that I can read. Keep preaching, Jack.

Finally, I send my love and gratitude to Toni and Kenneth Brooks and my other friends in Florence, Alabama who make room in their fellowship for Mildred and me.

ABOUT THE AUTHOR

DAPHNE SIMPKINS

Daphne Simpkins has been writing about life in the South for most of her adult life, and now that journey has extended to write about the life of a fictional retired Alabama school teacher, Mildred Budge who is also a full-time church lady. This series of books includes a collection of short stories and two novels—the third novel due out soon.

Prior to writing the Mildred Budge books, Daphne wrote essays and short stories about life in the South and many of these were published in many fine newspapers the United States and Canada. These included *The Chicago Tribune, The Atlanta-Journal Constitution, The Baltimore Sun, The St. Petersburg Times, The Miami Herald* and *The Christian Courier.* She has also been published in *The Christian Century.*

In addition to writing, Daphne is an active member of the Alabama Humanities Foundation's speakers' bureau. You can connect with her on Facebook, Twitter, or Linkedin.com.

BOOKS BY DAPHNE SIMPKINS:

Blessed—a collection of stories about caregiving and being a good neighbor

The Mission of Mildred Budge—a second collection of short stories about church ladies of the South featuring Mildred and her friends

Christmas in Fountain City—a feel good holiday story set in a fictional city in Alabama

What Al Left Behind—a follow-up to *The Long Good Night*. This collection of essays recounts the positive changes that being a caregiver of an Alzheimer's patient created in the author's life

A Cookbook for Katie—A Southern memoir masquerading as a cookbook, this collection of recipes and essays will encourage a new bride who will need to answer the question "What's for supper?" with good spirits, courage and perfectly cooked pan of cornbread

Mildred Budge in Embankment—the second novel in the Mildred Budge series. This story follows the pulpit committee as it works together to find the new preacher. But first they must survive flying off an embankment together. It's a long climb back up to church life and civilization. Originally published as *Embankment*.

Miss Budge in Love—a collection of early short stories that were published before the novels; This volume explores the inner life and faith of Southern church women.

The Long Good Night—a memoir of taking care of her father while he was suffering with Alzheimer's

Nat King Cole: An Unforgettable Life of Music—a biography for children about Nat King Cole, who was born in Montgomery, AL

Daphne Simpkins

Connect with Daphne on Facebook, Twitter, or Linkedin.com

Made in the USA
Las Vegas, NV
15 July 2021